THE FORBIDDEN LIBRARY

DJANGO WEXLER

KATHY DAWSON BOOKS
an imprint of Penguin Group (USA) LLC

KATHY DAWSON BOOKS
Published by the Penguin Group
Penguin Group (USA) LLC
375 Hudson Street
New York, New York 10014

USA / Canada / UK / Ireland / Australia / New Zealand / India / South Africa / China

penguin.com
A Penguin Random House Company

Text copyright © 2014 by Django Wexler
Illustrations copyright © 2014 by Alexander Jansson

Library of Congress Cataloging-in-Publication Data

Wexler, Django.
The forbidden library / Django Wexler.
pages   cm
Summary: When her father is lost at sea shortly after meeting a very unusual visitor, Alice must leave her home to live with an "uncle" whose rural Pennsylvania estate includes a massive and mysterious library that holds much more than books.
ISBN 978-0-8037-3975-8 (hardcover)
[1. Magic—Fiction. 2. Wizards—Fiction. 3. Libraries—Fiction. 4. Books and reading—Fiction. 5. Fairies—Fiction. 6. Cats—Fiction. 7. Orphans—Fiction.] I. Title.
PZ7.W5358For 2014
[Fic]—dc23
2013015285

Printed in the United States of America

1   3   5   7   9   10   8   6   4   2

Book Design by Jasmin Rubero
Text set in Lomba Medium

For Sakaki and the Tomoes,
who are 100% cat and proud of it

CONTENTS

CHAPTER ONE
THE FAIRY

MUCH LATER, ALICE WOULD wonder what might have happened if she'd gone to bed when she was supposed to.

It was a fluke, really, because she was the sort of girl who almost always followed the rules. But she'd been doing schoolwork and she'd lost track of time.

It was a Saturday night, and her tutor, Miss Juniper, had assigned her another chunk of algebra for Monday morning. Alice excelled in all her subjects—she never would have allowed it to be otherwise—but in algebra her excellence was born of hard work and long hours rather than natural talent, so she'd determined to make an early start. She wouldn't be bothering anyone, either. Her room had its own little writing desk and even its own electric lamp, which her father had had installed three years before with the boast that no daughter of *his* was going to ruin her eyes scribbling by gaslight.

Her father had been working late again. When Alice heard the telltale creak of the front door, she weighed the odds and decided he'd probably be happier to see her than angry that she was still up. She shrugged into her robe and padded into the hall and down the stairs.

The late-night silence was a little unnerving. Alice had grown up in a house that had practically bustled with servants and guests, even in the middle of the night, and she was used to seeing strangers about. But the servants had departed one by one as times had grown mean, until only Cook, Miss Juniper, and her father's man were left, and the visitors were less common than they used to be. The guest rooms that lined the hallway were all shut up now, with sheets draped over the furniture.

She passed the doors quickly, tugging her robe a little tighter, and ducked into the servants' stairs that led to the kitchen. Her father would probably be there, fixing himself something hot to drink.

Sure enough, the swinging door at the bottom of the

steps was outlined in yellow light. Alice put her hand out to push it open, but as her fingers brushed the wood she heard the voices, and realized her father wasn't alone.

". . . you have to know what we can do for you, Mr. Creighton," said someone who wasn't her father. "Someone is going to take advantage of it sooner or later."

Alice turned away at once. Being up late was one thing, but eavesdropping on her father's business conversations was quite another. She'd put her foot on the first step when the sound of her father's voice brought her up short.

"Don't you dare!" he shouted. "Don't you *dare* threaten my family."

The words hung in the air for long seconds, like a fading firework.

Her father never shouted, at least not in her hearing. He was a quiet, honest man who dealt fairly with everyone, put flowers on her mother's grave once a month, and went to church every Sunday. Hearing him talk like that was like watching a teddy bear yawn and reveal a mouth full of fangs. Alice stood perfectly still, not daring to move even her eyes. She wanted to run, knew she *ought* to—whatever was being said was obviously not for her ears—but her feet felt like lead weights.

"Mr. Creighton," said the other man. "Nobody's *threat-*

ening. I'm just stating a fact. Nothing wrong with stating a fact, is there? No law against it."

His voice was odd, high and nasal. Alice could hear a strange sound as well, a kind of urgent *thrum-thrum-thrum*.

"Don't mess me around," her father said, not shouting now but still angrier than she'd ever heard him. "We both know what you're here to say, and I'm sure you know what my answer's going to be."

"I strongly recommend you reconsider your position, Mr. Creighton." The thrumming grew louder. "For the sake of everyone involved."

"By God," Alice's father said. "So help me, I ought to break your ugly head against the wall."

"You could do that," the other man said. "You could do that, Mr. Creighton. But you won't. You know it would be unwise." His voice dropped a fraction. "For the girl, most of all."

Slowly, ever so slowly, Alice turned around. Her heart was still beating so hard, it seemed a wonder that her father couldn't hear it. She stepped back down to the door, carefully avoiding the creaky step, and pressed her fingers into the crack of light. It was wrong, possibly the most wrong thing she had ever done in her entire *life*, but she had to see. She gave the swinging door the lightest touch, and the crack widened into a gap big enough for a garter snake, to which she applied her eye.

The light made her squint. On one side of the room was her father, still in his suit, looking rumpled. His hair was damp with sweat. One of his hands was curled around the handle of a cast-iron frying pan sitting on the range, as though he meant to swing it and make good on his threat.

Across from him, hanging in the air, was a fairy.

When Alice had been a little girl, her father had given her a book called *The Enchanted Forest*. It was a big book made with thick paper, and had large type with pen-and-ink illustrations on each facing page. She'd probably been a bit too old for it, truth be told, but she'd read it anyway, as she read every piece of printed material that fell within her reach. It was the story of a rather stupid little girl who wandered into an enchanted forest, and caused a good deal of havoc among the creatures who lived there.

One of those creatures had been a fairy. It was a slim, child-like figure with wide eyes and a button nose wearing flowing robes, held aloft by gauzy insect wings—Alice had always imagined the wings in translucent greens and blues, like a butterfly's—and it had looked down at the little girl with an air of amused benevolence while it stood daintily in her raised palm.

At that age, Alice had grasped the idea that some things in books were real, and others were not. Questioning her father had revealed that there were such things as lions, tigers, and elephants (he'd promised a visit to the zoo, which had yet to happen), while trolls, centaurs, and dragons were the figments of writers' overactive imaginations. Alice remembered feeling vaguely annoyed at the author of *The Enchanted Forest,* who had clearly intended to deceive little girls possessing less penetrating intellects than her own.

There was, her father had told her, no such thing as fairies, either.

The thing hovering in the air in Alice's kitchen was similar enough to the picture in the book to be instantly recognizable, but he was larger, for one thing. The creature in the book had been insectile, six inches high at most, while this creature was a good two feet from head to heel. His wings were enormous, considerably bigger than his slender body, and beat the air so fast, they were a blur, like a hummingbird's. They were colored, not in greens and blues, but yellow and black, which put Alice in mind of something nasty and poisonous.

The fairy's skin was off-white and gnarled with warty growths sprouting clusters of thick, black hair. His scalp was bare and bald as an egg, gleaming wetly in the electric light. He had no nose at all, and his eyes were wide but black from edge to edge. When he spoke, she could see a mouth full of needle-like teeth, and a long red tongue like a snake's.

Alice closed her eyes. *This*, she thought, *is ridiculous. There are no such things as fairies.* She gave herself a pinch on the arm, which hurt, and counted slowly to ten.

When I open my eyes, she thought, *he will be gone.*

"I really wish you'd at least hear my offer," said the nasal voice.

Alice opened her eyes. The fairy was still there. He had hovered closer to her father, his wings *thrum-thrumming*, one tiny finger wagging in under his nose.

"I will not," Alice's father said. "I will not entertain any sort of *offer*. Go back and tell your master that. And tell him, if he troubles me again, I'll . . ."

The fairy waited, lip curled in a cocky grin that showed his teeth. "You'll what, Mr. Creighton?"

"Get out!" he shouted. "Get out of my house!"

There was a long moment of silence. The fairy hovered, impudently, as if to demonstrate that he didn't *have* to go

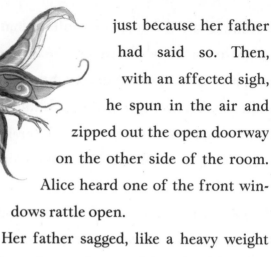

just because her father had said so. Then, with an affected sigh, he spun in the air and zipped out the open doorway on the other side of the room. Alice heard one of the front windows rattle open.

Her father sagged, like a heavy weight had been fastened around his shoulders. He let go of the frying pan and leaned on the range for support. Alice wanted to run to him, but she didn't dare. Whatever she had just seen—and she was still not certain *what* she had just seen—it was something she had not been supposed to witness.

Alice's father took a long breath, closed his eyes, and blew it out slowly, tickling the edges of his mustache. Then his eyes snapped open, full of panic.

"Alice," he said, under his breath. "Oh God."

All of a sudden he was running, struggling to get his feet under him, caroming off the kitchen doorway and out toward the main stairs. Alice was caught for a moment in stunned surprise, then started running herself, back up the servants' stairs, heedless of the creaking. He made it to her door only a few seconds before she arrived.

Finding the door slightly open, he flung it ajar, and stared wide-eyed at the empty room. His expression, bathed in the glow of her electric desk lamp, was the most terrifying thing Alice had ever seen.

She hurried to his side and grabbed his arm. "Father! Is something wrong?"

"You—" He gestured weakly at her empty room, then down at her. "I thought—"

"I was studying," Alice said, "and I got up for a moment. I'm sorry if I startled you."

All at once his fierceness melted, and he wrapped his arms around her in a hug so tight, he lifted her off the ground.

"Alice," he said, his scratchy cheek pressed against her forehead. "Alice."

"I'm here, Father." She squirmed until she worked her own arms free, then put them around him as far as they would go.

"It'll be all right," he said. She wasn't sure if he was talking to himself or not. "Everything is going to be all right."

"Of course it is," she said.

When he let go, there was something new in his face, a strange, wild determination so far out of the ordinary that it made Alice feel scared and proud of him, both at once. Her set her down gently, put his hands on her shoulders, and looked her in the eye.

"I love you," he said. "You know that, don't you?"

Alice felt herself blushing. "Of course."

His eyes were already miles away. He patted her shoulder, absently, and then hurried toward his study. Alice looked after him, wondering about the decision she'd seen in his eyes.

Then, because she was a girl who followed the rules, she went back into her room and went to bed.

The next morning, everything seemed so normal that Alice almost thought she'd dreamed the whole thing. Almost, but not quite.

She woke up in her familiar bed, under her warm, familiar quilt with its frayed edge. Her room was just her familiar room, with the heavy oak wardrobe in one corner and the framed picture of her grandmother looking down benevolently.

There was no elf sitting on her desk, and her books were just where she'd left them the night before. No troll in the heavy wooden chest at the foot of the bed, only the winter comforters and an ancient pair of stuffed rabbits she couldn't quite bear to throw away. She even, feeling intensely self-conscious, lifted the bedskirts and looked underneath, but there was no dragon there, only a thick layer of dust.

Nevertheless, she was certain what she'd seen had been real. The memory was bright and clear, not fuzzy and fading the way dreams were. When she sat down for breakfast with her father, she became doubly sure. He was acting normal, but it *was* an act, a little too sincere to believe.

"Earthquakes again," he said, paging through the *Times*. "First New Zealand, now Managua. Thousands dead, it says."

"That's terrible," Alice said, because she knew it was expected of her. She was trying to keep from staring at her father's face. He'd washed and shaved since last night, of course, but there was still something tight around his eyes. *It wasn't a dream,* she thought. *I'm sure of it.*

"Something ought to be done about it," he said, turning the page. "And still fighting in Spain. Seems like the whole world's coming to pieces."

"You always say they only print the bad news," Alice said.

Her father looked up and smiled, but it didn't reach his eyes.

Cooper, her father's man, appeared with a plate of toast and jam. Properly speaking, it wasn't his job to serve at table, but Alice's father had been forced to give the last of the footmen the sack when they'd caught him stealing from the pantry. Cooper insisted he didn't mind. In this day and age, he said, a man ought to be grateful to have work at all.

Her father put the paper aside and went to work on the toast, all in silence. Alice took a slice herself and carefully covered it with jam, right to the edges, working carefully with the butter knife to spread it evenly. The longer neither of them spoke, the more the silence grew and grew, like some monstrous thing squatting on the table between them. When her father finally cleared his throat Alice gave a little start.

"Alice."

"Yes, Father?"

"I'm going on a trip." He paused, and took a deep breath. "Something's come up. It's important, I'm afraid."

"When?" Alice said. "And how long will you be gone?"

"I'm catching a steamer tonight."

A ship? Her father's business took him all over New England, and occasionally as far as Chicago or Washington, D.C., but he'd never been gone for more than a week, and never on a steamer. "And where—"

"Here." He folded the paper and pushed it over to her. "It's the *Gideon,* bound for Buenos Aires." The schedule, a set of stops all down through the Caribbean and South America, was printed in a neat box beside the ticket prices and number for inquiries. "This way you'll be able to keep track of me."

Alice put one hand on the paper and swallowed hard, trying to sound as normal as she could. "When should I expect you back?"

His expression cracked. Just for a moment, but Alice was watching him closely, and she knew him better than anyone. His mouth turned down, pulling at his mustache, and his eyes glittered with tears.

"It'll be some time," he said. "I'm sorry, Alice. I wish there was another way."

Something was wrong, very wrong. Alice fought a growing thickness in her throat.

"Perhaps I should come with you," she said. Ordinarily she wouldn't have dreamed of offering such a suggestion unbidden, but desperate times called for desperate measures. "You've always said I need more experience in the practical side of business—"

"No," he said, a little too quickly. "Not this trip. When I get back . . ." He forced a smile. "Maybe then it'll be time for you to start making the rounds with me. But I'll make sure to send you a postcard from every stop."

The following day, Miss Juniper moved into one of the guest rooms and added looking after Alice to her tutoring duties, although in truth Alice didn't take much looking after. She worked on her French, and her algebra, and completed everything she was assigned on time. When Miss Juniper asked her what she wanted to do for her day off, Alice told her that she wanted to go to the Carnegie Library. She spent eight solid hours there, a solemn girl alone at one of the great wooden reading desks, working her way through a stack of books that represented everything the library had on the subject of fairies.

Her father needed her help, she was certain of it. She wasn't sure why, or how, but the brief glimpse of the fairy in the kitchen was all she had to go on. She took home a notebook full of references and scribbles, and as many books as the librarian would let her have. She stayed up late reading that night, and the night afterward as well. Alice was not a girl who believed in half measures.

Two days later, Cooper brought her the *Times* with breakfast. The front page told her that President Hoover had given another speech promising that the worst was over, that the stock market had taken another tumble, and, below the fold, that the steamer *Gideon* had gone down in a freak storm off Hatteras, with all hands.

CHAPTER TWO
MR. PALLWORTHY

AFTER THE STORM OF telegrams—the messenger boy kept bringing stacks of them, and Alice piled them unread inside the door to her father's study—came an inundation of relations. They were mostly cousins, none of whom Alice had ever seen before and none of whom paid her more than perfunctory attention. They trooped through the big old house like visitors to a museum, offering her halfhearted pats on the head while giving the furniture appraising looks.

After the cousins came the accountants, who were more open in their appraisals and didn't bother with Alice at all, and after the accountants, like a Biblical plague building up to a big finish, came the lawyers. They belonged to several different firms and seemed to have come to argue with one another, and for the most part they paid no attention to Alice either. She stood grimly in the dining room, in her short-sleeved black dress, feeling like an overlooked decoration.

Eventually, one of the lawyers came and told her they were going to have a chat. She wondered if he was their leader. He was certainly the largest, his coal-gray suit straining to contain his girth, and he had an enormous gray mustache that drooped past the corners of his mouth, the ends stained nicotine-yellow. When he came to fetch her, he affected a jolly, avuncular manner that made it clear it had been years since he'd dealt with anyone under the age of thirty.

She followed him up to her father's study, and seethed quietly as he seated himself behind the desk in her father's chair. It creaked alarmingly beneath his bulk. Alice stood in front of the desk, as she had so many times before, and fought the illusion that her father had somehow *transformed* into this smoke-stinking whale of a man.

"So, my girl," he said, "you have my sincerest condolences. Terrible business. A terrible business. You understand what's happened, don't you?"

I'm twelve, Alice thought, *not five*. She made herself nod. "I understand."

"My name is Mr. Pallworthy. I'm here to look after things on behalf of your father's business partners, that sort of thing."

Alice, feeling that a response was called for, nodded again.

"I don't imagine you know very much about your father's business"—his deep-set eyes flicked to her, as though to confirm this—"but that's fine. We'll take care of everything, don't you worry." He reached under the desk and brought up a heavy briefcase, from which he extracted a thick sheaf of paper. "Now, your father's primary interests had suffered, unfortunately, from our current market conditions—"

He went on, his tone changing from the jolly talking-to-children voice to a going-through-the-motions drone. Alice could follow what he was reading, possibly better than Mr. Pallworthy himself could—his voice faltered when he came to some of the more arcane financial terms—but the gist was clear from the outset. There was nothing left, nothing at all, and it was only by the extreme generosity of the creditors represented by Mr. Pallworthy that Alice would be allowed to leave the building with the clothes on her back.

Under other circumstances, she would have taken some pleasure in going through the paperwork herself to figure out how he was cheating her—he was, of course, cheating her, that was what lawyers were *for*—but at that moment she couldn't bring herself to care. When he'd wound down, he asked her if she had any questions.

"What is to happen to me?" she said.

"Eh?" Mr. Pallworthy frowned, his mustache bouncing. "What do you mean?"

"I can't stay here, I assume," Alice said.

"No, of course not," the lawyer said. "The house will be sold at auction, the arrangements are already being made." He seemed to remember he was speaking to a child, and put on his jolly-old-boy face again while he rummaged through the stack of papers. "Arrangements have been made for you too, of course. You're to stay with family, I believe. One moment." He found the paper he was looking for and peered at it. "Ah, yes. I see you'll be moving in with your uncle Jerry."

Alice blinked. "I haven't got an uncle Jerry."

"Of course you do." Mr. Pallworthy tapped the paper. "It says so right here."

"But—" She bit back her protest. It was no good to say that her father had had only one brother, and that his name had been Arnold and he'd died in the War before Alice had been born. Her mother's family she'd never known at all. Mr. Pallworthy wouldn't particularly care, and he would believe his piece of paper. "I see. Uncle Jerry."

"He lives in Pittsburgh, it says. Or near Pittsburgh. Arrangements are being made to get you there." He seemed to like the phrase. "Taking the train all the way to Pennsylvania, all by yourself! Won't that be an adventure."

"I suppose," Alice answered politely.

"Did you have any other questions?"

Alice just shook her head. Something about her expression must have finally registered with him, and the lawyer's face clouded as he dredged his memory for something to reassure grieving children. "Chin up, you know. I'm sure things seem awful, but . . ." He faltered, then brightened up. "Just remember, it's all part of God's plan!"

Courtesy of the extreme restraint of the creditors represented by Mr. Pallworthy, Alice was allowed to pack two trunks full of her clothes, books, and a few odds and ends, after one of the lawyers had looked them over to make sure there was nothing too expensive among them. She tucked the threadbare rabbits deep inside the trunk, underneath her nightshirts. She knew it was childish, but it made her feel better; and anyway, she couldn't bear the thought of leaving them for Mr. Pallworthy to toss in the trash. The picture of her grandmother stayed—it had been taken by someone famous, apparently, and would have to be auctioned—so Alice stared at her for a few moments in silent farewell before letting a lawyer escort her to the door.

A footman in a big black Ford delivered her to Penn Station, and handed her an envelope containing a one-way, coach-class ticket to Pittsburgh, a local ticket to a station called North Landing, and two ten-dollar bills. She had to break one of these almost immediately, at the station ticket window, in order make change to tip the porters who dragged her trunks down to the side of the track.

The long ride on the train barely registered. She spent it with her chin in her hands, staring blindly out the window as endless farms and pastures rolled past and the sun crossed overhead and sank behind the western horizon. The other passengers in her compartment, as though by common agreement, struck up a lively conversation and completely ignored the gloomy girl in the mourning dress.

Alice's father had taught her that when she had problems, she ought to list them carefully, one by one, and see what could be done about them. She did this now, using an imaginary pencil and the endless Pennsylvania farmland as a sketchpad.

The first problem was, Alice felt like she was living in a dream. Ever since the night in the kitchen, when she'd watched her father arguing with a fairy, the world had acquired a dangerously *thin* quality, as though it were only as substantial as a soap bubble.

The second problem was, Alice hadn't cried when she'd read the newspaper. She hadn't cried when the telegrams had arrived, or all the way through the funeral. She hadn't cried when Miss Juniper hugged her good-bye, though the tutor's eyes had been brimful of tears. She certainly hadn't cried while the flocks of vultures picked through the house. She kept expecting to, but she hadn't.

She supposed this was because of the third problem, which was that she didn't really believe it had happened. In a sane, normal world, when the *Times* reported that a ship had gone down, it had almost certainly gone down. The *Times* had ways of checking on these things. Sane, normal Alice would have accepted it as fact, and cried (quietly, alone, and in the dead of night, but cried nonetheless) and then squared her shoulders and tried to deal with whatever life offered her next, because that was the kind of girl she was.

But something had gone wrong. If fairies were real, then the world was not sane and normal anymore. If *magic* was real, then what she read in the *Times* didn't have to be true. Her father might not be drowned after all. He could be—she cast through her limited repertoire of fantastic fiction—a castaway, on an enchanted island. Or spirited away to a crystal palace to be entertained by an elfin court. Or *anything*. That was the point. If fairies were real, then anything could happen.

Alice realized, as the sun was setting, that she would never be able to leave things where they were. It was as though she had hold of a loose thread at the end of a sweater. She had to give it a tug, and find out if the whole garment unraveled, and if so, what was underneath.

The last problem, in this case, was that she had no idea what to do next. But that was all right. The difficult part was usually deciding where you were headed. After that, in Alice's experience, getting there was just a matter of hard work.

Not that I have very much choice where I'm headed, Alice thought, *for the moment.* She leaned back in her seat, eyes closed, and listened to the rails clicking endlessly past.

The two-car local pulled into North Landing station, which turned out to be little more than a wooden platform, a sign, and a gravel lot. A sullen attendant lugged Alice's trunks off the train, frowned at the nickel she gave him, and climbed back aboard the train without a word.

It was long after dark, and without the city lights to interfere, the sky was a riot of stars. Alice, who had never spent more than a fortnight outside the confines of New York City, looked up at them and felt very small and very alone. To the south, across the river, the city of Pittsburgh proper gave off a muted red-and-yellow glow, but to the north there was nothing but darkness.

She was just feeling the chill and wondering what she would do if no one arrived to meet her when she heard the rattle of an engine and the crunch of tires on gravel. A pair of headlamps blazed, and then an ancient car—a Model T that looked like it was older than Alice—circled around the lot and pulled to a stop in front of the platform. The driver got out, leaving the engine idling, and came up the short steps to meet her.

He was a huge man, tall and muscular, dressed in a leather motoring jacket. His beard, sideburns, mustache, and hair all merged into a wiry black mane that completely surrounded his head and hid his face, apart from a small patch around dark, sunken eyes and a protruding, scabby knob of a nose. If this was "Uncle Jerry," Alice decided, he was certainly not any relation of her father's.

"You'll be Miss Creighton," the man said. His voice rumbled deeper than the car's engine, and Alice half expected the same coal-black smoke to leak from his mouth.

She drew herself up and nodded. He stared at her for a moment, and managed to give the strong impression that he didn't like what he saw.

"Right," he said eventually. "Get in."

"You—" Alice began, then reconsidered and spoke more politely. "Have you been sent to bring me to my uncle?"

For some reason this made the huge man smile, flashing discolored teeth through the bristling hedge of beard and mustache. "That's right."

If she'd hoped for more information than that, she

was disappointed. Alice stepped down from the platform toward the car, and the big man followed closely behind. Halfway there, she stopped and looked back at her two trunks, which were now sitting unattended on the platform's edge.

The man halted, followed her gaze, then looked down at her. Something in his hairy face twitched, but he turned around with exaggerated care and climbed back up to the platform. He gathered the handles to her trunks in one hand—a hand, Alice couldn't help but notice, that was broad enough to wrap around a coconut—and lifted them without even a hint of effort. She stepped aside as he brushed past her and affixed her things to the car's luggage rack.

"Thank you," Alice said, and received only a grunt in return. "Can I ask your name?"

"You can call me Mr. Black," the big man said. "Now get in. Your *uncle* wants to see you."

CHAPTER THREE
GERYON

Mr. Black said nothing further, but anything he might have had to say would have been lost anyway in the putter of the Ford's engine and the rush of the wind. He drove the old car at a pace that struck Alice as distinctly unsafe, especially on the unpaved road, roaring down the straightaways and sending up sprays of gravel and dirt on the corners. She gripped the door handle so hard, her knuckles went white, although she was well aware that if Mr. Black lost control and went careening off the road, holding on wouldn't make the slightest bit of difference.

The winding road was hemmed in on either side by

trees, only occasionally opening out to reveal the distant glow of house lights. Each building was set well back from the road on considerable grounds, and separated by a fair distance from its neighbors.

She caught a blurred glimpse of a pair of mammoth stone beasts, lounging on tall plinths, as Mr. Black wrenched the car through a nearly right-angle turn and onto a long gravel drive, not slowing until the bulk of a building came into sight. Then, mercifully, he let the car coast to a halt, leaving the engine pinging softly and Alice's heart hammering like a tom-tom. It took an effort to pry herself from the handle, and her fingers went tingly as blood flowed back into them.

"The Library," Mr. Black announced, as though that was supposed to explain something. Alice heard gravel crunch, and someone opened the door on her side. She got out, legs as wobbly as a newborn fawn. Mr. Black got out as well and started crunching away toward the building.

"Come on," he said, when Alice took a moment too long to follow. "Emma, take her things."

A girl of about Alice's age in a plain brown dress, standing by the car door, bobbed her head obediently. Alice glanced back at the heavy trunks and gave her a doubtful look, but she presumed that Mr. Black knew his business.

Several deep breaths, cool and pine-scented, had gone a long way toward calming her, and she looked up at the building Mr. Black had called "The Library." It was mostly dark, a black blotch against the starlit sky, but she got the sense of a long, multi-story structure. Directly in front of her, a pair of massive wooden doors stood half-open, set into a stone façade that wouldn't have looked out of place on a medieval church. Tall, multi-paned windows flanked the doors, and a pair of gaslights at head height provided a flickering illumination.

Once she'd regained control of her legs, Alice climbed the stone steps up to the entrance, and found herself in a long hall. A faded red carpet ran into the middle distance, and on either hand the walls were adorned with odd statuary, interspersed with more gaslights.

At the end of the hall, a staircase led up to a second floor, and an old man was picking his way down it. His hair was pure white, long gone from the crown of his head but sticking up in wild tufts around his ears and along the back of skull. His chin was clean-shaven, but he sported massive gray side whiskers, of the sort that had gone out of fashion sometime around the end of the Civil War. His face was wrinkled and jowly, with deep-set eyes with lines around them that might have come from

smiles or just from a lifetime of squinting. He wore dark trousers and a gray waistcoat over a white shirt, whose sleeves were black with splotchy stains.

"I thought I heard that awful machine screeching," the old man said. "You'll be Miss Creighton. Any problems, Mr. Black?"

"No problems, sir," Mr. Black rumbled.

"Good, good." The old man reached the bottom of the steps. "Well, come on, girl. Let's have a look at you."

Alice walked the length of the hall. She would have liked to examine the statues more closely—they were marble, sitting on oaken stands, and each one seemed to depict a fantastic beast of some sort—but the old man was tapping the banister impatiently. Alice curtsied as best she could—it had never been her strong suit—and met his level glare.

"Are you my uncle?" she said. She couldn't see any resemblance herself.

"Not precisely," he said. "It's a bit more complicated than that. But all you need to understand is that we're family, and that you're welcome here. My name is Geryon."

"Alice," said Alice, trying to remember her manners. "It's very kind of you to take me in."

"Think nothing of it." Geryon gestured, one stained sleeve flapping. "After I heard what happened to your father, it was the least I could do."

"Did you know my father?"

"Not well, I'm afraid. But I've always kept track of him, and you, with a certain—affection. Please think of The Library as your home for as long as you like."

Alice looked around. "The Library?"

Geryon chuckled. "The estate is called The Library. A reference to my own peculiar habits, of course. I'm a great collector of books. Do you like books, Alice?"

"Very much," Alice admitted.

"I'm sure we shall get along, then. Though I must warn you, I'm a bit . . . particular about my books. You should never go into the library building on your own. For your own safety, you understand?" Before Alice could reply— she'd never found anything more dangerous in a library than a paper cut—Geryon slapped the banister with a sound like a gunshot. "But here I am keeping you talking in the hall when you must be exhausted. Let's get you squared away. Emma!"

Alice turned to see the girl from outside manhandling her luggage through the doorway, awkwardly trying to hold open the heavy doors with one foot while wrapping both arms around a trunk. At Geryon's call, she dropped it with a *thump* and straightened up.

"Yes, sir?"

"Show Alice to her room, would you? Mr. Black can bring her bags."

Mr. Black's lip twitched, and he shot a glare at Alice, but he said nothing.

Emma hurried over to Alice, lowering her head respectfully. "Of course, sir," she said. "Follow me, miss."

Emma started up the stairs, setting a rapid pace, and Alice had to scurry to keep up through a bewildering maze of corridors, T-junctions, and wood-paneled passages. Most of the house was dark, with only one gaslight out of three or four burning, but Emma seemed to have no trouble. Eventually they found another staircase, steeper and uncarpeted. At the top was a short corridor with a line of closely spaced doors, the first of which was open.

"This is your room," Emma said, stepping aside. She kept her eyes on the floor.

It was a servant's room, Alice thought, with space for a bed and a dresser but very little else. A massive leaded-glass window occupied much of the far wall, and a cheerless gray rug covered the floor.

"Toilets are down the stairs. Left, then right, then left

again," Emma went on, in a singsong tone, as though reciting something she'd memorized. "Breakfast is at seven in the dining hall, lunch at noon, dinner at six." She went silent, as though she'd run out of things to say, like a record player reaching the end of its groove.

"Emma," Alice said. "That's your name, right?"

"Yes, miss."

"Alice is fine."

"Yes, miss."

"I mean," Alice said carefully, "you can call me Alice. Not 'miss.'"

"I..." The girl paused, then gave a little bob of the head, automatic as a well-oiled mechanism. "As you say, miss."

Another awkward silence.

Alice cleared her throat. "Did you want something else?" she said, trying to be polite.

Emma blinked, placidly. "No, miss."

Alice looked at her more carefully. She was skinny, taller than Alice, but she hunched her shoulders and kept her head low. Her plain face was scattered with freckles, and her mouse-brown hair was tied in a tail at the back of her neck. Her cast-down eyes gave Alice the overpowering urge to check and see if her shoelaces were untied or her dress unbuttoned.

"I mean," Alice said, abandoning politeness in favor of making herself understood, "why are you still standing there?"

This question seemed to perplex Emma. Her forehead wrinkled, and after a moment she said, "Nobody told me where to go next, miss."

"Could you fetch some things for me?"

"Yes, miss."

Again, the silence, as though the conversation had fallen into a pothole.

"I'll need some light," Alice said carefully. There was a gas lamp in the hall, but it only provided a sliver of illumination through the doorway. "Please bring me a lamp, and some matches."

"Right away, miss."

Emma sprang into motion, animated by the words as if by a magic spell. She curtsied politely and went out, only to be replaced in the doorway by a scowling Mr. Black. He dropped Alice's trunks to the floor a bit harder than she thought was necessary, inclining his head the tiniest fraction in acknowledgment.

"The girl tell you about meals and such?" he said, in his deep, rumbling voice.

"She did." Alice hesitated. "Has my uncle said anything about what I'm supposed to *do* here?"

"Not to me." The big man smiled, his teeth a patchwork of gray and brown. "I'm sure he'll send for you when he wants you. Meantime, you can ask the girl if you need anything. And you remember what the master said about the library?"

"That it could be dangerous?"

"Right. That goes for the basement as well, 'cause if I catch you down there, then I'll stripe your hide. Got it?"

Alice nodded. Mr. Black grunted, looked around the room for a moment, then turned away and shut the door behind him. His heavy footsteps made the floorboards in the corridor pop and groan.

Alice felt, suddenly, very tired indeed. She decided that unpacking could wait until morning, and sat down on the bed. The mattress was stiff, and the sheet was splotchy and fraying at the edges. She undid her laces with a sigh and kicked her shoes across the room, then swung her legs onto the bed and put her head on the lumpy pillow without bothering to undress. Only the faintest light came from the gaslight in the hall through the crack under the door, and the ceiling was invisible in the gloom. Alice closed her eyes and pretended she was in a cave, some hermitage at the top of a mountain a thousand miles from anything.

CHAPTER FOUR
THE EMPTY HOUSE

W HEN SHE OPENED HER eyes again, daylight was filtering in through the grimy window. The fading remnants of a dream chased themselves around her skull for a moment, the fairy laughing at her and gibbering incomprehensibly. Then it was gone, and she was staring at the spiderweb of cracks across the ancient plaster ceiling.

After a drawn-out expedition to find the toilet that involved at least three wrong turns, Alice, feeling sticky and disheveled, went back to her room and stripped off her mourning dress. She rummaged through her trunks and changed into a gray blouse and a long skirt, both creased and rumpled from their bumpy journey. Emma had left an oil lamp and a box of matches, and Alice set it up on the dresser in front of the cloudy mirror. She dug a brush out of her things and did the best she could with her hair, though it really needed a proper wash. At the bottom of her trunk, she found the pair of ancient rabbits, and after a brief internal debate she pulled them out and sat them on the windowsill, where they could keep watch on the door.

They must have a bath here somewhere, she thought. At least the toilets proved they had running water. This far from New York, she wouldn't have been surprised to find outhouses and hand-drawn wells.

There was no clock in her room, but she was fairly sure it was well after seven by the time she made her way downstairs. The long train ride with only a packet of crackers from the station store had left her with a healthy appetite, and she hoped there was something left of breakfast. Finding the dining room turned out to be easier than locating the facilities, and as she pushed open a pair of big swinging doors, the rich smells of bacon and eggs wafted out to greet her.

The dining room was built on the same gargantuan scale as the rest of the house. The long wooden table could have seated at least sixty, flanked by threadbare, rickety-looking upholstered chairs. It was entirely bare except at one end, where a single chair had been pulled back, and three large, covered platters leaked delicious-smelling steam. Apart from Alice, the huge hall was empty.

Has everyone else eaten and gone, then? Alice hadn't thought she was *that* late. She sidled around the table—it was perfectly clean, and so gleaming with polish that she could see a cloudy reflection of her face in the surface—and made her way to the chair in front of the platters. In addition to the food, there was a pitcher of water and another of orange juice, so cold that drops of water beaded on the sides.

"Hello?" Alice said. "Is this for me? Anybody?"

The smell of the food was overwhelming. Alice put a hand on the back of the chair and made a last effort to be sure she wasn't somehow breaking the rules.

"If I'm not supposed to eat this," she said loudly, "someone please tell me."

There was no answer. Several more doors led off from the dining hall, including a big one that she guessed went to the kitchens, but there was no sound of movement or conversation from any of them. Still feeling a bit like Goldilocks trespassing in the bears' house, but unable to ignore the rumbles from her stomach any longer, Alice took a seat and lifted the covers.

She revealed a breakfast that wouldn't have been out of place at the Ritz. In addition to the bacon, there were thick slices of ham, swimming in juice, and big plates of hashed potatoes, toast, and scrambled eggs with bits of green stuff she couldn't identify. Alice loaded her plate with a bit of everything, then looked up instinctively for her father, expecting one of his gentle admonishments. *He always said that no one likes a pig at mealtimes.*

The room was still empty, of course. Alice's throat went tight, and she felt like something was rattling around loose in her chest. She wanted to cry, to let the feeling out, but the tears wouldn't come. After a moment she attacked the ham with knife and fork, making a bit of a mess of it and daring anyone to complain.

When she'd eaten her fill, and truth be told a little extra, she pushed her chair back from the table and got to her feet. The big house was still as quiet as a graveyard, but she couldn't escape the feeling that *something* was watching her, and so she spoke aloud again.

"Should I take the dishes in myself?"

It was something she'd learned to do in the past few years. After her father had had to let the maids go, he'd told her it was too hard on poor Mrs. Voule to expect her to cook *and* clean, so they'd done the washing together,

her father with his shirtsleeves rolled up past his elbows.

There was plenty of food left, though, and she didn't think she ought to just throw it all away. Alice went to the kitchen door and put her hand against it, pushing it inward just a crack.

"Hello?" she said, more quietly. "What should I do with the rest of this?"

When there was no answer, she opened the door all the way. The kitchen made the one in her father's house look tiny. There was a long central counter, spotlessly clean, and a row of shelves with plates, bowls, dishes, and tureens all stacked in regimented ranks. Against the other wall was a bank of stoves and ovens that looked big enough to handle a cow all at once. They were clean too, every burner scraped free of grime and even the metal frames polished to a dull sheen. Another door, with a heavy dead bolt, let onto the backyard, and there was corridor Alice guessed led to a pantry.

And it was all *empty*. The huge kitchen could have housed a dozen cooks comfortably, but there was not so much as a pot-boy in sight, and no sign that anyone had been there. Alice let the door swing back into place and turned around, shaking her head.

The platters were gone. Her plate was gone, and the

pitchers. Someone had wiped up the table where she'd let a bit of the ham juice drip. The whole thing gleamed, polished and perfect, as if it had never been used at all.

All right, Alice thought. She felt a fluttery, nervous feeling in the pit of her stomach, and that in turn made her feel irritated. *Something very strange is going on here.* She squared her shoulders and went to find out what.

Over the next several days, Alice explored the mansion from top to bottom, except for the parts that were behind locked doors. The dining room and kitchens, she discovered, were typical. The house was enormous, scrupulously clean, and *empty.*

There were rows of guest rooms on the third floor, all dusted and turned out as though visitors were expected at any moment. The corridor near her own room had quarters for an army of servants, none of which gave any sign of being lived in. Drawing rooms, sewing rooms, laundry rooms, rooms full of armchairs and small rickety tables of no obvious purpose, all as neat and uninhabited as an after-hours movie set.

Geryon lived in a suite of his own on the ground floor, and came out only rarely. Periodic awful stinks emerged from under his door, sometimes sick-sweet like something rotten, sometimes a vicious, bitter vapor that stung Alice's eyes and made her nose run. When the old man did show himself, it was usually to speak to Mr. Black, and he spared only a few, curt words for Alice.

Mr. Black's domain was the basement, which was reached via a passage from the kitchen. He spent nearly all his time down there, where he had something to do with maintaining the house's gas and heating. More than that, Alice didn't know, because he refused to answer any of her questions. If Geryon was curt, the huge man was downright rude, glowering at Alice whenever he spotted her as though she'd done something to offend him. Of course, his face seemed made for glowering, with its shaggy rough of hair and huge bushy eyebrows.

Emma, by contrast, seemed to have no secrets, but Alice found her the hardest to understand. All her attempts to engage the girl in conversation had gone the way of their talk the day she'd arrived, tailing off quickly into uncomfortable silence. At first Alice had thought Emma was putting her on. After a few days, she dismissed the idea, and decided the girl was just simple, but that didn't quite fit either.

She would do what she was asked, quickly and without hesitating, and was capable of executing quite complicated tasks flawlessly. She could read and write—Alice watched her go through a stack of newspapers for Mr. Black, page by page, noting down some detail from each into a little notebook. And she was unfailingly polite, even when Mr. Black fumed and glowered.

But she seemed, for lack of a better word, *empty*, like the house itself. A friend of Alice's father had described someone by saying: "The lights are on, but no one's home." In that case, he'd merely meant the poor man had gone mad, but it seemed to Alice that this was more literally true as a description of Emma. When no one gave her anything to do, she would simply do nothing, standing in the front hall or sitting alone in her room for *hours* without any sign of discomfort. She was more like a mechanism than a person, Alice thought, and wondered if there was a secret catch at the back of her head that would open up her skull and reveal whirring gears and pistons.

Emma was a servant, in that she did what Geryon or Mr. Black—or Alice, for that matter—told her to do, but she didn't do what Alice thought of as servants' duties. As far as Alice could tell, *no one* did, and yet things did get done, in a clandestine way that started out creepy and ended up as plain infuriating. There were no cooks in the kitchens, but meals were laid out on the table when she arrived and whisked away when her back was turned. When she returned to her room in the evening, the linen had been laundered and the bed made. The floors were always mopped, the windows scrubbed, the gaslights cleaned and lit and the lintels dusted. But it all happened out of sight, when she wasn't looking, and no matter how fast she raced from one room to the next or how suddenly she turned around, she could never catch any of the mysterious cleaners at work.

It felt like an enormous practical joke, or possibly a determined effort on the part of whoever-it-was to drive Alice insane. The suspiciously mindful silence around every corner made her want to run through the house screaming, fling her dishes against the wall, or break some windows, just to see what would happen. She didn't, of course, because her father hadn't brought her up as the sort of girl who broke windows, and also because she was gloomily sure they would only be made whole while she wasn't watching.

By the fourth day, she felt like she would soon go mad even without the mysterious servants. There was nothing she was supposed to be *doing,* and no one to talk to, except for Emma, and that was worse than talking to herself. She'd have given anything to have Miss Juniper assign her some algebra, or a French passage to translate, if only so she could look forward to being done with it.

When Emma turned up at her door just after lunch, therefore, Alice was glad to follow. Her sense of relief even survived the sight of Mr. Black, who was waiting for them in the front hall and regarded Alice as though she were something he'd had to scrape off the bottom of his shoe.

"Mr. Wurms asked for help in the library," he rumbled. "He's got a bit of a disaster that needs sorting out. The two of you go and do whatever he needs."

Alice's ears pricked up. The one thing she *hadn't* found in her explorations of The Library was, in fact, a library. She'd been assuming it was locked away somewhere, probably in Geryon's private suite, and she'd been hoping to catch him long enough to ask if she might visit. *At least then I could find something to read.*

Still, against her own best interests, she couldn't help raising an objection. "Geryon said I wasn't supposed to visit the library."

Mr. Black scowled. "He said you're not supposed to go in there *unaccompanied.* But you'll have Emma with you, so that's all right. Emma, make sure to tell Alice the rules and show her how not to get lost."

"Yes, Mr. Black."

Alice bit back a further argument. She wasn't honestly sure Emma counted as a proper escort, given that the girl would do whatever Alice asked her to. But those had, technically, been Geryon's words, and if it was good enough for Mr. Black, Alice thought she could accept.

Besides, Geryon had a library that was so big, you could get *lost* in it! *This*, Alice thought, *I have to see*.

CHAPTER FIVE
THE LIBRARY'S LIBRARY

To Alice's surprise, Emma led her, not to Gery-on's suite, but out the kitchen door and down a gravel path into the backyard. It was a gray, overcast day, not quite raining but thick with the threat of it, and the air smelled clingy and damp. The wind cut through Alice's shirt and raised goose bumps on her skin.

Alice hadn't paid much attention to the grounds thus far. For all that it was nearing summer, there hadn't been a proper sunny day since she'd arrived, and the air was still cold enough that she had to wrap up to go outside. From the upstairs windows, she'd gotten the impression of a vaguely rectangular lawn surrounded on all sides by dense, leafy forest, and she hadn't bothered to investigate further. She wasn't much for the outdoors at the best of times, and whenever her father had taken her on some rural outing, she'd always been secretly eager to return to the well-organized life of the city.

Now she found that her impression had been mostly correct, but for one important detail. There was another building on the other side of the lawn, its facade barely protruding from the thick surrounding greenery, its sides disappearing back into the forest so that it was difficult to get a proper sense of its size.

The gravel path led right up to its unornamented stone face, in which was set a single door of ancient, greening bronze. There were no windows that Alice could see, and no embellishments or decorations at all.

"This is the library?" Alice said.

"Yes," Emma said, as always without elaborating further.

It looks more like a fortress, Alice thought. *Or else some kind of bank vault.* Emma grabbed the heavy bronze ring attached to the door and pulled, grunting with effort, and the door swung slowly open with an anguished scream of corroded metal.

Inside was a little anteroom, dark except for the dim trickle of sunlight through the doorway. A set of heavy

hurricane lamps hung from pegs in one wall, beside another bronze door.

"You must use a lamp when you're inside, never a candle," Emma said. Alice was startled to hear her speak unbidden, until she remembered that Mr. Black had told her to explain the rules. "And you must always close the outer door before you open the inner."

"Got it," Alice said.

Emma lit one of the lanterns, dropping the match into a bucket of water apparently provided for the purpose. The flame flickered weakly inside the double layer of glass, like a caged spirit. She handed the lamp to Alice and lit another for herself, then pushed the outer door closed. It swung slowly, giving another grinding shriek of protest, and closed with a forbidding *boom*. Darkness closed in at once, broken only by the faint flicker of light from the lanterns.

Emma opened the inner door and raised the lamp over her head, revealing a wooden-floored space flanked by enormous bookshelves. Stretching back from the entrance—

Alice stifled a gasp. There were *eyes*, a forest of eyes, from the floor to up above her head. Every one of them glowed a brilliant yellow in the lantern light, and every one was focused on the two of them.

Emma went through, paying no mind whatsoever. After a moment, the closest pair of eyes came forward to greet her, sauntering into the circle of lamplight in the form of a small gray-and-white cat. Alice let out her breath.

"Cats," she said to herself. They'd had a cat, back in New York, a brown-and-white mouser that kept mostly to the storerooms. Alice had always left her alone, and she had returned the favor.

Emma bent down on one knee and held out her free hand. The little cat sniffed it for a moment, then permitted itself to be scratched behind the ears.

"I like cats," Emma said. There was a note in her voice that Alice hadn't heard before, something that, if she hadn't known better, she might have called human feeling.

The gray-and-white cat, having concluded that Emma had not brought it anything to eat, padded over to Alice. It met her gaze with unblinking eyes, yawned for a long moment, then wandered off. As though this were a signal, eyes disappeared from the bookcases all around them, and there was the faint susurrus of two dozen cats returning to their interrupted business.

Now that she'd recovered from her surprise and her eyes had adjusted to the semi-darkness, Alice got a better sense of the space around her. The library seemed to be a single vast room, cluttered with bookcases that rose almost to the low stone ceiling. They were arranged in rough rows, but irregularly, with gaps at random intervals. Each shelf was stacked high with books, some so heavily that they were bowing in the center.

The books themselves were of every possible description, from ancient leather-bound tomes to cheap cardboard-covered novels. The majority looked like they dated from the previous century or even earlier. Most of the titles were in foreign languages Alice didn't understand, and some were even in letters she didn't recognize.

There was no organization whatsoever that she could see, and a dense layer of dust covered everything. The air was absolutely still, and on the nearer shelves she could see where the cats had left trails of neat, feline footprints through the grime.

It's so . . . big. Alice had been to the Carnegie Library in the city, which was much larger, but that had been bustling with busy people. This place had the same dead, silent feeling as the house. It felt less like a library than a tomb, or a dragon's hoard. What would drive someone to collect so many books and stash them *here*, miles from anywhere, where they could do no good for anyone?

As they started to walk, the sliding shadows gave the unsettling impression that the bookcases were *shifting* behind them. It was comforting to spy a distant glow, vanishing and reappearing, like the pilot light of a distant ship on a stormy night. Alice kept looking over her shoulder at their dusty footprints disappearing into the darkness behind them.

"Mr. Wurms is working there." Emma pointed to the glow.

"I haven't seen him in the house," Alice said. "Does he live in here?"

"Yes," Emma said. Whatever spirit had briefly animated her was gone, and she was back to answering in monosyllables. They walked on in silence for a few moments.

"What do I do," Alice said after a while, "if I get lost?" It was easy to imagine in this huge, dark place.

"Look at the ceiling," Emma said.

She raised the lantern as she spoke, so Alice could see the stones that made up the roof. Something glittered among the irregularly shaped blocks—a chunk of obsidian, roughly triangular and about the size of her fist.

"The narrow end always points toward the front door," Emma explained tonelessly. "You should always be able to find your way back"

Unless your lantern goes out, Alice thought. But she kept that to herself.

They seemed to have walked for miles by the time Mr. Wurms' table came into view. It was set amid the bookcases, and volumes were piled up around his lamp. Beside them, in a rickety-looking chair, was a bespectacled man in a black suit.

He was middle-aged, Alice guessed, but he *seemed* old. His hair was still deep brown, but it had receded enough to leave him with a broad crown of shiny forehead. His face was thin and sallow, with sunken cheeks, and his hands had long, thin fingers with thick knots at the joints. He dressed in shabby black, like a clerk or an undertaker, but he sat so still that dust had settled all over him, like snow, and turned him a dirty gray. When he stirred at the sound of Alice's footsteps, it puffed up and rolled off him in waves.

"Ah," he said. His voice was as dry as a corpse. "Emma. And you must be Ms. Creighton, though I don't believe we've met."

Alice nodded politely. "Yes, sir."

"My name is Wurms." He had a slight German accent that turned it into *Vurms.* "Otto Wurms. It's a pleasure."

His tongue, shockingly soft and pink, rasped across his dry, cracked lips. The thick glass of his spectacles turned his eyes into huge, distorted pools, but she could nonetheless feel something unpleasant in his gaze. It felt . . . *hungry,* somehow. When he smiled, she could see his black, rotten teeth.

Alice decided she did not like Mr. Wurms.

She cleared her throat. "Mr. Black said you needed some help?"

"Yes." He turned his gaze away from her with some reluctance and pointed off into the shelves. "There's been another collapse. The rot gets into the shelves, you know. Mr. Black has promised me he'll see about getting another set, but in the meantime I need you to bring all the books back here. We can't have them lying on the floor, can we?"

"No," Emma said, apparently unable to tell if a question was rhetorical.

"It's quite a load," Mr. Wurms said. "You'd do best to fetch the trolley."

With that he turned away, back to his reading, as though the two girls were an electric light he'd switched off. Alice wanted to say something, just to make him turn around again, but she thought better of it.

She turned to Emma. "Come on. We'd better get to work."

The trolley was an ancient, squeaky-wheeled monstrosity that required both of them tugging to steer. It seemed almost sacrilegious to push the rattling, screeching thing through the deadly quiet of the library, and Alice fancied their progress was preceded by a vanguard of fleeing cats. Following Mr. Wurms' directions, they found a place where an ancient set of shelves had given way under the weight of books, spilling fragments of rotten wood and hundreds of volumes across the stone floor.

When she saw it, Alice sighed. "This is going to take all afternoon."

Emma didn't express an opinion one way or another, just set to work picking up the fallen books and stacking them in piles on the floor. Alice hesitated for a moment, distracted. She felt a peculiar itch between her shoulder blades, an odd sensation of being *watched*. Something moved, at the corner of her eye, but when she turned to look it was only a thin gray cat, slinking through a gap between the shelves.

"There's no percentage in hanging about," she said aloud. It had been something her father had told her, whenever he'd needed to get her moving; she'd said it automatically, but the memories it called up made her chest clench tight. She squeezed her eyes shut for a moment, then forced herself to take a deep breath. *Maybe if we finish early, I can ask Mr. Wurms if it's all right to take something back to read.* "All right. Try and pick out the biggest ones first, we'll need to put them on the bottom."

Emma followed Alice's instructions dutifully, and once she'd gotten started, she worked tirelessly. The biggest books were a set of huge, linen-bound folios, yellowed and musty with age, which the two girls extracted and laid on the trolley like foundation stones to support the rest of the pile. It was heavier work than Alice had expected, and after an hour her back was aching. Her blouse was damp from the exertion, and the dust mixed with sweat to form a gray paste that covered her skin like the marks of some horrible plague.

And someone was still watching her. She was certain of it, in the pit of her stomach, but no matter how fast she turned around, she could never catch a glimpse of the observer. She wondered if it could be Mr. Wurms, secretly checking on their progress.

Probably, she thought, *it's just the cats.*

It was difficult to keep track of time in the windowless library, but she thought it was getting on toward evening by the time they'd loaded the trolley with the last few springy pamphlets. Alice's stomach was reminding her it was nearly dinnertime, in any case, and she was more than ready to get out of the old library and find a basin to wash off the clinging, all-pervading dust. *For a library one mustn't go into, this has been a real disappointment. There must be some interesting books in here, surely, but with nothing organized, they would be impossible to find. And there's certainly nothing* dangerous, *unless Geryon was worried about the shelves collapsing on me.*

There remained the task of piloting the trolley back to where Mr. Wurms was waiting, which turned out to be no simple endeavor. The pile of books was taller than Alice's head, so if she pushed from the back she couldn't see where she was going, much less attempt to steer, and the thing weighed so much, it took ages to shove into motion and an equally long time to stop. Emma, at the front, walked in a sort of rolling crouch to drag the thing along and keep it pointed in the right direction, with Alice alternately shoving against the unyielding weight and hauling backward when they were about to run into something.

Between them, Alice imagined they made quite an amusing spectacle, and she was privately glad there was no one to see them but the cats. It was therefore with some surprise that she heard, through the squeaking rattle of the metal beast, the definite sound of a snicker.

At first she thought she'd imagined it. It had been a long day, and she was hungry and getting cross. But it came again as they were rounding a corner, which entailed both girls hauling sideways on the trolley like cowboys wrestling an unruly stallion, and this time the sound was absolutely unmistakable. Alice thought briefly of the cats, and her feeling of being watched. But—though she was not an expert on cats—she was fairly certain that they did not, as a rule, snicker. She waited a few heart-beats, until they'd gotten the trolley straightened out, and then, fast as she could, looked over her shoulder.

There *was* a cat, a gray one, standing on a low shelf. It sat quite still, staring directly at Alice and looking extremely pleased with itself.

Something went *thump* up ahead. Alice spun around and pulled back on the trolley as hard as she could. Once she'd gotten it stopped, she hurried around it, and found Emma on the floor and doing her best to keep from being run over.

"Sorry!" Alice said, automatically, putting out a hand to help her up. "Are you all right?"

"I am," Emma said. She got to her feet and took hold of the front of the trolley again, without even dusting herself off.

Alice looked over her shoulder. The cat, to her surprise, was still there. Its tail flicked back and forth, raising little puffs of dust.

The cat did not *snicker at me*, Alice thought. *I'm losing my mind.*

But, underneath that, the ever-present refrain: *If my father can talk to a fairy over our kitchen table, who knows what a cat can do?*

"Emma," Alice said, without taking her eyes off the feline. "Can you take the trolley the rest of the way to Mr. Wurms?"

"I can," Emma said. A moment passed, and she remained still, waiting for Alice to resume her place at the back. Alice sighed.

"Emma, take the cart to Mr. Wurms. Tell him I will be along shortly."

Emma nodded and started pulling. Alice felt guilty for a moment for making her haul the heavy load by herself, but it wasn't that much farther to Mr. Wurms' table and there was only one more corner. Once the squeaking, rattling trolley had made a little progress, Alice walked back toward the cat, moving slowly so as not to startle it.

The cat raised its head, and its eyes rolled in an excellent imitation of an impatient look. It raised one paw and started to wash itself daintily.

"Hello," Alice said quietly. She did not wish to be seen trying to talk to cats. "Was that you I heard laughing at me?"

The cat did not reply—honestly, Alice would have been startled if it had—but after a moment it stood up, stretched, yawned, and jumped to the floor. It sauntered a few steps, through a gap between shelves that led away from Mr. Wurms' table, then stopped and pointedly looked over its shoulder.

"You want me to . . ." Alice paused. *This is crazy.* But what was the worst that could happen? She glanced upward, to make sure the markers in the ceiling were still there. No matter how much of a maze the place was, it couldn't be *that* hard to find her way out.

The cat cocked its head inquisitively. Alice raised her lantern a little higher and went after it, and it turned away from her immediately and led the way through the gap in the shelves and down a little lane, small footprints trailing behind it in the dust.

They walked for some time. The distant noise of the trolley's progress vanished almost at once, and there was no sound in the library except for the soft padding of her own footsteps. The darkness seemed to close in around her, no matter how high she lifted the lantern. The cat looked over its shoulder from time to time, to make sure she was still there, and its eyes glowed yellow in the dim light.

Very gradually, Alice became aware that something strange was happening. They were walking in a straight line, not turning any corners or going around any bends, but she had the odd feeling they'd changed directions several times. She looked up at the markers, and tried to remember which way they'd been pointing before. And the aisle they were following went on and on, without ever reaching a wall or an intersection. She already felt as though she'd walked so far, they should have been at the edge of the building.

And, out of the corner of her eye, she thought she could see the shelves *changing*. Shifting their positions, rearranging themselves in her wake. When she looked at them, they remained reassuringly still, as bookshelves ought to, but as she turned away she could have sworn she saw gaps appear and vanish again, books and shelves sliding apart and together again.

It reminded her of the invisible servants in the house, and all at once she went from being a little afraid to flushed and irritated. She was sick of everything happening behind her back, sick of whatever *joke* was going on. *It's about time they let me in on it.*

Alice walked a few more steps, picking her moment, then whirled abruptly on one foot.

"What is going . . ."

She trailed off. The path behind her was gone. The aisle continued for a few feet, then dead-ended in a heavy-looking shelf whose layer of dust clearly showed that no one had touched it for decades.

Anger drained away, and fear came flooding back. Alice turned back to the cat. "Listen—"

The cat was gone too.

Ahead of her, the aisle came to a row of backless steel shelves, more like pantry shelves than proper bookcases, that were made into a nearly solid wall by stacks of heavy leather-covered volumes. The path turned right, paralleling this row for a few feet before turning again to head back in the direction it had come.

What caught Alice's attention, though, was the light. It came through the tiny gaps and cracks between the books ahead of her, casting vivid shadows. Someone, on the other side of those shelves, had a lantern much brighter than her own. And there was a sound, a very faint one, that Alice found maddeningly familiar.

Slowly, she set her own lantern on the floor, and crept closer to the shelves. The sound grew louder, a deep droning, almost like an electric fan—

It clicked. How could she have ever forgotten it? The *fairy* had sounded like that in her kitchen, its horrible yellow-and-black wings buzzing to keep him aloft. Alice put her hands against the wall of books and searched frantically for a crack to put her eye against. Small pinholes were everywhere, but all she could see through them was the floor or another row of books. She noticed a shaft of light from higher up where the lantern shone through, and stood on her tiptoes to try and reach it.

"All right," came a voice, and Alice froze, because it was the familiar rumble of Mr. Black. "What have you got that's so all-fired important? You know it's dangerous for me to come here."

"You worry too much." The other voice was high and nasal. It *sounded* like the fairy, Alice was almost sure it was, but "almost" wasn't good enough. *I need to see.* "It's worked out so far, hasn't it? As long as I have this, *she* won't be able to lay eyes on me."

"She's not the only one that needs worrying about," Mr. Black grumbled. "Get on with it."

"My information confirms what we suspected. The book *is* here, I'm sure of it."

"I hope your information is more specific than *that*," Mr. Black said. "I don't know if you noticed, but there are *a lot* of books here."

"Patience, my friend."

"I'm not your friend. And I'm not patient." Mr. Black's voice was low and dangerous. "You tell your master that he had better come through on his end of the deal."

Alice couldn't quite reach. Her eyes were just below the level of the gap in the books, giving her a view of the ceiling but not the speakers. She grabbed the bookshelf and pulled, testing to see if it would support her weight. It didn't so much as wobble, but the steel edges dug painfully into her fingers when she tightened her grip.

"All in good time." The *thrumming* increased in volume. "I'll begin my search, and when I catch the scent—"

"Send me a message first," Mr. Black said. "This place has too many eyes."

Alice took a deep breath, held on to the bookshelf, and pulled herself up. Her feet scrabbled for purchase, but the book she'd been planning to stand on shifted underneath her and slid out of the way, leaving her to hold herself up with her hands alone. The steel bit into her skin, but just for a moment she could see. There was the short, misshapen body, and the fast-beating yellow-and-black wings. The fairy was moving away, following Mr. Black, and for a mad moment Alice wanted to shout after him. Anything that would keep him in place long enough for her to find a way through this bookshelf, grab hold of him, and demand to know—

The pain in her hands was too much. She let go and fell, feet slipping from underneath her so she sprawled on her bottom in the dust. Alice lay there for a long moment, listening to the receding sound of the fairy's wings and Mr. Black's footsteps, and clenched her fists where the steel edge of the bookcase had rasped them raw. She was breathing hard.

More footsteps made her look up. Emma was approaching, gray with dust.

"Mr. Wurms told me to find you," she said. "And bring you to him. He said to tell you that you should not go off by yourself, and that he is very cross."

The response that bubbled to Alice's lips was very rude, and would have shocked her father. She bit it back, closed her eyes, and tried to steady her breathing.

He's here. The fairy is here, in the library.

It wasn't the time for anger, or wild notions. *Calm, collected action.* Alice got to her feet, carefully, and followed Emma back toward Mr. Wurms' table.

I'll figure out a way to find him. Make a plan.

Then I'll grab the damned thing and shake him until his teeth rattle, unless he tells me what he did with my father.

CHAPTER SIX
SNEAKING OUT

T HE PRUDENT THING TO do, Alice knew, would be to wait. She still knew too little about the library, and even less about the fairy. She hoped that Mr. Black would send her there again to help Mr. Wurms, but he didn't, and by the next day Alice was frantic. All she could think about was the fairy, and what she was going to ask him when she finally got her hands around his neck. By that night, she realized it was a choice between sneaking out to the library right then and there, or lying awake until dawn staring at the ceiling, and Alice gave in.

She left her usual clothes behind and crept out her door wearing only a nightshirt and slippers. Mr. Black sometimes walked the halls at night, and a little shivering would be a small price to pay against the possibility that he'd catch her on her way out. It would be easy to say that she'd gone to the toilet and gotten lost in the dark—it had actually happened to her twice already—but that excuse wouldn't fly if she had her coat and hat on.

She brought with her a box of matches, a candle, a pencil, and a few folded sheets of paper. The latter, she thought, might come in handy if she needed to take something down, or perhaps copy something from out of a book. She'd considered arming herself with one of the pokers from the downstairs hearth, but she couldn't imagine a situation where that would really make a difference.

Getting outside turned out to be anticlimactic. The big house was silent as a tomb after the gaslights were turned out, and Alice found the back door beside the kitchens unlocked. She eased it open, gasping a little at the blast of chill night air. Gravel crunched softly under her feet, but that was surely too quiet for anyone inside the house to hear. She let the door close gently, touched the matches and her candle in her pocket, and looked across the lawn at the low, dark shape of the library.

In the back of her mind, all the way from her room, had been a voice telling her she shouldn't be doing this at all. It wasn't just worry about being caught, by Mr. Black or Mr. Wurms. This was against the *rules*, a boundary Alice had carefully stayed on the right side of nearly her entire life. Just the thought of it brought up a picture of her father, and the look he'd given her on the very few times she'd strayed. It hadn't been an angry look, just a sad, disappointed one, and Alice would rather have torn her heart out with her fingernails than see it on his face again.

But, she reminded herself, her father was gone. He was *gone*, and if there was any possibility of getting him back, it lay across the lawn in that dark, windowless building. *Some things are more important than following the rules.*

Aren't they?

She shook her head and started across the lawn, avoiding the path—it was visible from the house—and staying close to the edge of the woods. Not *too* close, though. The forest frightened her more than she cared to admit. The only forests Alice had ever visited had been tame, gentle things, airy well-tended parks, and of course she'd never gone at night. *This* forest was different, ancient and dark, and all she could see was a solid wall of black foliage rising into the sky to blot out the stars. Each gust of wind brought a rush of whispering leaves, rising and falling like the sound of surf on a beach. The wind was *cold* too, cutting right through the thin cotton of her nightshirt. Her skin rose in goose pimples, and Alice hugged herself and wished she'd been a little less cautious in her planning.

The library seemed almost a part of the forest, a great black hump of a building looming up among the trees like an ancient standing stone. She could see the gleam of moonlight on the great bronze door, and she hurried over to it. The big metal ring was so cold, her hand burned where she touched it, but she gritted her teeth and hauled, expecting the scream of protesting hinges.

Nothing happened. The door was stuck fast; Alice might as well have been hauling on a ring set directly into the wall.

Locked. But it couldn't be locked, she thought. Emma certainly hadn't opened it with any kind of a key, and she didn't remember seeing a keyhole.

She hauled again, harder. The door remained obstinately closed, without a hint of movement.

Alice let the ring slip from her numb fingers, and it fell against the door with a *clack*. For a long moment she stared at the unyielding portal, not quite ready to believe how easily she'd been thwarted. A particularly fierce gust of wind tore through her nightshirt as though it weren't there and made her shiver violently. Alice sank into a crouch, hands jammed in her armpits and teeth chattering, and felt tears springing into her eyes.

It's just the cold, she thought. She hadn't cried when they'd told her her father was dead. *I won't cry just because of a stuck door. I* won't.

All she had to do was walk back to the house, climb back into her warm, scratchy bed, and figure things out in the morning. Get Emma to tell her the trick to getting in. She turned, wiping her eyes with the back of one shaking hand. The path back looked even darker and more forbidding than it had from the house, barely a glitter of moonlight penetrating the canopy to show the way. The trees shivered and shook in the wind, like something alive, leaves and branches rustling with a hollow, skeletal sound.

Something else was moving too, low to the ground, visible for just an instant as it crossed a patch of moonlight. It was a cat, a calico cat, whose white patches glowed like shining silver until it slipped back into shadow. It was heading along the wall of the library, back through the underbrush and into the trees.

Cats, Alice thought. *There are cats in the library, quite*

a lot of them. Are they cooped up in there all the time? Or is
there a way for them to get in and out?

Before she was quite aware of it, she was crashing through the bushes at the corner of the building, following the cat back along the overgrown side of the building. It was, she had to admit, a stupid thing to do. She lost one slipper almost immediately, and branches snatched and tore at her nightshirt and left long welts and scratches on her legs.

At one point her ankle got stuck on a snag, and she had a sudden, horrid vision of being trapped there till morning, when Emma or Mr. Black would stumble across her frozen, half-naked body. All this flashed through her mind in less than a second, as it took her only that long to free herself, but it left her heart hammering. The only thing that kept her moving forward was the thought of all the brush *behind* her; going back would be just as painful as keeping on.

Ahead, there was a brief flash of yellow, a pair of eyes glowing in the moonlight. The cat observed her crashing, clumsy progress, but it didn't seem perturbed. Breaking into a small clear space where she could see it clearly, it wandered up to the wall of the library—

— and vanished.

Alice stopped in her tracks, blinking. She could have

sworn she'd seen the cat step *forward,* into the wall, as though it were no more substantial than fog. But that was impossible.

Fairies are impossible, she thought angrily, ripping her nightshirt free of a grasping branch and leaving a chunk of fabric behind. *But I saw one, and now I'm here. What's wrong with a cat walking through walls?*

She broke free of the brush and stumbled into the clear space, leaning against the rough stone wall of the library. Her legs were a mass of pain, and something had cut the sole of her left foot so that it hurt to put much weight on it. The hem of her nightshirt was in tatters, and her hair was a tangle of leaves and broken twigs. Her breath came fast, and in spite of the chill of the night, her skin felt hot and flushed.

After a moment's rest, she pushed herself into motion, feeling her way along the wall to where she thought the cat had been. The stone was solid under her fingers, all the way from the ground to as high as she could reach. In desperation, she slid her fingers in the cracks between blocks, looking for some kind of catch or hidden mechanism. Which is ridiculous, she thought, because how complicated could a secret door be if a *cat* figured it out?

There was nothing but flaking mortar in the joints. Alice gave the wall a kick with the sole of her slipper, lost her balance, and landed heavily on her bottom among the stones and weeds.

Somebody laughed, just behind her, nasty and mocking. Alice's heart lurched, and she scrambled forward on hands and knees and pressed herself against the wall. It was suddenly very cold again.

"It's not going to work," a voice said. "You can't get in that way. Because you're not a cat, you see?"

Alice tried hard to make her tongue work, without success. It seemed to have fused to the roof of her mouth.

"There wouldn't be much sense in having a cat door if just anybody could use it," the voice said. It sounded like a young man, with a pleasantly superior accent she couldn't quite identify. "A cat door should only admit cats. It seems obvious, if you ask *me*."

Alice swallowed hard, pressing one hand to her chest in an effort to calm her frantic heartbeat. When she was sure she had enough breath, she whispered, "Who's there?"

"I am. Look up. That's it, a little to the left, now up a little more, too far to the right, no, *up*, you stupid girl. There."

Trying to follow these directions, Alice stared up into the overhanging canopy of branches. One twisted, leaf-less limb crooked a few feet over her head, and she found herself looking into another pair of shining yellow eyes. A sleek feline body was only barely visible behind them.

"You're a cat," she said automatically.

"Your powers of perception are astounding," the cat drawled. "Although I feel obliged to point out, in the interests of ontological exactitude, that I am in fact only *half* cat. Personally, though, I have always considered it the better half."

"And you can talk," Alice said, working her way through the situation.

"Better and better! With brains like that, I can see how you monkeys took over the world."

Alice closed her eyes for a moment and took a deter-mined hold on herself. *You followed a cat in the library and it led you to the fairy,* she admonished. *Hearing one talk should not be such a shock.* She could feel a tiny worm of ecstatic excitement, deep in her gut, and she tried to fight it down. The thing to do, she thought, is think about this logically.

She opened her eyes, and realized she had absolutely no idea what to say.

"I must say, if you're practicing for an 'impressions of lower life-forms' contest, you're a shoe-in. That 'slack-jawed cow' look is spot on. Can you do a giraffe?"

"All right," Alice said. "All right. You're a cat, and you can talk. What are you doing here?"

"A vocal reaction at last! But still not a very clever one. Under the circumstances, don't you think it is I who should be directing that question to you?"

"Me?"

"I, after all, live here. I am a library cat, and this is the library, and so I am in my domain. You, on the other hand, do not belong. So allow me to put the same question on the table, in reverse: What are *you* doing here?"

"I live here," Alice said. "There, anyway. In the house. My name is Alice Creighton."

"I know that. But what are you doing *here*?"

There was a moment of blurred motion as the cat dropped to the ground, landing in a crouch. In the moonlight his fur was a dull, rippling silver. His yellow eyes stayed fixed on hers, but she noticed that his mouth remained closed when he spoke, the clever voice emerging apparently from nowhere.

"Politeness demands," he said, "that I introduce myself. You may call me Ashes."

"Ash?" Alice repeated.

"Ash*es*." The cat bristled. "Or, in full, Ashes-Drifting-Through-the-Dead-Cities-of-the-World, but Ashes will do."

Alice dropped to her knees, to put herself closer to the cat's level. "Pleased to meet you."

"If you try to shake my paw, be warned, you're getting a smack on the nose," Ashes said.

"Are you the cat I saw in the library this afternoon?" It was hard to be sure, but she thought he was the right color.

"If I answer your questions, will you answer mine?"

Alice sighed and stood up, putting one hand on the cold stone of the wall. "I'm trying to get into the library. The front door wouldn't open, so I thought there might be a way in I could use around here."

"Not unexpected. It wouldn't be much of a fortress if you just left the doors open." Ashes yawned, showing tiny white teeth. "And what are you planning to do, once you get inside?"

"I'm going to find that fairy with the yellow-and-black wings." Alice decided not to volunteer what she planned to do to the thing. For all she knew, the cat could be on his side.

"I see." His fur rippled. "Well, fair is fair. Yes, it was me you followed."

"You laughed at me!"

"You were making such a spectacle of yourself, I couldn't help it."

"Why did you lead me to the fairy?" Alice said. "What do you know about him?"

"Lead?" Ashes chuckled. "Cats wander where they please. Whether or not anyone follows is not our business."

"You—" Alice clenched her teeth and let a moment or two pass in silence. "Look. Can you help me get inside?"

He gave her a long, yellow-eyed stare. "Of course."

Alice blinked. "Really?"

"I *am* half cat." He cocked his head, an oddly human gesture. "The operative question, young lady, is *will* I help you?"

Alice felt like giving him a kick. The excitement of meeting a talking cat was starting to wear off, and she was reminded once again that she was a mass of cuts and scrapes, and also very cold.

"*Will* you help me? I would appreciate it very much."

"I will," Ashes said. He sounded as though he'd made the decision on the spot. "But only because you have aroused my curiosity. Don't expect me to stand up for you if you get in trouble."

"Thank you."

The cat gave a little sigh. "You can go ahead and say it. I know you want to."

"Say what?"

"The proverb. About cats, and curiosity, and its effect thereon."

"I wasn't going to say anything like that," Alice said.

"No?" Ashes yawned again. "What a strange girl."

Getting through the wall turned out to be a much simpler procedure than Alice had expected. Ashes strolled past her, rubbing idly against her leg as he went, and then stepped into the stonework as though it were no more substantial than smoke. For a moment all she could see was his lashing tail. Then his face popped out again, producing the somewhat gruesome effect of a cat head mounted on a stone wall, like a hunting trophy.

"You can come through," he said. "As long as I'm in the doorway. Hurry up, though. If it stays open for too long someone may take an interest."

Alice extended a hand cautiously. Where her fingers expected to meet stone there was nothing, not even a tingle or a ripple in the air. Her hand was gone, as though she'd thrust it into inky black water, but she could still feel her fingers. She wiggled them and pulled her hand back, obscurely relieved to find it intact.

"Come on, come on," Ashes said.

Alice took a deep breath, closed her eyes, and shuffled forward. The transition was detectable only as a change in the air: It was suddenly much warmer, and her next breath carried the overwhelming smell of dust and old paper that permeated the library. She felt something soft and warm brush against her ankle, and panicked for a moment before she realized it was only Ashes.

She opened her eyes, but nothing happened. The blackness remained absolute.

"I can't see," she whispered.

"That's because there's no lights." Ashes sounded smug. "Not enough for a human, anyway. *I* can see just fine."

"Hold on."

She fumbled for her supplies, found the matches, and after a few tries managed to strike one on the floor. She transferred the flame to the candle, which gave a wan glow that was barely enough to show her the bookshelves on either side of her. Behind her was a stone wall. She put a hand on it, and felt only cold rock.

"Fire in the library?" Ashes chided. "Master Geryon would not approve."

"If I'd been able to get in the front door, I'd have borrowed one of the lamps," Alice said. "I'll be careful."

"I'm sure," the cat said. "Now. Thanks to my good graces, you're inside. What next?"

"I . . . I'm not sure."

She pursed her lips and looked down at the cat, who was only a gray smudge in the flickering light of the candle. She was feeling, frankly, a little peevish. Ashes' smug superiority was grating, no matter how helpful he was, and it was irritating that he had the advantage of her, so she had to gawp like a slack-jawed idiot in his wake.

"Let me guess," Ashes said. He couldn't grin, like a human might, but she could hear it in his voice. "You thought you'd just poke around and somehow you'd happen across this 'fairy' you're looking for?"

"I wasn't sure I'd even be able to get inside," Alice told the cat. "Forgive me for not having a long-term plan."

"It's not *my* forgiveness you should be worried about." Ashes walked around Alice in a circle, his tail caressing her bare shins. "Right. Follow me."

"Where are we going?" Alice had to move quickly to

keep the cat in view. The library shelves loomed up on either side, dark and cave-like in the inadequate glow of the candle.

"To see someone who may able to help you find what you want to know," Ashes said. "If you're polite."

CHAPTER SEVEN
ISAAC

F OLLOW ME VERY CLOSELY," Ashes said. "If we get separated, you'll never find your way back out again."

"Emma taught me a trick for that," Alice said, trying to assert a modicum of independence. "You just need to follow the glass arrows in the ceiling."

The cat snorted. "You can follow them, all right. Where they'll lead you is something else entirely."

They'd been walking for at least a quarter of an hour. Alice had removed her remaining slipper—wearing only one made her walk with a limp—and her feet were now coated with library dust. Ashes never hesitated when he came to an intersection, so she assumed he knew where he was going. But the shelves all looked alike, and she wondered briefly if he was leading her in circles for a laugh. That couldn't be, though. When she looked behind her, her footprints in the dust were clear even in the dim light of the candle, and the dust ahead of them was always pristine and undisturbed.

Then the character of the library started to change. Instead of neat alleys, the bookshelves stood in tight little groups, enclosing small spaces almost like little rooms. In these interior spaces, Alice glimpsed things that were not bookshelves—statues, suits of armor, even what looked very much like a living tree. There were flashes of movement too, and shadows that were definitely un-feline dancing on the floor.

Ashes' formerly confident steps took on a decidedly cautious air as they wove through the clusters of shelving. At times he would suddenly stop, tasting the air while his ears twitched, as though listening to a distant noise Alice couldn't hear. Once, without explanation, he backtracked and led her in a circle, giving wide berth to an apparently empty passage. When she tried to ask why, all she got was a peremptory *shush*.

By the time they arrived at their destination, Alice felt like she'd walked for miles. Their path had to have been a twisting one, she thought, because the library building simply couldn't be that large. They'd never even come in sight of one of the outer walls.

Ashes stopped at a particular group of shelves, five heavy wooden things arranged in a pentagon with only slim gaps between them. As they'd penetrated deeper in the library, the books themselves had grown fewer and fewer, and these shelves were entirely empty. Dust lay so thick on them that they seemed to have been there for centuries.

"All right," Ashes said. "Wait here. I won't be long."

"But you said—"

The cat was already gone, slipping lithely between two of the bookcases. Alice stared after him, seeing nothing but darkness beyond, and felt utterly foolish.

Perhaps he's abandoned me here, she thought. *For a joke? Or is he really trying to make sure I never come back?* She was starting to question the wisdom of following a talking cat in the first place. Cats were notoriously fickle creatures.

Ashes re-emerged into the candlelight. "He's not here yet," he said. "Come in, but move carefully, and don't touch anything."

She looked dubiously at the gap between the shelves.

"You'll fit," Ashes said. "Although you'd fit better if

you were a cat." He turned and slipped easily through the narrow crack.

Alice edged sideways into the angle formed by the two bookshelves, pushed her arm through the space between them, and tried to force her shoulders through. To her surprise, it wasn't difficult. She got the distinct sense that the shelves were moving apart, or actually bending back as though they were made of clay. Something passed across her skin, a faint tingle like a wall of warm mist, and her next breath brought a lungful of air so unlike the dry, dusty smell of the library that she stopped short, wedged halfway between the bookshelves.

"Don't just stand there," came Ashes' voice. "You'll let the damp out."

Alice dragged herself through with a final effort, carefully bringing the candle in last of all. When she turned around, she discovered she didn't need it, and nearly dropped it in surprise.

Inside, the little cluster looked nothing like the library beyond. The backs of the shelves were enormous, shadowy things, more like stone than wood. The space they enclosed was much larger than it had appeared from the outside, as big as a good-sized garden. The floor had changed from dusty stone to a rich, soft loam, damp and clingy on her feet. The air smelled wet, warm, and thick with the scent of rotting, growing things.

In the center of the place was a circular pond. It was the only way Alice could think to describe it, in spite of the ridiculousness of having a pond inside a library. In the middle of the pond was an island, only a few feet across, and on the island a small fire of sticks and dry leaves crackled merrily. Balanced on an iron stand above the fire was a small iron cauldron, of the sort a witch in a story might use to boil unwary children. Something was bubbling in it, and the rising steam mixed with the smoke of the fire as it rose toward the invisible ceiling.

All around, growing out of the soil in incredible profusion, were mushrooms. These ranged from whole banks of familiar-looking fungi a few inches high, topped with caps or puffballs, to truly enormous specimens taller than Alice was. The bigger they were, the stranger their shapes, dividing into many quivering branches or forming neat, concentric rings like a wedding cake. They came in all colors too, not just the drab gray and brown of ordinary mushrooms. She could see streaks of green, red, violet, and royal blue in the light of the bonfire.

Ashes stood at the edge of the pond, back arched, trying to keep his body as far away from the ground as possible. He caught Alice's eyes with his yellow ones and gave an exaggerated sigh.

"I don't know how he stands the damp," the cat said. "It's a nasty little hole, if you ask me."

"Who is 'he'? Is someone living in here?"

"All in good time."

Alice gave the cat a cross look. "You're not being very helpful."

"No," Ashes said, sounding pleased with himself. He yawned. "However, perhaps a little *quid pro quo* is in order. Do me a favor, and I'll answer your questions."

"A favor?" Alice narrowed her eyes. "What kind of favor?"

"Let me ride on your shoulder," Ashes said, holding up his front paw. "This stuff mats my fur something awful."

Ashes was lighter than he looked. She lifted him to her shoulder and he shifted around until he found a comfortable position, the tips of his claws pricking through the thin fabric of her nightshirt. His tail flipped back and forth against her shoulder blades.

"All right," Alice said. "So where are we?"

"Hmm?" Ashes said. "We're in the library, of course."

"You don't have to be clever about it," Alice said. She pushed a foot into the ground, which squelched. "This doesn't look like any library I've ever been in. And it certainly doesn't look like the library out"—she gestured vaguely—"there."

"I've never been in another library, so I wouldn't know," the cat said. "But you're right. 'Out there' is what you might think of as the front parlor. This is Master Geryon's private collection."

"But—"

"He keeps his really important books here. But they start to . . . leak, after a while, and you end up with places like this."

"Leak?" Alice frowned. "Books have always seemed fairly solid to me. Paper, leather, ink. How can they *leak*?"

"I can see that you're an expert," Ashes said, with injured pride.

"Sorry," Alice said. "What books are we talking about?"

"Look at one of the big mushrooms," the cat said. "Like that one just there, see?"

Alice squelched over to it. It was of the classic shape, with a long white stem and a dark red cap with green spots, and about four feet high. Lying on top of the cap, Alice was surprised to see, *was* a book. It was a big, flat volume, leather-bound, that wouldn't have looked out of place in her father's collection. The title was picked out in gold leaf on the cover. It said *The Swarm*.

"It looks like an ordinary book," Alice said. "Why would you store a book *here*? You'd think the damp would get to it in no time."

"I told you, the damp leaks *out* of the books," Ashes said. "It probably likes it that way."

"*Likes?* It's alive?"

"Not exactly. But it's not exactly *not* alive, either."

Alice reached out and laid a finger on the cover. It felt normal enough.

"Can I look inside it?" she said.

Ashes chuckled. "Go ahead, but you'll only give yourself a headache."

"It doesn't look all *that* difficult to me—"

"Who's there?" a voice said from behind her. "What are you doing here?"

Alice turned around, fast enough that Ashes had to grip a little tighter to keep his perch. There was a boy standing by the edge of the pond, his back to the fire and his face in shadow. He wore a long, heavy coat, almost like a wizard's cape with pockets. What she could see of his face looked thin and unfriendly. It was hard to guess his age exactly, but from his height he couldn't be much older than she was. He held his hands in front of him in a sort of boxer's stance, as though he expected to be attacked.

"Finally," Ashes said. "We've been waiting."

"Ashes." The boy sighed and let his arms fall. "You might have warned me."

"I might have," Ashes agreed.

The boy frowned. "But what's *she* doing here?"

"I'll do the introductions, shall I?" Ashes said. "Alice, this is Isaac. Isaac, Alice."

"I know *who* she is," Isaac said. "But why did you bring her here?"

"Just being polite." Ashes sniffed. "You told Mother you needed help, didn't you?"

"From *her*?" Isaac looked incredulous. "She's just a . . . a girl! Geryon's niece, or something. What am I supposed to do with *her*, use her as bait?"

"Maybe," Ashes said. "You can never tell, with Mother."

"All *right*," said Alice, who had had just about enough of being discussed as though she weren't there. "First of all, I have no idea what you need help with, but you can forget it. Second of all, nobody *brought* me anywhere." She turned her head to glare at Ashes. "This cat said that you might be able to help *me*, but apparently he had something else in mind. Someone in his position ought to be a little more forthcoming, or else he might find himself tail-deep in the mud."

"There's no need for *that* sort of thing," Ashes said, alarmed.

Isaac chuckled. "Right. You haven't been told much, have you?"

"He's a Reader," Ashes blurted.

94

"So am I," Alice said. "What's so special about read-ing?"

"No, you're not," Ashes said. "He's a *Reader*. A wizard. A magician. A wielder of arcane forces."

"What is that supposed to mean?"

"It means he can use these books," Ashes said. "Or try to, anyway."

Isaac shot Ashes a cold glance, then turned back to Alice. "I know this may be hard to accept—"

"I'm standing by the side of the pond in the middle of a library with a talking cat on my shoulder," Alice dead-panned. "What's so special about these books?"

"Take a look and see," Isaac said. It was hard to tell with his back to the fire, but she thought he was smirking.

Alice turned back to the mushroom. Ashes dug his claws into her shoulder a little harder.

"I really wouldn't," the cat said. "Trust me. Your head will hurt for hours."

"I don't think so," Alice said. "Anything *he* can read, I can read."

"It's not like that, I told you—"

Alice flipped the cover open and looked down at the first page. It was a solid block of text, but the characters were in a language she didn't recognize, all strange curls and crossed lines. There was something *off* about them, as though they were out of focus, and she felt herself going cross-eyed. Then the print *moved,* with a crawling sensation that seemed to go straight from the page to the back of her eyeballs, and formed itself into familiar English words.

"Wait a minute—" Ashes said.

Alice read:

Alice opened her eyes in another place entirely. It was dark after the brightness of Isaac's fire . . .

CHAPTER EIGHT
THE SWARM

ALICE OPENED HER EYES in another place entirely. It was dark after the brightness of Isaac's fire, with only faint glowing patches on the walls. She could feel brickwork underfoot, cracked and crumbling with age.

Ashes dug in all four sets of claws at once, hard enough to draw blood. Alice gave a screech and grabbed for him, but he jumped, landing with a soft *thump* on the bricks and vanishing into the darkness.

"Ashes?" she said quietly, one hand clapped to her lacerated shoulder. "Where are you?"

"Right here, you half-blind two-legs," the cat said. She felt his tail brush against her shin. "All right, very clever, you put one over on old Ashes. I like the 'clueless little girl' act, it's quite good. Now, I assume you've got a plan?"

"A plan?"

Alice blinked and held up a hand, trying to find the outline of her fingers. Her eyes were adjusting to the gloom, and she could just make out that they were in a small room, like a cellar, with arched doorways in all four walls. The light was coming from something growing on the brickwork, hanging in great glowing strips, like tattered wallpaper painted with the guts of lightning bugs.

Ashes sounded annoyed. "Yes, a plan! For getting out of here."

"I don't even know where *here* is," Alice said. "How could I possibly have a plan?"

"It's no good trying to keep up the act *now*," Ashes said. "You're one of them, obviously. A Reader. Very clever of you to have Geryon go around telling everyone you're his half-wit niece."

"I have no idea what he tells people," Alice said, a bit testily. "And I *don't* know what's going on, and I don't have a plan. You told me the book would only give me a headache!"

"I didn't think you could Read it!" Alice could hear the capital letter. "Isaac was only making a joke!"

"If you explain it to me," Alice retorted, "maybe I'll start laughing."

She reached out to the closest wall. The bricks felt real enough under her fingers, with rounded corners and ancient, flaking mortar. She ran a hand along the glowing moss and found her skin coated with flakes of dust that shimmered a brief, brilliant green and then faded. She could see now that each of the four doorways led to a narrow corridor with a low ceiling and a central gutter full of a few inches of stagnant, fetid water.

"It feels like a sewer," she said aloud. "I saw pictures of the New York sewers in a book once. Are there sewers under the library?"

She could see Ashes staring at her, two brilliant rings in the darkness. His yellow eyes were tinged with green in the glow from the walls.

"You're serious, aren't you?" the cat said. "You don't know what's happened."

"No! For the last time, you . . . *stupid* cat, I don't know *anything*!"

"Well." Ashes blinked and paced around in a circle, tail whipping. "I should probably tell you, then, that we're definitely going to die."

There was a long moment of silence.

"Die?" Alice said. "What do you mean?"

"Expire. Cease. End. Shuffle off this mortal coil. I assume you're familiar with the concept. Although at this point I suppose I shouldn't assume you're familiar with anything."

"Ashes," Alice said, in a tone of extremely strained patience. "Where *are* we?"

He sighed, which was an odd sound to hear from a cat. "We're inside the book, of course. The one you Read. *The Swarm.*"

Alice laughed. "You're not serious."

"Don't ask questions if you don't want to hear the answers," Ashes said. He swished his tail, offended, and started off down one of the corridors. Alice, feeling the first thrills of fear, hurried after him.

"All right, all right," she said. "We're inside the book. How did we get here?"

"You brought us," the cat says. "You have the gift, apparently. You're a Reader."

"I've read a lot of books," Alice said, "and nothing like this has ever happened."

Ashes sniffed. "It doesn't work with just any book, *obviously*. This is one of Geryon's. It's special. This particular kind of volume is called a prison-book, because it's what Readers use to lock up all sorts of nastiness."

"Nastiness?" Alice looked over her shoulder, but saw only darkness. "There's something in here with us, you mean?"

"Of course. The Swarm, presumably."

"What's that?"

"How should I know?" Ashes said. His voice was strained. "I just know that if Geryon shoved it in a prison-book, it probably isn't friendly!"

Alice thought about that for a moment. The corridor they were following bent slowly to the right, so that their original room quickly passed out of view. More strips of moss glowed on the walls, and here and there iron fittings of no obvious purpose were hammered between the bricks, weeping long, rusty stains.

"So," Alice said eventually, "how do we get out?"

"I thought you'd get around to that," Ashes said. "There are at least two ways out of a prison-book. Another Reader on the outside can pop you out again, if he knows the book well enough."

"Could Isaac do that?"

"Maybe with a year's study," Ashes said. "And a good deal more power than he's got."

"What's the other way?"

"You find the prisoner," Ashes said, "and kill it."

"Excuse me?"

"It's the way the prison-books are written," Ashes said. "The Reader goes *into* the prison book, conquers the prisoner, and the book lets him out. Or her out, in this case."

"But," Alice said, "I don't want to kill anything."

"Unless the Swarm is something you can *argue* to death, I doubt it's going to matter. The Reader is supposed to be prepared for this kind of thing, with magic fire and silver swords and so forth. Normally you don't just wander into a prison-book in your nightshirt and carpet slippers."

"I haven't even *got* carpet slippers," Alice reminded him. The bricks underfoot were worn with years and slimy with damp, but the occasional sharp corner still scraped painfully against her bare feet. "So what are we going to do?"

"I suppose I could try to kill the prisoner," Ashes said, "but if it was something *I* could kill, I doubt it would be locked up. I'm only half cat, after all. So when we find it, it will probably kill us."

"You don't seem too upset at the prospect," Alice said. "If you're half cat, have you got four and a half lives?"

"No, I haven't," Ashes snapped. "And I'm absolutely

terrified." There was a long pause. Alice swallowed hard. The cat looked back at her, eyes glowing yellow green, and sniffed. "It just wouldn't do to show fear in front of any *human*, Reader or not. Mother would skin me alive if she heard about it."

Ashes padded on, and Alice hurried after him. They walked for a moment in silence down the apparently endless corridor.

"Maybe it's not as bad as that," Alice said slowly. "Maybe the prisoner is something we can ... talk to, or—"

"Shh," Ashes said.

"It's not *impossible*," Alice protested. "You can't just assume—"

"I mean *be quiet*," the cat hissed. "I hear something coming."

Alice stopped. Ashes was nearly invisible in the gloom, a gray-on-black shadow, but her eyes had adapted surprisingly quickly to the faint green glow. Ahead was another arched doorway, with some sort of room beyond it. From that direction she could hear a faint, fast sound, *tik-tik-tik-tik*, like a small dog running across marble. Something scurried out of the doorway in their direction, low and fast. Alice looked around for Ashes, uncertainly, but the cat had vanished.

In a few moments the thing entered the nearest pool of light. It was about the size of a large rat, but it put her more in mind of a bird, though admittedly the oddest-looking bird she'd ever seen. It stood on two bird-like legs, covered in dark fur or feathers except for splay-toed feet. A roughly oval body was angled forward, like a picture she'd once seen of an ostrich, but there was no neck, no head, and no wings, not even vestigial ones. Two black eyes glittered above a long, pointed beak that looked as sharp as a sewing needle.

The *tik-tik-tik* noise came from the claws on its feet, which blurred in a rapid, pigeon-like gait. It stopped a few yards away, body tilted so it could look up at her, and made a short, interrogative *quirk*.

Alice couldn't help laughing. After all the dire pronouncements from Ashes, fear had begun to settle somewhere deep in her gut. But this little thing, while certainly odd, looked more like a creature you'd shoo out of the basement than any kind of a threat.

It might even be tame, she decided. Certainly it didn't seem afraid of her. She crouched slowly and beckoned to it.

"Come here. That's right. I'm not going to hurt you." Reflecting, she added, "If you can talk, I'd appreciate if you'd tell me now, before I make myself look foolish."

The thing didn't seem inclined to talk. It did venture forward, however, a few feet at a time, veering slightly from side to side as though to study her from new angles. Eventually it came within arm's reach, and Alice extended a hand in case it wanted to sniff. She managed to keep herself from starting when it darted forward, all in a rush, and hopped into the hollow of her palm. Its claws were painful pinpricks, but they didn't break the skin. It *quirked* again.

"You *are* friendly, aren't you?" Alice said. She lifted the little creature to look it in the eyes. It was surprisingly heavy, like a little lead weight, not bird-like at all. It settled back on its haunches, claws flexing. "What are you called, I wonder. You don't belong to any genus *I* can think of, that's for certain."

The little thing shifted its weight. Then, when it was close enough that it could nearly touch her nose with its beak, it lunged.

Alice had a split second of warning from the pressure of its claws on her palm. Some instinct made her jerk her head backward, so the little creature's needle-sharp beak missed spearing her eye and instead scored a line across the cheek just beneath it. Alice gave a screech and tried to back away, up against the tunnel wall, but the thing's jump had landed it on her nightshirt and it clung to the fabric for all it was worth.

It lunged again, this time at her shoulder, and the pointed beak went through shirt and skin like they were gauze and nipped at her flesh. When it pulled back, blood welled, and the beak parted to reveal a long, black tongue, skinny as a snake's, that darted out to lap delicately at the wound.

Shaking her arm only made it grip tighter, but Alice finally got a hold of the thing with her other hand and pulled. It came free with a rip of fabric, and she could feel it squirming under her fingers. She hurled it at the wall, as hard she could, and it tucked in its legs and *bounced* like a softball. For a moment it lay still, and she thought she'd killed it, but its legs shot out again and scrabbled at the floor until it righted itself. It stared at her again, with another *quirk*, and this time it didn't sound nearly so friendly. Alice, one hand on the wall for support, felt a bloody tear dribbling down her cheek and wondered if she should run.

Before she could decide, something else moved in the darkness. Ashes, a blur of gray fur on the pounce, hit the thing and bowled it over, trapping it between his paws before it could get back to its feet. Ignoring its scrabbling claws, he sank his teeth into the little creature and gave it the quick shake cats give mice to break their necks. This failed to produce the desired effect, but the squirming thing was quite helpless, and Ashes turned to face Alice triumphantly.

"I've got it!" His voice was not, she noted, impeded in any way by having a mouthful of squirming bird-thing. "Pfeh! It tastes like coal." He shook it again, and the thing gave a high-pitched *quirk*. "Have you got something heavy we could drop on it, perhaps?"

A few moments earlier, Alice wouldn't have entertained the idea; now, cheek and shoulder burning, she would have gladly bashed the little terror with a poker.

"Maybe I can get one of these bricks loose," she muttered. "Or else—"

She paused. Ashes, intent on his prey, was batting it playfully with his paws without releasing his stranglehold. Underneath the frantic *quirks*, though, she could hear something else, almost like the sounds of rain on a tin roof.

Tik. Tik. Tik-tik. Tik-tik-tik.

Tiktiktiktiktiktiktik—

"Ashes, let it go," Alice breathed.

"But—"

"Run!"

She took to her heels. Ashes, relinquishing his prize, followed. A few moments later, small creatures filled the passage, the staccato *tiks* of their claws on the brickwork merging into a rising crescendo.

CHAPTER NINE
TRAPPED!

ALICE POUNDED DOWN THE tunnel as fast as she had ever run in her life. She skidded back into the room with four doors, and looked frantically from one to the other, uncertain. The *tik-tik-tik* echoed off the bricks and seemed to come from every direction at once.

Deciding that one door was as good as another, she took off straight ahead, into another corridor. More halls branched off from it at random intervals, with no sign of anything solid she could put between herself and the approaching swarm.

Rounding a corner into a four-way intersection, she turned left and drew up short at the sound of *quirking*. A pair of the little creatures sidled out to block the path, so Alice backed up and ran down the opposite corridor. It split into a T-junction a dozen yards on, and from one of the arms she heard the scrape of claws on stone. She took the other way, heart slamming against her ribs and breath rattling in her chest.

"They're herding us," said Ashes, who apparently had no trouble running and speaking at the same time.

"Herding?" Alice gasped.

"Pushing us toward something," Ashes said. "Probably a dead end."

Alice had a sudden image of turning down a corridor and finding noth-ing but a blank wall

ahead of her, then turning back to find the exit full of tiny, beady eyes. She pictured them coming at her, all in a rush, covering her in a carpet of vicious claws, needle-beaks pecking—

She tasted bile at the back of her throat, and gritted her teeth. There had to be a way out, somewhere.

At the next intersection, she stopped to listen. Ashes, halfway to the opposite tunnel, skidded to a halt and looked back at her.

"Are you—"

"Shh!" After a moment, she closed her eyes. "Do you hear water?"

"Yes," the cat said. "That way." He gestured with his head. "Which is all the more reason to go the other way—"

"Come on."

Alice ran toward the sound, and after an instant's hesitation Ashes followed.

"But," he said, "I can hear them coming this way!"

"Just keep going!"

They turned a corner and found a small platoon of swarmers blocking their path. The little bird-things looked taken aback to find their prey rushing at them, and Alice took advantage of their hesitation to bull through. Her foot came down heavily on one of them, bouncing it to one side as though she'd stepped on a tennis ball. She stumbled sideways, hit the brick wall hard enough to scrape her palms, but spun away from it and kept running. Another swarmer managed a wild stab as she went past, and she felt a bloom of pain at her ankle.

Then she was past them, and the skitter of claws behind her was almost drowned under the clearly audible rush of water. She turned another corner and saw—praise God—a *door,* a rusted iron bulkhead of the kind one might find on a steamship, half-open and with the sound of water coming from beyond it. Alice slid sideways through the gap, and Ashes bounded through right behind her. Once he was through, she put her back to the door. For a horrible moment it resisted, and she thought her weight wouldn't be enough. Then it swung a few inches, rusty hinges shrieking at the abuse, and stuttered through the rest of its arc until it hit the metal doorframe with a *clang.* Something in the mechanism clicked.

Alice leaned against the door, panting. She thought her lungs would collapse. After a moment her legs gave way, and she slid down the rough surface of the iron until she was sitting on the slimy brick floor.

"Are you all right?" said Ashes.

Alice was too busy gulping air to reply for a while. Taking stock, she found herself a mass of cuts, scrapes, and bruises. Her cheek was smeared with blood, and she'd skinned her palms badly when she'd hit the wall.

When she could spare the breath to speak, she said, "I'm alive, I think. What about you?"

"I'm filthy," Ashes said. "And I think one of them may have nipped off a bit of my tail."

Alice closed her eyes and blew out a long breath. All her limbs felt shaky, but she managed to climb to her feet and look around.

The results of her survey were disappointing. She'd been hoping for a barrier she could put between herself and the Swarm, and she'd found one, but the space on this side was barely larger than a closet and there were no other exits. In one corner was the source of the sound of rushing water: A fat pipe on the ceiling gushed a continuous torrent into a brick basin, which drained away through a cast-iron grating. Alice gave this last a long look, but even if she'd been able to remove the rusty grate, the hole was too narrow for her to squeeze into.

A hollow *bong* filled the room for a moment, making her jump. It was repeated a moment later, then twice more, and when she put a hand on the door she could feel it reverberating from the impacts. She pictured the corridor outside filling with swarmers, hurling themselves into the air like living missiles, hammering at the portal . . .

She gave it a tug, and it seemed secure. The bangs continued, but Alice breathed a little easier.

"I hate to say this," Ashes commented, "but our situation has not materially improved."

Alice gave the door a bang. "This seems like an improvement to me."

"Only if you intend to remain here until you starve to death." The cat, in the corner farthest from the falling torrent of water, bent and began to lick his fur. "And while I might be able to survive for some time by eating your corpse, in the end the same applies to me."

Alice closed her eyes and gave a hysterical giggle. "Who says you get to eat me, and not the other way around?"

"It's only logical, given our relative sizes," Ashes said, still grooming. "I'd be barely a mouthful."

Alice took a deep breath for the first time in what felt like hours.

"Nobody is eating anybody," she said. "We'll just have to think of something."

A short while later, after a detailed examination of the room, she had the beginnings of a plan.

A brief inspection of the walls had turned up a brick that had cracked in half, and from the loose section Alice had broken off a vaguely wedge-shaped fragment. With this she attacked the mortar around some of the bricks beside the doorway, at about head-height. Her tool was crude, but the mortar was so old, wet, and rotten that some of the bricks were loose to begin with. After a little bit of work, she managed to lever a couple out of their sockets, and went to work on another pair a little farther down.

"If you're planning to tunnel through the wall," Ashes said, looking on curiously, "I don't think it's going to help."

Alice ignored him. When she'd pulled out two more bricks, she tossed them aside and clambered up onto the wall, using the spaces she'd made as hand- and foot-holds. It wasn't exactly comfortable, but she was able to climb a good four feet off the ground, without any immediate danger of losing her grip. She dropped back to the floor, wincing at the pain in her abused feet, and shrugged out of the cotton nightshirt with its shredded sleeves and stains. The shift she wore underneath was thin, and the air here was chilly enough to make her shiver. She climbed up onto the edge of the basin and tested the water with one finger. It was frigidly cold.

Gritting her teeth, she thrust the shirt into the water and spread it over the grille at the bottom of the basin. The suction held it in place, but just to be sure, she retrieved a couple of the bricks and dropped them on top. Water was escaping through a few tears in the fabric, but not enough to balance the flow from the pipe, and the water in the basin was already rising fast. Ashes looked on, aghast.

"Come on," Alice said. "You're going to have to sit on my shoulder."

"I should say so," the cat said, hurrying to her side. She lifted him up as the water reached the edge of the basin and spilled out onto the floor. Alice perched him on her shoulder and then, feeling the frigid water lapping around her feet, turned to the door.

This was the hard part. The banging on the door had not relented, and when she put her hand on the inner latch she could feel it vibrate with each impact. She spent a moment mentally rehearsing what she had to do, while Ashes balanced precariously on her shoulder, the pinpricks of his claws digging through her shift.

"Right," she said aloud. "Here goes nothing."

She pushed the latch and gave the door a tug, pulling it inward a fraction of an inch. Almost immediately the swarmers on the other side pushed forward, shoving the portal open and spilling into the room with triumphant *quirks* while a flood of water flowed around their legs and into the corridor. Alice jumped for her handholds on the wall, felt her fingers slip on the wet brick for a heart-stopping moment, and managed to hang on by digging her nails into the mortar. She risked a look down—the door was half-open now, and more and more of the little black creatures came into the room, carpeting the floor until it was a seething, *quirking* mass of swarmers. The ones closest to her started to jump for her exposed feet, but they couldn't quite get the height they needed to reach her, and their beaks rasped against the brickwork.

"I don't mean to be a bother," Ashes said, his claws now gripping tight enough to draw beads of blood, "but I fail to see how this has helped."

"Hang on," Alice said.

"I wouldn't dream of doing anything else."

The water pouring out of the basin was now flowing

into the corridor in a steady stream. The edge of the door was only a foot away, but it still required all of Alice's courage to reach out to it, endangering her precarious position by shifting her weight. A bit of mortar crunched under one foot, and she stopped breathing, but she didn't slip free. Her fingertips found the door and pushed. Slowly at first, hinges protesting, the door started to close. The swarmers in its path *quirk*ed indignantly and pressed into the room, climbing atop the living carpet of their fellows. Alice pushed harder, and the door swung shut with a resounding boom and a *click* from the latch.

The iron door wasn't quite watertight, but it was the next best thing. The flood that had been escaping into the corridor now had nowhere to go, and within moments Alice could see the water level in the little room rising. Inch by inch, the frigid stream spilled over the lip of the basin and started to climb up the walls.

Ashes eyed it balefully. "Do you think they float?"

"No," Alice said. "I picked one up earlier, and they're much too dense."

The rising water covered the swarmers' legs now. The living carpet writhed, trying to escape, and more and more of them threw themselves at the brickwork by her feet. A few even managed to find scrabbling holds, digging their beaks into the mortar, but they couldn't hang on for more than a few seconds before falling back into the mass.

"We used to have rats in the house," Alice said, staring at the bricks a few inches in front of her face. "They would put traps down, but sometimes they wouldn't work properly, and the poor things would still be alive. Father would have the servants take them outside and drown them in the rain barrel." She swallowed hard. "I always felt sorry for them."

"Better them than us," Ashes said. The water was now at least a foot high, covering the swarmers, but it still boiled with the swarmers' struggle to escape. "You realize it *is* going to be us in a few minutes?"

"I'll open the door and let the water out," Alice said.

Ashes thought about the geometry of that for a moment. "And where will *I* be standing when this happens, pray?"

"Cats can swim, can't they?"

"I've never had occasion to find out! Besides, I'm only *half* cat."

"It'll be a learning experience, then."

"I absolutely refuse!"

"You've got a couple of minutes to think of another plan, then."

They waited in silence as the water rose. The surface no longer boiled, but Alice wasn't sure if that meant the swarmers had drowned, or if they were just too deep underwater. To be safe she gave it until the rising tide was nearly at her toes.

"Have you thought of anything?"

"I'm still thinking," Ashes said desperately.

"Too late." Alice drew in a breath and dropped off her handhold.

She had learned to swim in the beaches along Long Island, on summer vacations and visits to her parents' friends. The Atlantic was always cold, even on a sunny day, but this was something else entirely. It hit her like a punch to the gut, driving the air from her lungs. She managed to kick enough to keep off the bottom—the thought of putting a foot down among the mass of drowned swarmers turned her stomach—and fumbled for the latch on the door. Behind her, Ashes had taken a flying leap from her shoulder, tried to get a hold on the brick-work, and ended up in the water anyway. He paddled desperately, shrieking incoherently.

Alice tried to work the latch, but her fingers had gone instantly numb. Her hands felt as though they were encased in blocks of ice. She pressed down with the palm of her hand and gave the handle a hard tug, but the door didn't so much as budge. Sudden realization dawned.

"Too much water on this side." Her teeth were chattering. "I can't . . . open it . . . too heavy . . ."

Ashes didn't hear, or didn't answer. Alice pushed weakly away from the door, in the direction of the basin. If she could remove the nightshirt, the water might start to drain—not fast enough, she suspected, but it was all she could think of. But the cold was in her now, stealing along her limbs and clutching icy fingers through her chest. Her legs felt like they'd been strapped to concrete blocks, and keeping her head above water was all she could manage. Presently, even that seemed impossible. Her jaw was so tightly locked, she thought her teeth would shatter, and her arms had gone completely numb. She tried to paddle, but only managed a weak thrashing. There was a stinging pain from the wound in her cheek as it went below the surface.

She wondered if her father had felt like this as the *Gideon* came apart around him. She could see him, clinging to a rail as the ship slipped below the waves. She couldn't breathe.

Something shifted, as though a hole had opened in the floor and the water was streaming out, sucking Alice down with it. But the water wasn't moving, only Alice, and she was moving not down but *away*, in a direction perpendicular to the usual three dimensions. She felt something strain, and then *snap*—

Chapter Ten

THE WIZARD OF THE LIBRARY

SHE OPENED HER EYES to the familiar flicker of gaslight.

She was in a bed, under thick covers, soft and heavy and above all, *warm*. It felt wonderful, and for a while she simply luxuriated in the sensation. She was wearing a fresh nightgown, and someone had attended to her cuts and scrapes. Her hands and feet were wound with linen, and a bandage was affixed to her cheek with sticking plaster.

The room was not one she recognized, but by the rich décor she guessed it was somewhere in Geryon's private suite. Bookcases lined the walls, and a fire glowed from a small hearth. A high-backed armchair had been positioned beside the bed, as though someone had been sitting beside her.

Alice lay back, covers pulled up to her chin, and savored the warmth and the simple sensation of being *alive*. After being nearly devoured, drowned, frozen, and stabbed, she was content to let matters take their course for a while.

As it happened, she didn't have long to wait. The wood-paneled door opened to reveal Geryon himself, carrying a steaming mug in both hands. He padded across the room in his carpet slippers, looking just as he had when she'd first seen him, in ratty clothing and old-fashioned whiskers, but something indefinable had changed. The way he moved carried a sense of purpose, of power, and the air fairly crackled as he passed.

"I see that you're awake," he said, setting the mug on the nightstand. He settled himself in the chair beside the bed and gave a brief smile. "I can only imagine you're very confused."

"You're a wizard," she said flatly. He raised one eyebrow, and she shook her head violently. "You're a wizard, and you've got a magical library, and if you try to tell me that I've been . . . ill, or hallucinating, or anything like that, I swear I'm going to scream. That was *not* a fever-dream."

"I wouldn't insult your intelligence with the suggestion." Geryon stroked his whiskers.

"I'm sorry," she said. "I just—I wasn't sure if you would—"

"It's all right." Geryon settled back in the chair. "As for 'wizard,' I have certainly been called such a thing. Also a sorcerer, a magi, a saint, and a devil. Among ourselves, we tend to use the term 'Reader' for those who have the gift. It is a little more . . . accurate."

"Ashes said something like that," Alice said. She paused. There were a thousand questions that leaped immediately to mind, but one shouldered the others aside. "Do you know what happened to my father?"

Geryon pursed his lips. "I'm afraid that is a long story, and not a pleasant one."

"Please. I have to know." Alice looked away from his face, almost afraid to ask. "Is he really dead?"

"I . . . do not know." Something of Alice's feelings must have shown on her face, because Geryon sighed and shook his head. "Oh, I don't wish to give you false hope. He is dead, almost certainly. All I meant is that the manner of his death might not be that which was reported to the world."

Alice's throat was suddenly tight. "What really happened?"

"To understand that, you must understand a little bit about Readers." He glanced at the mug on the nightstand. "You should drink that before it goes cold, by the way."

"Why?" Alice eyed it suspiciously. "Is it a potion?"

Geryon chuckled and shook his head. Alice picked up the mug and took a sniff, then a cautious sip. It was cocoa, thick and sweet.

"There aren't many of us," Geryon went on. "Readers, I mean. The talent is a rare thing, and of those who have it, the vast majority go through their whole lives without ever realizing their potential. There are perhaps two dozen fully trained Readers in the entire world. Most of them, I'm sorry to say, prefer things this way, and to them any talented newcomer is either a prize to be possessed or a threat to be eliminated."

"You mean me, don't you?" Alice said.

Geryon nodded. "You have the potential to be a great Reader, Alice. Perhaps the greatest of the age, with the right training. Unfortunately, this puts you in danger.

Ever since you were a little girl, I have been doing my best to protect you."

"Why?" Alice said. "Are you really my uncle?"

"It would be more accurate to say that I am your great-great-great-grandfather, although it's possible I have left out a generation somewhere. At times the records are a bit muddled. Nevertheless, I make a point of looking after my family. I am a sentimental man, in my fashion."

"But . . ." She wanted to say "That's impossible," but realized how foolish it would sound. Instead she took a sip from the cocoa. "Was my father a Reader? Did he know about any of this?"

"He was not a Reader himself, that is for certain. The gift runs in families, but only fitfully, and it will often skip several generations. As for how much he knew, I'm not certain. What I do know is that my efforts to keep you secret eventually failed, and one of my . . . colleagues, another Reader . . . learned of your potential. I believe this person contacted your father."

"I saw something like that." Alice swallowed hard. "Why would he go off and leave me behind after that?"

"Again, I can only speculate. Maybe your father thought he could draw attention away from you by leaving, and he may have succeeded. My guess is that this other Reader took your father from the *Gideon* and sank it to cover himself. When I heard what had happened, I realized I had to bring you here at once."

"Then he could still be alive," Alice blurted. "My father. If someone took him . . ."

Geryon closed his eyes. He looked weary, and somehow *ancient* beyond the years that showed on his face. "I don't pretend to know for certain. But I do know the nature of my fellow Readers, and they are not the sort of people who would keep a tool around when it had lost its value. We are, I'm afraid to say, a rather callous fraternity."

"All right." She squirreled the idea away for later examination. "Why bring me here and not tell me any of this? You must have known I would find out eventually!"

"I thought you might," Geryon said. "Although you have not had as gentle an introduction as I had hoped for."

Alice bristled. "You might have warned me."

"I believe I did," Geryon said mildly. "Simply having the talent is not enough. I brought you here in part to find out what kind of person you were. Some minds—*most* minds, I should say, most of humanity—are so closed to the idea of the supernatural that they wrap themselves in a blanket of normality, and when anything leaks through they make up little stories to explain it. 'I was dreaming,' say, or 'I imagined it all.' If you confront such a mind with incontrovertible proof, there is always the risk that it will simply crack." Geryon spread his hands. "I had no wish to bring you here simply to drive you mad."

"Are you sure you haven't?" Alice said, a bit testily. Privately, though, she was relieved to discover that Geryon had known all along she would sneak into the library. In a way, it meant that she hadn't *really* broken the rules after all.

Geryon smiled. "Quite sure," he said.

Alice paused, considering. "What about Emma, and Mr. Black and the others? Are they . . ."

"Readers? No. They are my servants, as they claimed to be."

"And they know about all this?"

Geryon nodded. "Don't blame them for not letting you in on the secret. I gave them very strict instructions. If you're angry, be angry with me."

"I don't think I'm angry," Alice said, examining her own feelings with mild curiosity. "But what happens now?"

Geryon's face was suddenly grave. "Now," he said, "you have a choice to make."

"Choice?" The mug of cocoa was empty. Alice set it

aside and gripped the blanket a little tighter. "What kind of choice?"

"A Reader's life is a dangerous one, for herself and everyone around her." Geryon scratched his whiskers. "It is not, truthfully, a life I would wish on anyone, and I will not force it on you. But neither can I leave you untrained and helpless, blundering about with the power to open doors and no idea what lies behind them."

"It doesn't sound like I *have* a choice," Alice said. "If I have the talent, I have it, like it or not."

"Not necessarily. I could erase your memories of what happened, and ensure you never stumbled onto the secret again. Your life would go on as before, and you would always have a place here. I would make certain that you were happy."

Alice felt her skin crawl. "You mean you'd cut my skull open and fool around in my brain?"

"In a manner of speaking. But you would feel no pain, I assure you. It is the only chance for a normal life you have left."

Alice closed her eyes. It ought to sound attractive, she guessed. *If I could just forget about all of this, forget every-thing and just be a normal girl...*

But this was the way the world was. It was deeper and stranger and scarier than she'd ever imagined, but it was *real.* To forget, to give up now, would just be giving in to her fear. And Alice's father hadn't raised her to give up.

You'll be afraid, he'd told her once. *It's nothing to be ashamed of. The important thing is what you* do *about it.*

"What's the other choice?"

"You become my apprentice," Geryon said. "You work here, and I train you until you're ready to defend yourself."

"How long will that be?"

"Years. Maybe decades. And even when you're trained, you'll be a Reader, with all the dangers that implies. The mundane world will be closed to you forever." He shook his head. "I know you did not ask for this, and I know it must be difficult for you. But there is no other way, I promise you."

Alice's brow furrowed, but in the end it wasn't such a difficult choice after all. Forgetting about magic would mean forgetting the fairy in her kitchen, the last memories she had of her father, as well as giving up any chance of finding out what had really happened to him. *If I train to be a Reader, then maybe . . .*

"I'll do it," Alice said. "Be an apprentice, I mean."

"I thought you might." Geryon gave a little sigh. "Even now, you do not appreciate what may be required of you. Remember that the other option remains open, if you are ever inclined to give up. Or," he added, almost offhandedly, "if you fail."

CHAPTER ELEVEN

THE SORCERER'S APPRENTICE

ALICE SPENT THE REST of the day resting in her room. Meals were delivered to her door by the familiar invisible servants, and dirty dishes whisked away in the same fashion. Before she got into bed, she peeled off the bandages and looked at herself in the mirror. Her bruises were fading, and her cuts had scabbed over. The one on her cheek was still an angry red, cutting across her pale, freckled skin as straight as a grid-rule.

The following morning, when she smelled breakfast cooking downstairs and opened the door, she found a small gray cat sitting in the doorway. Alice frowned at him.

"Ashes? What are you doing in the house?"

"I'm being punished for my sins," the cat sighed. "Can I come in? We need to talk."

"I suppose." Ashes slunk past her ankles, and she shut the door behind him. "I ought to be angry with you, though."

"Why?"

"What do you mean, *why*? You nearly got me killed!"

The cat hopped up on her bed. "I could say the same about you."

"That's not fair. *I* didn't even know what a Reader was, much less that I was one. At least I got us both out alive."

"And wet," Ashes muttered.

"Isaac is really the one to blame," Alice said. The thought of his smug, dismissive expression brought heat to her cheeks.

"That's what I wanted to talk to you about," Ashes said. "Did you say anything about Isaac to Geryon?"

Alice frowned, replaying yesterday's conversation in her mind. "No. I don't think so. I didn't really have the chance."

"That's something, anyway." He sat down, folding his forepaws under him. "Listen. You can't mention him to Geryon, or Mr. Black, or *anyone*."

"Why not?" Alice's eyes narrowed. "What's he doing living in the library, anyway? Is he supposed to be there?"

"It's complicated—"

"He's not, is he?" Alice grinned. "You're keeping secrets from Geryon."

"It's not *me* keeping secrets. I just do what I'm told. As for *why*, you'll have to take that up with Mother."

"You mentioned her yesterday. Do you mean your real mother?"

"Yes," said the cat. "She guards the library for Geryon. Letting Isaac stay there was her idea."

"If she guards it *for* him, then why would she—"

"I don't know, all right? You just have to keep quiet until she gets a chance to explain it to you herself."

Alice considered. She really *ought* to say something to Geryon. But Ashes had helped, in the world of the Swarm. Without his explanation, she might never have survived.

Besides, said a sneaky part of her mind, *if Ashes and Isaac are breaking the rules, maybe they'll be more likely to help me.* She hadn't given up on finding the yellow-and-black fairy, though she was starting to appreciate that it might be more difficult than she'd originally thought.

"All right," she said. "For now. But no promises. Does Geryon know you're here?"

"Actually," Ashes said, "since I let you get into the book, he's given me the job of being your minder when you're in the library. We're supposed to go there after breakfast and see Mr. Wurms."

"We'd better get to breakfast, then."

Ashes waited while Alice finished dressing, and padded at her side to the main stairs. Halfway down, he froze, back arched, and a moment later the massive form of Mr. Black came into view from the second floor. His expression, usually sour at the sight of Alice, was positively pinched this time, but it twisted into a sneer when he noticed Ashes.

"I'm going to have to get Emma to put down traps," he said. "The *vermin* are getting into the house again."

Ashes gave a low growl, and Mr. Black snorted. Alice glared at him. It had been his voice she'd heard talking to the yellow fairy, and now she wondered if Geryon knew anything about it. They certainly hadn't *sounded* like they were doing anything aboveboard.

"Have you been in the library lately, Mr. Black?" Alice said, doing her best to sound innocent. "I could have sworn I heard your voice the other day."

Mr. Black fixed his gaze on her, bushy black eyebrows rising.

"Maybe I have and maybe I haven't. I go where I please on the master's business, and it's no concern of yours." He leaned closer, voice dropping to a low growl. "If I were *you*, I wouldn't go poking your nose where it doesn't belong. Just because you're a Reader doesn't mean you've got the run of the place. And you ought not to hang around with *cats*. You might get fleas."

Without waiting for a response, he straightened up and brushed past her, his bulk forcing Alice and Ashes to squeeze to one side of the stairway. Alice stared after him until he'd gone out of sight, then looked down at Ashes.

"What an awful man," she said. "He doesn't seem to like you."

"He doesn't like anyone he can't order around," Ashes said. "And I only take orders from Mother, not from the likes of him. But I think it's mostly you he's angry with."

"Me? Why?"

"You're Geryon's new apprentice," Ashes explained. "That puts you above him, or will eventually. What did you mean about hearing him in the library?"

Alice frowned. Ashes had vanished just before she'd started eavesdropping on Mr. Black, and apparently he hadn't overheard the conversation . . .

"Nothing," she said. "Just . . . trying to needle him."

"You ought to watch yourself around him," Ashes said. "He's dangerous."

"I'm not afraid of Mr. Black," Alice said, though she was, a little. "Come on. Let's get something to eat."

After breakfast, Alice and Ashes walked over to the library. This time the door opened easily when she pulled on the ring, and she lit one of the hurricane lamps and went inside. The neat rows of bookshelves by the entrance bore little resemblance to the weird geometries she'd seen that night, and she ran one finger along the scab on her cheek to remind herself that she hadn't made any of it up.

Mr. Wurms was right at the long table where she'd last seen him, surrounded by piles of books. He looked up as she approached, and favored her with a brief smile, showing a mouthful of rotten teeth.

"Ms. Creighton," he said, with his soft, buzzing accent. "How nice to see that you've recovered from your . . . adventure."

Alice nodded. "Ashes tells me I'm to work with you."

"Indeed. You will assist me, and begin picking up some of the . . . ah . . . tricks of the trade, as it were. If you have any questions, feel free to ask."

"Thank you." She hesitated, then said, "Are you a Reader, then? Like Geryon?"

"Course not," Ashes said, jumping onto the table and sending up a little billow of dust. "He's a servant, like the rest of us. Go on, ask him what he really is."

Mr. Wurms glared at the cat. Alice swallowed.

"That doesn't seem like a very polite question," she ventured.

"A very astute judgment," Mr. Wurms said. "I'm glad you have more sense than this . . . rat-catcher."

"Rat-catcher! *Rat-catcher?!*"

"So," Alice said, over the sounds of Ashes' indignation, "I'm eager to get started. What am I to be doing?"

"Looking for magic," Mr. Wurms said. His licked his lips, his tongue disturbingly pink and agile. "Has Master Geryon explained it to you?"

"He hasn't explained anything," Alice said.

Mr. Wurms blinked behind his enormous spectacles and gestured vaguely at the bookshelves all around him. "What do you see here?"

"Books?"

"Indeed, books. They are the ocean in which magic swims."

"These are magical books?"

"Not in themselves, no. But every so often, somewhere among them, a particular word or phrase or sentence achieves a meaning that goes beyond the natural. If *I* were to look at it, I would see only dry letters on paper, but to *you* they would express a flicker of power."

"But if you can't see magic, then how can it be your job to find it?"

"One thing at a time. Now, those fragments must be extracted as a surgeon might extract a foreign body from a patient. Then they can be combined to serve as the raw material for magic. Master Geryon can weave them together, one to the next, and create new books of the sort you mentioned."

"Prison-books?"

"And portal-books, and world-books, and books that lead to the bottom of the ocean, and a hundred other things. What he does with his books and why he does it is not for us to know. Our task is to comb the library for the fragments so that he might do it."

Alice frowned. "Haven't you looked through all these books already? They have to have been here for ages."

"Magic is not something stamped into a book by a printing press, girl! Where it takes root and how long it lasts, no one can say. Have you never picked up a book you've read before, and found it speaks to you in a new way?"

Alice nodded.

Mr. Wurms shrugged. "Books age, they yellow, the pages dry and crackle and tear. Who can tell what tiny defect will change simple paper and ink into true meaning? Certain authors, certain printers, even certain binders or typesetters are more likely to generate magic than others. We suspect that those who have a bit of the Reader's talent leave little traces of their passage wherever they go, like a man with paint on his shoes. Master Geryon's collection is among the finest. But even here, we must dig carefully to find the scraps of value."

"So I should . . . what? Just grab a book at random and flip through it?" Alice had a sudden vision of spending the rest of her life in here, paging patiently through ancient folios while she grew old and gray and wrinkled and the library dust settled on her like a cloak.

"We're not so primitive as that," Mr. Wurms said, with a smile that suggested he understood her private horror. "Let me introduce you to your new friend."

He bent and fumbled under the table, then came up with an open-topped wooden crate half-filled with straw. Nestled amongst the brittle stalks Alice could see something black and glistening. Mr. Wurms reached in and lifted the thing out onto the tabletop with a squelch.

Alice had to fight two very strong instincts. The first was to run; the second was to find the heaviest book on the shelves and bash the horrid thing until it was a puddle of goo. It looked vaguely like a leech, but the largest leech she had ever seen, black with gray stripes and the size of a small dog. One end, which she assumed was the head, was equipped with a round, puckered sphincter of a mouth and two parallel ridges, along which were dozens of hard black dots that might be eyes. Rousted from its box, it wriggled helplessly for a moment and then rose slightly on its rippling flanks.

Vomiting also presented itself as an option to Alice, and she fought down bile at the back of her throat. She tried to tell herself it was no more awful than an earthworm, even though it was big enough to stretch its gummy mouth around her fist.

"What *is* that?" She was unable to keep a faint quiver out of her voice.

"It hasn't got a proper name, I'm afraid," Mr. Wurms said, looking at the creature affectionately. "I call them 'seekers,' after their function. They have the nearly unique talent of being able to find a book with a scrap of magic in it even from a distance. I suspect they can smell it, somehow, or perhaps they have some other sense that we lack. You can use it like a bloodhound."

"Does it respond to commands, then?" said Alice, feeling a little hysterical. "'Stay' and 'heel' and so on?"

"No," Mr. Wurms said, "I don't believe it has ears."

He took a leather cord from the box and threaded it into a metal eyelet screwed directly into the leech-thing's back. Mr. Wurms knotted the cord neatly and presented Alice with the other end.

"Just give it a tug, and it will get the message. When it starts trying to climb the shelves, you're getting near the book you want. Then just show it the nearby volumes until it likes one of them, and flip through that one until you find the scrap. You'll know it when you see it, I assure you."

"Fine," Alice said distantly. "All right."

"By the by, the moisture on the seeker's skin is its own secretion. There's no need to keep it wet."

"That's . . . good to hear."

CHAPTER TWELVE
ENDING

I'M WALKING A LEECH, Alice thought. *I've got a leech on a leash.* She had to suppress mad giggles.

The "seeker" gave a steady pull on the leash, like an eager puppy, and Alice let it go where it liked. Ashes followed, trotting along the bookshelves and occasionally gathering himself for a leap from one to the next.

"Did you know all that?" Alice asked him. "About the books and scraps of magic and so forth?"

"Mother may have mentioned it once or twice," the cat said, "but I wasn't really paying attention. It doesn't make much difference to me. Not my job description, you might say."

"What *is* your job description? Aside from taking care of me."

"Keeping things out of the library that ought not to be in it."

Alice chuckled. "No wonder Geryon was angry with you."

"Yes. Well." Ashes bristled and lashed his tail for a moment. "It'll teach me to have a sense of humor."

They walked for a few moments in silence.

"Where did this thing *come* from, anyway?" Alice said, nodding toward the seeker. "I've never heard of anything like it."

"It came out of a book, of course," Ashes said. "From another world."

"Another *world*? Like another planet?"

"Maybe. Who knows? You saw the shelves in the back of the library. Every one of those books is a portal to another place. It could be somewhere on Earth, or it could be somewhere else."

"And the Readers create the books?"

"Or they find them, or steal them from other Readers."

"Are these other worlds *inside* the books? Or do they exist anyway, and the book only opens a doorway to them? If nobody had written the book, would the place it goes to still exist? Or—"

"They exist," Ashes said. "You'll drive yourself mad thinking like that. People have, believe me. It's like wondering whether the inside of your closet still exists when you shut the door. Keep on down that path and you end up thinking the whole universe is a dream of someone in someone else's dream, or some such nonsense. All you need to know is that Master Geryon keeps the books here, and sometimes they *leak*. There are things prowling this library that you wouldn't like to meet on a dark night."

"Not the things from the prison-books, though."

"No. Those are different."

Alice considered for a moment. "What about Mr. Wurms? If he's not a Reader, does that mean he came out of a book as well?"

"Certainly. So did Mr. Black. Even Mother came out of a book, though that was so long ago, I doubt even Geryon can remember. You and Geryon are the only real humans here." Ashes hesitated. "Oh. And Emma, I suppose."

"Why does Mr. Black work for Geryon? He doesn't seem to like doing what he's told." The idea of the big furnace-keeper drawing a salary suddenly seemed ludicrous. *He never leaves the house, so how could he spend it?*

Ashes gave an irritated flick of his tail. "A Reader can draw up a sort of magical contract with his servants. As long as he can get the creature to agree to it, they're both bound by the terms until something breaks the magic. Mr. Black might not be happy about his job, but there's nothing he can do about it, unless—"

Alice stopped and held up a hand as the seeker gave a tug on its leash. "I think it's found something."

The leech-like thing was indeed straining toward a particular shelf, a cheap, cracked wooden one groaning under a mountain of old paperbacks. Alice didn't have any way of telling *which* book the seeker was pointing her toward, so she began the long and tedious process of holding each one up for the creature's inspection.

It was twenty minutes before she found the right book, a thick, half-rotten volume with a title she didn't understand in what looked like Dutch. When she held it up, the seeker pressed its sticky body right against the cover, so she tied the creature up and started to page through. The text was incomprehensible to her, and some of the tissue-paper-thin pages fell to pieces when she touched them. It felt like a thoroughly pointless exercise, and she had almost concluded she was doing it wrong, somehow, when she found what she was looking for.

Toward the back of the book, one half-torn page bore a solid block of text that looked different from the rest. It was printed the same, and the language was still incomprehensible, but when her eye fell on it Alice had a sudden feeling of *clarity*, as though the meaning of what was written was so apparent that it shone forth like a beacon through the faded ink and foreign words. She couldn't have explained what that meaning *was*, but it felt as obvious as the nose on her face, as though it had skipped her eyes entirely and sunk directly into her brain.

It was a feeling she realized that she'd had before, though very rarely. Alice had always loved books, and she'd devoured first the contents of her father's shelves and then whatever she was allowed to borrow from the Carnegie Library. Occasionally, she had come across a passage that made her feel like this, as though a light were shining out of the book and directly into her skull. She'd never been able to explain to anyone else *why* those particular pieces felt so meaningful to her. Even her father had only laughed when she'd tried to get him to see it, and said that books spoke to everyone in a different way.

It was also a faint echo of the sensation she'd had when she'd open the prison-book. If this was a faint whisper, that had been a full-throated roar, a *meaning* so strong, it grabbed hold of reality and tied it in knots. Alice looked down at the book in her hands, and couldn't help the smile spreading across her face. *So this is magic.*

She hurried back to Mr. Wurms, hoping he'd show her what to do with what she'd found, but the goggle-eyed scholar merely set the book on a pile and told her to go back out and find another. After her second trip out and back, Ashes decided he would be better employed napping underneath Mr. Wurms' table than tagging along with her. After her third trip, Alice was seriously thinking about joining him.

The seeker went on and on, apparently tireless. By the afternoon, her feet ached from walking and she was coughing from the omnipresent dust. Of all the ways Alice would have expected to describe her new life as a magician's apprentice, "boring" wouldn't have been on the list, but she was beginning to wonder if being a Reader's apprentice was all it was cracked up to be. She was just wondering if it was getting close to time to head in to dinner when a strange sensation on the back of her neck made her pull up short.

It felt like her first night in the library, just before she'd found the fairy. As though the shelves were *moving* around her, behind her back, somehow pushing themselves into new configurations while leaving decades of dust undisturbed. Her first impulse was to spin around to catch them at it, but she stifled this and simply stood very still, staring straight ahead. The seeker had halted, pulling itself into a tight little ball as though it was afraid of something.

"Hello, Alice."

It was a deep, sibilant purr of a voice, soft and rich. If velvet and silk could talk, they would have had a voice like that. It made Alice think of something dark and hidden, poised to spring.

She shivered, and forced herself to turn around slowly.

Behind her, where the aisle had been, there was now a dead end. It was shrouded in shadow, and no matter how Alice moved her lantern, the light refused to penetrate. All she could see was a pair of eyes, yellow-silver and cat-slitted. Like Ashes' eyes, but *this* pair was on a level with Alice's own.

"Hello," Alice managed.

"I thought," said the voice, "that you and I should have a little chat."

Alice swallowed and nodded. "You're . . . Ashes' mother, aren't you? The one he called the guardian of the library."

"Yesssss," she hissed. "You may call me Ending."

"What do you want with me?"

"Isn't it obvious, child?" Ending smiled. At least, Alice thought it was a smile. In the darkness, all she could see was the faint glint of the lantern on bone-white teeth, as long as knives. "I want to help you."

There was a quivery feeling in the pit of Alice's stomach that she'd never felt before, not even when she'd thought the Swarm was going to get her. She pulled herself together.

"Help me?" she said, proud that she kept any quiver out of her voice. "Help me how?"

"You have chosen a dark path," Ending purred. "I would like you to walk it with your eyes open."

"You mean by becoming Geryon's apprentice?"

"Yesss. You do not yet know what he will do to you, child."

"But Geryon *helped* me. I might have died after I got out of the Swarm, if not for him."

"Yes," Ending said, "but he is a Reader. His magic is based on cruelty and death. It is his nature. He will hurt you, bend you, break you, and tell you it is for your own good. He will send you to do his bidding, and you will fight for him, bleed for him, *kill* for him. He will teach you just enough to be useful, but never so much that you might surpass him. And in the end, when your usefulness to him is done, he will cast you aside like a knife that breaks in his hand."

There was a long silence. Alice's mouth was dry.

"However," Ending continued, "I think you and I can be allies, Alice Creighton. I am trying to find something that I lost, long ago. A book. It is hidden somewhere in the library."

"What does that have to do with me?"

"I am not the only one seeking it. And one of the others is, I think, of great interest to you."

Alice thought for a moment. Then she remembered what the fairy had said, when she'd eavesdropped on his meeting with Mr. Black. *The book is here, I'm sure of it.*

"The fairy!" she blurted. "The yellow-and-black fairy. He's looking for this same book?"

Alice thought Ending's smile widened a bit. "Indeed. The 'fairy,' as you call him, is a poison-sprite named Vespidian. He serves another Reader, one of Geryon's enemies, who wants the book for himself."

"Then I have to find him," Alice said. "He may know what really happened to my father."

"That will not be easy," Ending said. "He is a clever

little beast. He has a charm of some kind that renders him invisible to me." Her voice took on a rumbling edge. "Otherwise, he would never have been able to set foot in my labyrinth without my knowing. But there may be a way to trap him. All we require is suitable bait."

"The book, in other words." Alice's mind was racing ahead. "If we had this book he wants so badly, we could get him to come to us."

"Indeed. And so you see our interests align."

"All right," Alice said cautiously. "But I don't see how I can help you find one book in a place like this."

"The nature of the hiding place prevents me from locating the book myself," Ending said. "But there must be a way to find it, or Vespidian would not be attempting the search. My first attempt to recruit someone to assist me has not been . . . fruitful. Nevertheless, if the two of you work together, I remain hopeful that you will discover something. I believe you have already met."

Alice tried to think who else she had met, during her brief time at The Library. Ending could hardly mean Emma, or Mr. Wurms, or—

"*Isaac?* You asked *him* to help you?"

"I did."

"Well," Alice said, "I'm not surprised you didn't get

anywhere. I only met him for five minutes, and he nearly got me killed." She paused. "That was you, wasn't it? You led me to where Mr. Black was meeting the fairy, and then you sent Ashes to lead me to Isaac."

"Clever girl," Ending purred. "Yes. The paths of the labyrinth are mine to command. They lead where I wish them to go."

"Why not just *talk* to me?" Alice said. "Why stay in the shadows?"

Ending gave a soft chuckle. "I suppose that is because that is *my* nature."

Alice pictured the library as a game board, with those eyes hovering over it, pushing the little pieces this way and that until she got what she wanted. It wasn't a pleasant image, no matter how much Ending said she wanted to help.

But if it gets me to this Vespidian . . .

Only, there was a question that nagged at her. "What about Geryon?"

"What about him?"

"You're his servant, aren't you? I mean, this is his library, and you're its guardian . . ."

She trailed off. The yellow eyes had gone very wide, and a deep, rumbling growl echoed off the bookshelves and rattled Alice's back teeth. She felt like a mouse, going about its business in the kitchen, who suddenly looked up and saw those eyes looming above it.

"I am *bound* to Geryon," Ending said in a low, dangerous tone. "By ancient contract. I keep his library safe in the coils of my labyrinth. I protect his precious books from his enemies. But I am *not* his servant. And someday . . ."

She stopped, staring into the distance.

Alice cleared her throat. "Sorry. I just meant, if someone is trying to steal his book, shouldn't we tell him about it?"

"It's not his book," Ending snapped. "It's mine."

"All right, all right," Alice said. "I was only asking."

The yellow eyes were gone, the shadows dark and empty.

"What is this book, anyway?" Alice said, half to herself. "What's so important about it?"

Ending's voice was a distant whisper. "The Dragon . . ."

CHAPTER THIRTEEN
THE EYES OF A WIZARD

ALICE TOOK A DEEP breath and knocked on the door to Geryon's suite. His voice answered at once.

"Yes?"

"It's Alice, sir," she said. "Mr. Black said you wanted to see me."

Finding the sour-faced servant at her door first thing in the morning was never a pleasant experience, but after a week of hunting through the library for scraps, Alice was more than pleased to receive Geryon's summons.

He opened the door to his suite wearing his usual shabby jacket and stained waistcoat. His beard and whiskers were freshly combed, though, and there was a gleam of anticipation in his eye.

"Come in, come in." He ushered her into the hall, past the bedroom where she'd woken up after the Swarm incident and a half-dozen other closed doors. At the end of the corridor, one door stood open, and Geryon waved her inside.

"Over here," he said. "Mind the pillows."

The room was small, the floor covered in a burgundy carpet so thick, Alice's shoes sank into it, the walls heavily hung with soft-looking fabric. There was no furniture, not even a bookcase, but tasseled pillows were scattered everywhere, gathered in the corners and built up into a kind of nest. Geryon sat in the middle of these, looking utterly out of place.

"I apologize for the way this place looks," he said. "Take off your shoes, please, and make yourself comfortable."

Baffled, Alice did as he asked, and sat where he indicated, just in front of him, her skirts folded neatly underneath her. The carpet was as soft as it looked, slipping through her fingers like thick, springy moss.

"How have you been finding your work with Mr. Wurms?" Geryon said.

Weighing her options, Alice decided that honesty was probably best. "On the dull side, sir."

"I suspected as much. Magic, you'll find, is nine parts dull to one part excitement, and the exciting bits usually hurt like the blazes." He scratched his cheek and smoothed his whiskers absently. "The same as anything else, I imagine."

"I just want to learn something, sir. If I'm to be your apprentice, shouldn't I be studying?"

"Learning magic is not like learning Latin or algebra. It's more like learning to swim, or to ride a bicycle. No amount of study will substitute for even a little bit of *doing*. Which is why you're here today."

Alice did her best not to look excited, but her heart beat a little harder. "Yes, sir."

"As in many things, the first step is the hardest. There is a certain—feeling, a perspective, a view of the world, perhaps, that in time will become utterly second nature to you. But getting that first glimpse of it is tremendously difficult."

He cleared his throat with a great *harrumph*. "For the same reason that it is difficult to explain in words, it is hard for me to prepare you for our work here. What you must keep in mind, above all else, is that nothing you experience while I'm working with you is *real* in the sense that you understand it. When we are done, you will find yourself sitting here in this room, without a mark on you. You have my word on that. Do you trust me?"

"I trust you, sir."

"Good. Are you ready?"

Alice nodded. "I'm ready."

"Give me your hands."

He extended his own hands, palms up, and took hold of Alice's wrists. His fingers were thin, but his grip was iron-hard. Sitting so close, she could smell him, warm and cloying.

"All right," Geryon said. "Now, if it helps, feel free to scream."

Alice's heart slammed in her chest. *Anticipation,* she thought, *is always the worst part. The moment* before *the doctor puts the needle in your arm is much worse than actually feeling it go in.*

Then Geryon did—something. Nothing she could see or hear, but she felt it nonetheless. Something invisible leaped across the space between them. It settled over her face like a mask, scrabbling at her skin like a living thing until it found the corners of her mouth and flooded inside her. She could feel it spreading out, like she'd inhaled a mouthful of hot gas, down into her lungs but also *up*, filtering through her sinuses and out through her skull until it found her eyes.

She'd been wrong. The pain was worse than the anticipation, worse than anything she'd ever experienced or imagined. It felt like someone had pushed jagged shards of glass into her eyes and was twisting them back and forth in the sockets, sending searing tendrils of pain all the way down her body. Her toes curled and her arms jerked, ready to claw at the offending orbs, but Geryon held her in a firm grip. Her vision had gone black, but she could hear someone screaming, a pathetic, little-girl shriek of terror and agony.

It was over nearly as soon as it began, a single telescoped instant of mind-numbing suffering, but it was a few moments more before she could form a coherent thought. Geryon's voice broke through the clouds of phantom agony still echoing in her skull, the gentle monotone of a hypnotist.

"Alice. Listen to me, Alice. You're all right. It's all over, and you're all right. Just listen to me. Listen to my voice..."

She drew a ragged breath and shuddered. Her fingers

had gripped Geryon's forearms so tightly that her nails had dug tiny cuts in his skin.

"You're all right," Geryon repeated. "Can you hear me, Alice?"

"I can hear you," she said. Her voice was a croak.

"It's all over. You never have to do that again."

"I'm sorry," she mumbled, realizing that the shriek had been her own. "I'm sorry."

"You did well," he said. "When I did it, I bit my tongue so badly, I couldn't speak for three days. Now. How do you feel?"

"I'm . . . all right." Tingles of pain still came and went, but they were fading.

"Open your eyes, then. But be careful. Remember what I said about what's real."

She hadn't realized her eyes were closed, or even still intact. When she opened them, her breath caught in her throat. The pillowed room was gone, Geryon was gone. Even Alice herself was gone. When she looked down at her lap, there was nothing to see, as though she'd been turned invisible. Her hands clenched tighter on Geryon's wrists.

In place of the room full of carpets was an enormous starry vista, utterly dark except for tiny pinpricks of light scattered both above and below her like grains of sand on black velvet. They weren't the stars of the real world—she couldn't see any familiar constellations, and they lacked the friendly twinkle of the stars she knew.

"You are still here," Geryon said in his calm monotone. "Sitting in a room in The Library, with me. What I have done is taken control of your vision and trained it a new direction, a way you've never looked before. Not up or down, left or right, but *inside*. This is the other half of magic, to look inside and see the essence of things. Now, don't be alarmed."

Alice's field of view began to rotate, as though she were being turned in place. Something huge came into sight, and soon it filled the world. It looked a bit like a fanciful drawing she'd once seen of a comet—a blazing fireball, trailing a long glowing tail—except that the tail continued on and on, into the indefinite distance, and the fire was a brilliant blue.

It seemed to be coming directly at her, or she was moving toward it, and Alice's breath caught in her throat. It seemed almost close enough to touch, but she felt no heat. She felt nothing, in fact; as far as her body was concerned, she was still sitting in the room full of pillows with Geryon.

"What am I looking at?" Alice said, when she found her voice again.

"Yourself," Geryon said. "Or the magical representation thereof. Your essence. Your soul, if you like, though I wouldn't read too much into the religious side of things. What we see here is very much shaped by our preconceptions, so one shouldn't leap to draw any deep conclusions."

"My . . ." Alice swallowed hard.

"What I would like you to do is look back, along the tail. There's something wrapping round and round—do you see it?"

It took her a few moments.

"I see it," she said. "A little silver thread."

"This part is a little tricky." He must have felt her tense, because he quickly added, "It doesn't hurt, though. I want you to reach out and grab it."

Alice nodded gamely, but when she released her grip on Geryon's wrists, he held her arms tightly. "Not," he said, "with your hands."

She opened her mouth to protest, then thought better of it. Instead she focused on the little thread, staring intently, trying to *will* it closer to her, or herself closer to it. She was surprised to find that she *could* reach out, extending herself in some dimension completely unlike the usual three. Her grip closed around the thread, and she could feel the tension shivering through it in her mind. It was like holding a fishing line with something jerking about at the far end.

"You've got it." Geryon sounded satisfied. "I should have known you would be a quick study. Now, hold on to it, and I'll let go of your eyes."

Something flowed out of Alice, down from inside her skull and out between her lips like a whispered breath. She blinked, and when she opened her eyes again the brilliant comet and the starlit night were gone. There was only Geryon, shadowy in the gaslight, still holding her wrists and smiling under his whiskers.

"Still got that thread?" he said.

Alice nodded. It tingled in her mind, a phantom limb holding a phantom line.

Geryon let go of her wrists and sat back. "Try giving it a little tug. Pull it toward *here*, toward the world. Just a touch."

"All right."

Alice's hands ached with cramps, but her mental grip was still strong. She pulled on the thread, tugging in the direction she thought of as "reality." It resisted at first, then gave a little, and there was a little *pop* from beside her. She felt a sudden pressure on her knee, and there was a well-remembered *quirk.*

The swarmer stood quietly, its claws dimpling her skirt, its body cocked at an angle that seemed almost quizzical. Its tiny black eyes gleamed. It took all of her self-control not to jump up, or to grab the vile little thing and hurl it against the wall.

"I thought I killed those things," Alice said, keeping her voice as calm as she could.

"And so you did. I'd quite like to hear how you managed it, incidentally. But that was inside a prison-book, and in there, matters are a bit different. Time doesn't progress, you see. It just goes round and round." Geryon shrugged. "Think of it like a novel. If a character dies on page four hundred, he'll still be alive if you flip back to the beginning."

"So it wouldn't have mattered if I'd drowned?"

"It would have mattered a great deal to *you*, I suspect. As far as the book was concerned, when it went round again, you would just be gone, never to be seen again. To follow the analogy, as a Reader, you're not part of the story, you just insert yourself into it for a while."

The swarmer shifted, its claws pricking Alice's thigh. She gritted her teeth.

"But what is this thing doing here?"

"You brought it here," Geryon said. "The thread you hold leads back to the prison-book. When you defeated the Swarm, you formed a bond between its essence and your own. It is yours now, and will be for all time. It will lend you its strength, fight your enemies, die for you if need be, and be ready to spring into action again afterward."

"But—" Alice looked down at the swarmer's glassy black eyes. Her stomach churned.

"This is the power of the Reader," Geryon went on. "The prison-books give us the power to bind another being to our will. You've taken your first step, and I congratulate you. But there's a long way to go yet."

CHAPTER FOURTEEN

A SECOND CHANCE AT A FIRST IMPRESSION

I STILL SAY THEY'RE CREEPY," Ashes said.

"I don't think you get to decide what's creepy," Alice said. "You're a talking cat. *You're* creepy. This whole place is creepy."

"Hmph." Ashes' fur bristled with indignation.

From where Ashes perched on top of the nearest book-shelf, Alice supposed she presented a rather odd picture, walking down the library alleys followed by a train of walking books, like a mother duck and her ducklings. One would have to peek underneath to see the quartet of obedient swarmers supporting each volume on their backs, legs moving in perfect synchronicity. They reminded Alice of ants working together to carry a pebble many times their own size.

Mr. Wurms, for reasons only he knew, had requested the contents of an entire shelf, so the string of books stretched for some distance behind her. Alice led at a cautious pace, a large portion of her attention devoted to keeping the swarmers moving. Ashes, sulking along beside her, didn't seem to approve of the way she was using the little creatures.

"What if you told them all to jump into the pond?" Ashes said. "Would they do it?"

"They would, but I wouldn't. I don't need to be cruel to them."

"True. They're already your slaves, how much crueler do you need to be?"

Alice shot him a sharp look. "I didn't ask for this, if you'll recall. Some brilliant half-cat decided it would be a good idea to show me a prison-book for laughs."

"And got soaked for his troubles," Ashes said, tail lashing. "Don't think I'm likely to forget it."

"Be quiet for a minute," Alice said. "This is a tricky bit."

They'd arrived at Mr. Wurms' table. The bespectacled

scholar didn't look up, so Alice began building a tower of the books beside him. This was a more difficult exercise than it at first appeared, since the swarmers had a tendency to unbalance the stack while placing the next volume on the top. She almost had it until one of the little creatures tripped on the slipcover of a Swedish dictionary and brought the whole lot tumbling down. The swarmers scattered like an exploding dandelion puff, except for the one the dictionary landed on, and Mr. Wurms looked up with an irritated expression.

"Sorry, Mr. Wurms."

He sniffed and went back to his work. Alice bent and lifted the dictionary off the creature, whose rubber-ball-like physiology had kept it from being seriously damaged. It gave a pleased *quirk* and hopped to its feet, then vanished with a tiny *pop* as Alice released her mental grip on the thread. She restacked the books with her actual hands, trying to ignore Ashes' snide chuckling. When she was done, she cleared her throat and said, "What's next, Mr. Wurms?"

He glared at her with eyes like pools of smeared paint behind his thick glasses. Alice wasn't sure it wasn't her imagination, but she thought Mr. Wurms' attitude toward her had gotten steadily worse in the days since she'd learned the first rudiments of her power from Geryon.

"Here," he said, handing her a scrap of paper covered in his neat handwriting. It was a set of directions to a shelf, and a list of titles. "Find these and bring them back."

"Are there magic scraps in them?" Alice said.

"Never mind what's in them," Mr. Wurms said. "Just do as you're told."

Ashes slipped past her, rubbing against her ankle, and curled up underneath the table for a nap. Alice turned away with an inward sigh and headed back into the maze of shelves.

After lunching on a packet of sandwiches she'd brought from the kitchen, Alice settled down in a quiet spot to spend some time practicing with the swarmers. A soft tug on the thread called one into being with a soft *pop*, and a harder yank created a cascade of the little things. They stood in a semicircle around her, bright black eyes staring, *quirking* softly and waiting obediently for orders.

Though it wasn't really like she gave them *orders*, exactly. It was more like she'd acquired another limb. All she had to do was think, and the creatures would rush to obey, though getting them to do *precisely* what she wanted was sometimes as difficult as threading a needle.

She made them rush one way, then another, running full tilt into a bookshelf and bouncing off in an explosion of rubbery little bodies. They were almost impossible to injure, Alice had found. Any attempt to squash them just sent them bouncing off in another direction, like a rubber ball, and they always rolled back to their feet in moments, ready for more.

Those beaks were *sharp* too. She'd thrown them the wrapping from one of her sandwiches as a test, and they'd torn it to shreds in seconds, filling the air with flying bits of paper. Alice shuddered to think what would have happened to her and Ashes if they'd been caught.

Today she was trying to get them to climb a bookshelf. The wood was too hard for their little claws to grip, and they weren't good jumpers, but Alice had hit on the idea of piling them up in a sort of pyramid. They climbed onto one another's backs readily enough, but keeping the whole structure stable required paying attention to all of them at once, and the first few times she tried it, they quickly collapsed into a pile of squirming, bouncing bodies.

Eventually she managed to keep them steady enough that a single intrepid swarmer managed to scurry up to the very top of the pyramid and clamber onto a shelf higher than Alice's arms could reach. She waved to it, grinning in triumph. The swarmer stood stolidly, looking back at her, waiting for further instructions.

Alice let all the rest of them vanish, with a noise like someone cooking popcorn, and regarded the one on the shelf.

"*They're already your slaves,*" Ashes had said. "*How much crueler do you need to be?*"

It wasn't like slavery, though. Not *really*. The swarmers didn't even *exist* when she didn't call on them, so it wasn't like they were waiting around and getting bored. *It's more like . . . having a dog. One of those clever dogs that can herd sheep and do tricks when you whistle.* For all she knew, the little things loved bouncing around and running into walls for her. *Maybe I should feed them.* Geryon hadn't mentioned anything about that; all his instructions had focused on making the swarmers do what she wanted them to.

Ending's voice purred at the back of her mind. "*He is a Reader. His magic is based on cruelty and death. It is his nature.*"

I'm a Reader too. So . . .

She shook her head, with a frown, and focused on the swarmer. According to Geryon, she ought to be able to reach into it and see through its eyes. Trying that with a whole batch of them had left her with an instant head-ache. *I ought to be able to manage* one, *though.*

Alice closed her eyes and reached out to the swarmer with her mind. She could feel it, a little silver mote in the inner darkness, connected to the shining thread that wrapped back around Alice herself and led back to the prison-book. Alice shifted her attention into that little mote, working hard not to open her real eyes and instead letting the swarmers' senses flow into her. All at once, she found herself looking down at a girl in a blouse and a dust-covered skirt, with a long straight scar cutting through the freckles on her cheek.

It works! Alice clamped down on her excitement, not wanting to lose the fragile connection, but she couldn't help a little giggle. *I'll never have to worry about having a mirror.*

She tried moving the swarmer. It was disorienting, swinging its point-of-view around while her real body insisted she was standing still, but she fought through a wave of something like seasickness and kept at it. Before long she had it scampering back and forth across the shelf, brushing dust from the books as it passed. She could do more than see through it too—the *tiks* of its claws on the wood sounded loud in the swarmer's own ears, and she even thought she could smell the dust up close.

I didn't even know they had *ears. They must be buried under the fur somewhere.*

Turning back to herself, she caught sight of something moving, farther down the aisle. Anything in motion was brighter and more obvious through the swarmer's eyes, while stationary objects faded slightly, like a painted backdrop. She made it run to the edge of the shelf and look down, expecting to see one of the ubiquitous library cats.

It wasn't a cat. It was Isaac, coming toward her.

Alice hurriedly let the swarmer disappear and opened her real eyes, wobbling a little as she settled back into her own body. She brushed some of the omnipresent dust off her skirt, squared her shoulders, and turned to face him.

Without the flickering light of a fire behind him, he was considerably less intimidating than he'd seemed that first night. His long, flaring coat was a shabby thing, a blue-gray trench coat so covered in tears and patches that it might conceivably have served in the trenches. It was several sizes too large for him, and the hem trailed on the ground, raising a slow-motion tsunami of dust.

He might be a little older than she was, Alice decided, but he wasn't any taller. He had a pointed nose, dark, intelligent eyes, and a mop of ragged brown hair.

She crossed her arms and glared at him the way Miss Juniper had glared at her when she'd turned in a page of bad French. To her delight, he wilted like a cut flower.

"Hello," he said. There was, Alice decided, something mouse-like in his expression, a quiver around the eyes that made him look like he was ready to flee at any moment.

"Don't you 'hello' me," Alice said, still channeling her old tutor. "I could have been killed!"

Isaac held up his hands defensively. "It's not *my* fault! How could I know you were a Reader?"

Alice sniffed. "That's still no excuse. You said you were going to use me as *bait*."

"That was a joke," Isaac said miserably. "More or less, anyway. Look, would it be any help if I apologized?"

"It would be a start."

"I'm sorry that I said I would use you as bait. And for the rest."

He wore such a kicked-puppy expression that Alice felt herself softening a little. It was true, of course, that he'd had no way of knowing she was a Reader, since Alice herself had had no idea at the time. *And it was all part of Geryon's plan, in a way.*

That thought made her a little uneasy. *Isaac* was not part of Geryon's plans. Ending had brought him to look for the book she called the Dragon, and she and Ashes were concealing him from the old Reader. Alice didn't know why, but the very fact that they were keeping it a secret meant that Geryon probably would not approve. She got that stomach-twisting feeling again.

"All right," Alice said, eyeing Isaac cautiously. "I didn't die, no thanks to you. But I'm still not sure I should be talking to you."

"Ending said she was going to explain," Isaac said.

"She did." The hair on the back of Alice's neck prickled at the memory of the deep, rumbling voice and the luminous feline eyes. She wondered if Ending was watching them right now, from some hidden shadow. *Pushing the pieces around the board . . .* "At least, she explained a little bit. You're looking for a book, and it's hidden somewhere in the library."

Isaac nodded eagerly. "Not just hidden, but guarded as well. Ending told me she'd find help, and she brought me you. I didn't understand at first, but once I realized you were one of *us* it all made sense."

"Who said I was going to help?"

Isaac blinked. "Ending did."

"She made me a proposition," Alice agreed, "but I haven't decided on it one way or the other."

"But you've *got* to help!" Isaac protested. "Otherwise—" He stopped abruptly.

"I'm not sure I should," Alice said. "I'm Geryon's apprentice, after all. What I really *ought* to do is tell him you're here."

"Listen." Isaac's voice dropped until it was almost a whisper. "You can't trust Geryon. If he made you his apprentice, it's only because he wants something from you."

"That's what Ending said. But as far as I can see, I haven't got any special reason to trust her. Or," Alice added, "you. Geryon's helped me, and I can't imagine what he could want from me that he couldn't get for himself."

"You don't know him," Isaac said darkly.

"And you do?"

"Yes!"

"How? From hiding in his library?"

There was a long pause. Isaac bit his lip, glancing side-long at Alice.

"What are you going to do?" he said.

"I'm not sure yet," Alice said, frowning. "I need to think about it."

"Well, think quickly, all right? I think we may be running out of time."

"*You* may be," Alice said. "I belong here." She sounded as haughty as she could, but the worry in Isaac's face took some of the sting out of it. She re-crossed her arms uncomfortably. "I'd better get back to work."

"If you do . . . make a decision, come and tell me, all right? Ending can help you find me."

Alice sighed. "All right."

A little color returned to Isaac's face, and he let out a long breath. Alice gave him a little nod and turned back the way she'd come.

"Alice?"

She looked over her shoulder. "What?"

"Was that your creature I saw on the shelf? From the prison-book?"

"The book you let me get trapped in, you mean?" Alice said.

Isaac winced. "Yeah."

"Yes. One of them, anyway."

"Ashes told me what happened in there." Isaac scratched the side of his head, further mussing his already ruffled hair. "He was still angry about getting wet, but I thought what you did was brilliant."

"Oh." Alice frowned again, not sure what to say. "Thanks?" she ventured.

Isaac smiled, quick and furtive, and turned away in a whirl of fluttering canvas and flying dust. Alice stared after him for a moment, before walking back toward Mr. Wurms' table.

CHAPTER FIFTEEN
EAVESDROPPING AGAIN

AFTER SHE FINISHED FINDING books for Mr. Wurms, Alice returned to the house for an early dinner. Her stomach was rumbling, in spite of the sandwiches. Geryon had told her that using magic took up a lot of energy, and that she would need to be sure to eat a healthy diet. It didn't make her *tired*, exactly, but spending too long at it without a break gave her mind the same dull, foggy feeling she got when she forced herself through too many pages of algebra drills.

She found Emma standing in the front hall. If it had been anyone else, Alice would have said she was waiting for someone, but in Emma's case it was probably because Mr. Black had parked her there after some task and forgotten to give her any further orders. Alice told her to go back to her room and lie down, then headed down to the dining room herself to get something to eat.

Since she'd discovered the true nature of Geryon's household, Alice had become more comfortable with the invisible servants who cooked the meals and cleaned the table while her back was turned. Whoever the shy creatures were, they were masters of their craft, though to Alice's tastes, their range of menus was a little old-fashioned. She wondered if she could ask Geryon to speak to them about a few modern touches, and perhaps a few more fresh vegetables.

Tonight, though, she found herself unable to enjoy her meal, and she finished quickly and went up to her room. Her mind was full of Ending and Isaac, both warning her that Geryon was not to be trusted and demanding that she trust *them* instead. But Geryon had been nothing but kind to her—except for that one moment in the room full of pillows, but that had been important for her training—and the thought of keeping secrets from him while living under his roof made Alice deeply uncomfortable.

On the other hand, Ending clearly knew something

about Vespidian, and the fairy was the only link she had left to her father. *If I don't help her, and he finds this book and leaves, I may never be able to track him down again.* Her father might be dead, though she hadn't been able to banish a tiny germ of hope from the darkest corners of her mind. But the thought of never *knowing* for certain made Alice want to scream.

In an attempt to quiet the tumult in her mind, she lay on her bed, closed her eyes, and summoned a single swarmer. Reaching in to see through its eyes was easier now; she surveyed her room from this new perspective: her trunks in the corner, the pair of stuffed rabbits on the windowsill, the haphazard stack of books she'd borrowed from the library on the nightstand. At her command the swarmer jumped off the bed, bounced, righted itself, and peeked out the half-open door and into the hallway.

I wonder how far it can go? Geryon hadn't said anything about it. Alice sent the swarmer out toward the servants' stair, its claws *tik tik tik*ing on the floorboards. From its low vantage point, all the doors looked like enormous, looming portals, and the gas lamps were distant glows far overhead. When she got to the stairs, Alice stared through the creature's eyes at slab-like steps descending, apparently endless, into a deep abyss.

She hesitated a moment, then determined to give it a try. It was liberating, being in someone else's body; no matter what happened to the swarmer, she had the snug certainty that she could always let it vanish and find herself lying in her own bed. In her mind's eye, she could see Ashes' disapproving glare, but she banished him with a thought. *I'm a Reader. This is what being a Reader* is.

The swarmer tried the first step, and Alice realized immediately that descending was going to be tricky. The step was nearly as tall as the little creature's whole body, and its short, bird-like legs didn't come close to reaching the first step. The best Alice could manage was to make it balance on the edge, then hop down, but the swarmer's natural instinct was to tuck its legs in and *bounce* rather than to land on its feet, and she felt it roll dangerously close to the edge of the next step before it popped back up again.

Maybe this isn't such a good idea, she thought, eyeing the mountain of steps. Still, she wasn't the sort of girl who gave up easily. Another hop took her down one more step, and another, until she thought she was getting the hang of it. She was just getting into a nice rhythm when the swarmer's claw slipped on a smooth spot in the wood, sending it tumbling. Alice was too surprised to right it in time, and the little thing curled itself into a ball and hit the next step hard enough that the bounce took it down two more and sent it bounding back into the air.

The view from the swarmer's eyes, spinning wildly as it caromed down the stairs, was enough to turn Alice's stomach, and she hurriedly abandoned its senses and opened her real eyes. For a few moments it was a struggle not to vomit, staring fixedly at the ceiling and reminding herself that it was not *her* who had been falling down the stairs. Once she had her rebellious gut under control, she reached out for the swarmer again, cautiously, ready to will it out of existence if it was badly hurt.

To her surprise, it was standing placidly on the second-floor landing, apparently no worse for wear. *They really are like little rubber balls*, Alice thought. Then she laughed out loud as another thought occurred to her. It seemed a little—undignified, perhaps, but after all, there was no one to see, and it would certainly be easier than going down the steps one at a time.

A moment later, the swarmer sprinted to the edge of the landing and took a flying leap off the first step, tucking its legs away and hitting the fourth step down with such force that it bounced nearly to the low ceiling. This time Alice stayed with it, laughing out loud at the sensation of caroming down the stairs like a stray tennis ball, bouncing at an angle off the landing wall and on down *another* flight of stairs, ricocheting wildly between the banister and the wall.

The swarmer was now three stories below her, on the ground floor, and as it got to its feet Alice noticed that the distance was having an effect. If moving the swarmer was like moving a limb she'd never known she had, it now felt as though that limb was wearing a lead weight. It wasn't painful, but it took effort, and the weight got heavier the farther away the creature got.

At the moment, it was still bearable, and she looked around with the swarmer's eyes to orient herself. The bottom of the servants' stairs let out into the passage beside the kitchen, and the door had apparently been open, because the swarmer had bounced right through it and off the opposite wall. In one direction, the kitchen was as dark and silent as always. The other way led to a door that was always closed, which led into the boiler-room domain of Mr. Black.

Except, tonight, it wasn't closed. There was a narrow gap between the door and the door frame, just wide enough to admit the body of the swarmer. Gaslight from inside spilled out of the narrow opening. Shuffling a little closer, Alice could hear voices, just on the edge of comprehensibility.

Vespidian! She was sure she could make out the fairy's nasal drone, and the deeper voice of Mr. Black. Before she could think about it, she'd sent the swarmer through the door, hopping over the lintel and pushing through the gap. The door swung where she brushed it, very slightly, and gave a creak that sounded very loud in the little creature's ears. Alice stopped, and spent a moment listening, but the sound of conversation drifted up undisturbed.

The feeling of weight was getting stronger the farther she went, but she could hear the drone of the fairy's wings now, and a crackling sound that might have been a fire. A short corridor led past a gaslight and turned a corner, and then she was facing another flight of stairs. At the bottom, outlined in a glowing doorway, stood Mr. Black, with the smaller figure of Vespidian hovering in the air in front of him.

". . . you're sure the map works?" the fairy said, in his high, nasal voice.

"I got it straight from the Bone Oracle," Mr. Black

rumbled. "It had better work, considering what it cost me. She drives a hard bargain, but I called in a couple of old favors. I couldn't try it in the library, but it shows the start of the path, no problem."

"That doesn't mean much," Vespidian said dubiously. "It's only inside the labyrinth that things get tricky."

"Don't use it, then," Mr. Black spat. "Search every book by hand, for all I care. As long as I get what's coming to me."

"All right, all right," the fairy said. "No need to get huffy. Let's have it, then."

"No."

There was a sharp intake of breath, and a long silence. Alice perched the swarmer on the edge of the first step, straining to hear.

"What do you mean, no?"

"I mean that it's about time for a show of good faith on your part." Mr. Black waved one huge finger in the fairy's face, and Vespidian buzzed backward. "I've done everything you wanted, haven't I? I got you in here, I kept you secret, and now I've got you the map. I even tipped you off about the girl and her father, for all the good it did you."

Alice's breath froze in her throat, and the swarmer wobbled.

"Once I hand it over"—Mr. Black waved at the door behind him, where the fire was burning—"there'll be nothing keeping you from grabbing this book you want so badly and scurrying back home. So you go and tell your *master* that Mr. Black wants what he's owed, and he wants it now. Once he delivers, then you can have the map, and good luck to you. Until then . . ." He crossed his enormous arms and waited impassively.

Vespidian buzzed from side to side in agitation for a moment before regaining his composure and hovering in front of the big servant's face. His voice had the snide tone Alice remembered from the night in her kitchen.

"I thought we had moved beyond this level of dealing," he said. "Haven't we learned to trust each other?"

"You may have learned to trust me. I don't trust you farther than I could throw you." Mr. Black grinned maliciously under his bristly beard. "Which might actually be some distance, now that I come to think about it."

"Very well," Vespidian said. "I shall have to consult my master. You realize, of course, that every day that passes increases the risk of discovery?"

"You'd better hurry, then, hadn't you? I'll be—"

That was when Alice, leaning the swarmer forward to catch every word, felt it lose its footing. It tumbled forward, automatically tucking into a ball, hit the step with a *thump*, and bounced high into the air. Alice hurriedly let go of the silver thread in her mind, letting the little creature snap back into nonexistence. Her world went black, and she felt a moment's panic before she realized she was only lying with her eyes closed. When she opened them, the cracked paint of her ceiling stared back at her.

Mr. Black had told Vespidian where to find me. She felt anger welling up inside her again. *He sold me to that vile little fairy, and that made Father go off on his trip, and then . . .*

She had to find the book Ending had called the Dragon. *And it sounds like Mr. Black has a way to do it.* She had to get hold of that map, whether it meant breaking the rules or not.

Alice rolled out of bed and hunted for her shoes, already working on a plan. She had an idea, but she thought she'd need help, and there was only one place she was likely to get it.

CHAPTER SIXTEEN
THE LAIR OF MR. BLACK

T HE SUN WAS DROPPING behind the encircling forest by the time Alice emerged from the library with Isaac in tow. He paused on the threshold, one hand on the great bronze door, and shivered. Alice looked over her shoulder.

"What's wrong?" she said.

"Nothing." He let the door close behind him with a hollow *bang,* and huddled deeper into his threadbare trench coat. "It's cold."

The chill was rising fast as the sun disappeared. Alice tried not to think about the last time she'd been out of the building after dark, and how that night had ended with her fighting for her life in the world of the Swarm. Gaslight shone from the windows of the house, glowing cheerily through the curtains.

"You're sure we won't run into anybody?" Isaac said.

"There's nobody to run into, aside from Mr. Black," Alice said. "Geryon stays in his rooms, and Emma doesn't go anywhere she hasn't been told to go."

"All right." Isaac took a deep breath and squared his shoulders. "Lead the way."

They were only stealing into the kitchens at night, not trying to sneak across enemy lines, and Alice felt that the theatrics from Isaac were a little unnecessary. But as they skirted the edge of the lawn, keeping them under the shadow of the trees, she admitted to herself that the stakes for Isaac were considerably higher than for herself. After all, if they were caught, she didn't *think* she'd get more than a stern talking-to, but she had no idea what would happen to Isaac if Geryon or Mr. Black found him in the house. *They wouldn't really . . . hurt him, or anything like that. Would they?*

Alice chewed her lip, and looked back at Isaac with a little more respect. Though she was loath to admit it, the thought of facing down Mr. Black alone made her knees a bit wobbly, and she was glad she'd been able to convince Isaac to come along.

Alice edged up to the back door, pulled it open a crack, and peeked inside. Isaac tensed up again, ready to bolt, and his nervousness threatened to infect her. She told herself not to be silly.

The kitchen was empty, as usual, with all the pots, pans, and utensils clean and hanging in their places. Isaac entered cautiously, staring around as though he'd never seen anything like it before, and Alice found herself wondering if he really hadn't. She knew nothing about him, she realized, not even where he came from, or if he was someone's apprentice or on his own. She shook her head and fought down the surge of curiosity. *Later. This is not the time.*

"All right," she whispered. "Mr. Black's rooms are down here. I *think* he'd keep the map in the furnace room, which is at the back. If we're lucky, he'll be in bed or something, and we can just creep by and find it."

"And if we're not lucky?"

"Then I'll cause a distraction, and you find the map and get out before he comes back."

Isaac frowned. "You're sure he called it a 'map'? We don't really know what we're looking for."

"He definitely said map."

"What if I can't find it?"

"Then we'll . . . have to figure something out." Alice had to admit it wasn't the best plan in the world, but it was all she'd been able to come up with on short notice. "Are you ready?"

He nodded.

Alice eased the door open, hoping it wouldn't creak. It swung inward silently, revealing a short corridor and the stairway where she'd perched the swarmer. In the flickering gaslight she saw a large, square room at the bottom, crowded with bushels and crates of stuff—baskets of nails, crates of soap-flakes, huge bottles of oil and cleansers, wrapped bundles of candles. At the back of it, the door to the furnace room was open, letting out a dull red glow that bathed the stone-flagged floor in crimson light. As she watched, a shadow moved across it.

"He's in there," she whispered to Isaac.

"All right." Isaac peered doubtfully down the stairs. "So you'll distract him, and I get in there."

"Right."

"Let's hope he hasn't hidden it, or locked it up." Isaac got an odd, faraway look in his eyes for a moment, as though staring at something on the far side of the wall. "I'm ready."

Alice nodded tightly. She took the staircase one step at a time, wary of any noise. Once she reached the bottom, she crept around the piles of supplies to the opposite corner of the room, where she'd be out of view from the furnace-room doorway.

She closed her eyes and reached out, and found the silver thread of the Swarm waiting. Gathering it up, she gave a gentle tug, and a half-dozen swarmers popped quietly into existence by her feet. They greeted her with a chorus of *quirks*, which she stilled with a hasty mental command.

Carefully, she extended her vision into one of them, keeping her real eyes closed. She navigated the swarmer around the pile of supplies and toward the door to the furnace room, ordering the others to follow a few paces behind. The little bird-like creature scurried across the floor until it had a good view of Mr. Black, sitting at his workbench and working on something with a pair of heavy iron clippers. From her point of view a few inches off the ground, she couldn't see the top of the table.

The swarmer crept closer, until it was only a few feet from the huge man. Before she could go any farther, he gave an enormous snort and shoved his chair back from the workbench, one enormous hand coming down with shocking speed to snatch the swarmer off the floor. Alice felt a moment of sheer terror and had to remind herself that it was not her actual physical body in danger. One of the swarmer's eyes had a close-up view of Mr. Black's hairy, pockmarked face, and the trails of smoke leaking from his nostrils.

"What have we got here?" he said, his voice echoing oddly as it came both through the swarmer and through Alice's real ears. "What in the Pit are you supposed to be?"

He gave the swarmer a squeeze. If he'd been holding a rat, the pressure of those sausage-thick fingers would have shattered its bones and crushed it into a gooey paste, but the swarmer was roughly the consistency of a hard rubber ball and it simply continued to stare at him. Mr. Black put his head on one side, then smiled.

"Tough little bastard, ain't you?" He turned toward the furnace. "Let's see how you like a little fire."

"Get him," Alice whispered.

The other five swarmers rushed forward, charging beak-first like a wedge of medieval lancers. The needle-sharp points struck Mr. Black around the ankles, piercing the thick leather of his boots. At the same time, the swarmer he was holding twisted in his grasp and sank its beak into his hand, in between his fingers and thumb.

The huge man roared like an animal, so loud that Alice retreated from the swarmer's senses and clapped her hands over her ears. He threw the swarmer he was holding against the wall, hard, and it ricocheted off like a tennis ball and rolled across the floor. The others ran for it, just ahead of his reaching hands, and scurried back toward the door.

As she'd hoped, Mr. Black followed. Alice kept the swarmers in a group until Mr. Black cleared the doorway. He charged, head lowered like an angry bull, and they scattered. He aimed a kick at one that moved a bit too slow, and sent it ricocheting off the wall to land among the crates with a crash of splintered wood. Mr. Black roared again and went after the others, who scurried and dodged to stay ahead of him.

Go, Alice willed Isaac, and she was gratified to catch a glimpse of him darting toward the furnace room. Mr. Black was in a rage, kicking over boxes and smashing neatly piled stores to get at the swarmers. Alice began to smile. It was almost fun, trying to keep ahead of him— the swarmers could get under and around things he would trip over, and even when he caught up, his swats and kicks did the durable little creatures no real damage.

It serves him right, she thought as he stumbled over a crate and crashed headlong into a sack of potatoes.

Mr. Black stopped thrashing about. He raised his head and gave a low, animal growl. Then he sniffed the air, like a hound catching a scent.

"Very clever," he rumbled. "Oh, *very* clever." He straightened up, extricating his feet from the ruin of the crate. "You thought you'd have some *fun* with poor old Mr. Black?"

There was a tremendous crash and clatter as Mr. Black hurled a box of flatware out of the way and closed the distance with Alice in two enormous strides.

"I—" she had time to say, before he was on top of her. He grabbed her arms, one in each hand, and her belated attempt to escape barely moved his fingers. When he was satisfied she was caught, he transferred both her wrists to one huge hand, pulling her arms up over her head.

"I knew my basement was infested with *vermin,*" Mr. Black said. "But this one is a bit larger than the others."

"I thought—" Alice tried again.

"I bet I know what you *thought.* You thought, *I'm Gery-on's new favorite, let's go amuse myself at the expense of poor stupid Mr. Black, who doesn't know up from down.* Is that what you *thought*?"

"No," Alice said. "I was just . . ."

She stopped, partly because she couldn't think of anything to say that wouldn't tip off Mr. Black there was someone else in the room, but mostly because he tugged her wrists upward, forcing Alice to stretch and then to stand on tiptoes.

"You were 'just,'" Mr. Black parroted. "I'm sure. And I'm sure you thought, worst comes to worst, what's Mr. Black going to do? Give me a paddling?" He snarled. "If that's what you think, you don't know Mr. Black."

He raised her, slowly, until her feet scrabbled at the dusty floor and then kicked helplessly in the air. Dangling like a shot hare from his one-handed grip, she felt her hands going numb, and her shoulders felt like they were about to tear from their sockets. She fumbled in the back of her mind for the thread that led to the Swarm, but every time she almost had it, she caught Mr. Black's eyes and it slipped from her mental grasp.

"When I tell you what I'm going to do, you'll piss your drawers," Mr. Black said. "And once we're done, well, you'd be surprised how hot that furnace can get. Hot enough that when Geryon comes looking, I'll just give him a little shrug, you see, and there won't be anything to tell him different. You won't be the first, not by a long way." He gave a savage grin, showing huge teeth, and then exhaled a puff of awful-tasting smoke into Alice's face. "But before that, we're going to—"

Someone started to sing.

The music filled the room, snatching her out of her sluggish body like the gentle hand of a benevolent god. It went on for eons, an eternity, and she wanted nothing more than to lie back and glory in it. It suffused her, soaking in through her pores and bursting out again. The whole universe spun around her and danced to that glorious voice.

And then it ended, as suddenly as it had begun. For a heartbeat Alice felt the staggering loss like a physical blow, but after an instant it faded, and the glory of the song dispersed and blew away like a fading dream. She opened her eyes, feeling oddly at peace.

Isaac was bent over her, one arm around her shoulders and the other hand on her chin, his dry lips pressed against hers. His eyes were open, and they locked gazes for a startled moment, before Alice's hand shot out palm-first and shoved him away so hard he stumbled.

Apparently satisfied, Isaac scrambled to his feet and beckoned. "Come on."

"But—" Alice felt like her brain wasn't quite working. "You—"

"Come *on*," Isaac said.

Alice clambered to her feet, a little shakily. As she turned she saw Mr. Black, still standing behind her. Alice had to clamp her jaw shut painfully hard to stifle a scream. His eyes were closed, enormous hands resting at his sides, his mouth half-open in awe.

Isaac was already halfway up the staircase.

"Isaac!" she hissed. "Did you get the map?"

"I couldn't find anything that looked like a map," Isaac said. "Come *on*, we haven't got long!"

We have to find it. If they left now, they certainly wouldn't get another chance, not with Mr. Black on his guard. She turned back to the huge, silent figure.

"He must keep it on him," she said. "I'm going to check his pockets."

"*Alice!*" Isaac's voice was strained. "We have to go!"

Alice ignored him and edged up to Mr. Black. The top of her head barely came up to his chest, and she had to stand on her toes to get into his side pocket. When she touched him, he shifted slightly, and Alice froze in place like a startled deer. But his eyes were still closed, and after a moment she let out a breath and carried on.

The pocket contained a handful of change and a couple of heavy iron keys. Alice left them where they were and went around to the other side, in spite of another desperate hiss from Isaac. Up close, Mr. Black smelled of coal and black smoke, as though he were a furnace himself.

His other pocket held a thick packet of something that crinkled under her fingers. Alice tugged it free carefully, and found herself holding a piece of parchment folded over on itself many times until it was a fat square.

"Let's go!"

Alice hurried after Isaac, taking the steps two at a time and slipping past him to open the door into the kitchens. Thankfully, all was still dark and silent, and they ran out the back door and into the night.

It wasn't until they'd attained the relative safety of the fringe of the woods, halfway to the library and well out of earshot of the house, that Isaac pulled up short, leaning against a sapling and puffing hard. Alice wasn't out of breath, but her shoulders and wrists ached where Mr. Black had held her, and her lips still tingled from Isaac's kiss. She felt herself blushing furiously, and was glad it was too dark for him to see it.

"What happened?" she said. "What did you do?"

"I saw that you were in trouble," Isaac said.

"So why did you *kiss* me?"

"I'm sorry about that," he said. "I had to, it's part of the spell. It makes you immune. Otherwise I'd have had to carry you, and I'm not sure I could have managed it."

"Oh." Alice brought her sleeve to her lips and absently wiped them. "What did you do to Mr. Black? How long will he stay like that?"

"I'll have to let him go pretty soon. If I use too much power, Geryon would feel it for sure. I probably shouldn't have done even that much." He paused. "Did you get the map?"

"I think so." Alice held up the paper square. "We can—"

"Later." Isaac grabbed the thing from her hand and tucked it in his jacket. "We'd better get back to the library before somebody comes after us."

"All right."

Isaac pushed himself away from the tree and started forward. Alice, following behind, hesitated for a moment.

"Isaac?"

"What?"

"Thank you."

"Oh." He gave an awkward shrug. "Don't mention it."

CHAPTER SEVENTEEN

A MAP OF THE LABYRINTH

ALICE HAD WORRIED THAT they would find the bronze door to the library stuck fast, as she had that first night, but it opened reluctantly when she gave a tug on the ring. With a sigh of relief, she ushered Isaac inside and pulled the squealing portal closed behind her. She lit a match and managed to kindle one of the hurricane lamps. She offered it to Isaac, but he only smiled and put up one hand. A softly glowing ball of white light materialized in his palm and drifted lazily upward to orbit around his head.

"That's handy," Alice said.

He shrugged. "It's just a little glow-wisp. I'm sure Geryon would dig one out for you if you asked him."

Alice stared at the thing for a moment. She hadn't realized it was a living thing, but of course it had to be. Geryon said a Reader's power comes from the creatures he has bound to service. So Isaac had found that tiny light in a prison-book, somewhere, and . . . killed it? Alice looked down uncomfortably.

"Geryon won't sense it?" Alice said.

"Not in the library," Isaac said. "Ending can keep me hidden."

She nodded. "Okay. Let's see the map."

Isaac pulled the square of parchment out of his pocket, and they examined it together. It was many sheets thick, folded in on itself in a complicated pattern. The outside was blank.

"I'm not sure this is it," Isaac said. "I'm not even sure you *can* have a map of a place like the library. It wouldn't stay put long enough to draw one."

"Let me see it," Alice said.

Isaac looked down at the map, hesitated for a moment, and handed it over. It looked as though it should unfold, but whenever she tried to tease the layers apart, it resisted stubbornly. She tried to work her little finger between

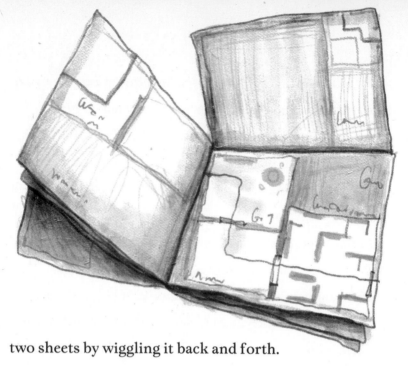

two sheets by wiggling it back and forth.

"Hey!" Isaac said. "Be careful! You'll tear it."

Alice frowned and worked her way around the edge. All at once, she found a place where she could get it apart, peeling two layers away from each other and opening the square like a tiny book. They felt slightly sticky, as though someone had spilled apple juice on it.

Where the parchment had been pressed together, drawn so small she could barely make out the details, was a perfect little map. In the center of one half of the paper was the anteroom in which they were standing, with its two thick doors. From there a thin green line ran down the length of the page, into the library and snaking through a maze of shelves, crossing the crease where the map had been folded and eventually going off the oppo-site end of the page.

Isaac looked down at it in the light of his glow-wisp, fascinated.

"It must be magic," Alice said. "Do you know how it works?"

"I have no idea."

Perversely, that made Alice feel a little better. "Mr. Black said he got it from something called the Bone Ora-cle. Have you ever heard of it?"

Isaac shook his head. "A friend of mine once told me that you can find practically anything, if you know which book to look in. Some world, somewhere, has what you need, and some Reader probably wrote down how to find it a thousand years ago. There have been Readers a long time, and they may lose things occasionally, but they never throw anything away."

"I've seen that for myself," Alice said, nodding at the door leading into the cavernous library. She traced the green line on the page with her finger. "I suppose we're meant to follow this. But what happens when we get to the end of the page?"

"I guess we'll find out," Isaac said. He seemed consider-ably happier now that they were back in the library, and she couldn't blame him. *At least in here he can always hide if someone comes after us.* "Come on."

Alice knew roughly where Mr. Wurms' table was, and kept a watch for his light, but the line went well to one side of the little clear space where the scholar worked. For a while they walked in silence, but eventually Alice examined the map and declared they were well past and out of earshot. The library was as quiet as ever, the dust thick and undisturbed except for the trail Isaac's coat left behind them. Alice didn't even see any cats.

Isaac checked the map from time to time, but less frequently as they moved on and it proved to be correct to the last particular. The path they followed ambled back and forth, apparently at random, but they stuck to it faithfully even when an invitingly wide alley offered an apparent shortcut. Whenever Alice's arm tired of holding up the lantern, she traded off map-reading duty with Isaac, and let him lead the way for a while down the silent, dust-shrouded aisles.

There were a hundred questions she wanted to ask him—what Ending had promised him in return for his help, for example, or how he had gotten in to the library in the first place—but she was wary of endangering their fragile alliance before they'd reached their goal. When the quiet had gone on too long to bear, she cleared her throat and said, "When did you find out you were a Reader?"

Isaac pulled up short in a billowing cloud of dust. "What?"

"Sorry. Is that not something I'm supposed to ask?" Alice hesitated. "It's just that I only found out a couple of weeks ago, and I wondered what it was like for you. You don't have to answer if it's too personal."

"No, it's not . . ." He shook his head. "You just startled me." He glanced down at the map and started walking again, and Alice fell in beside him. "I'm not really sure, to be honest. I feel like I've always known, so it must have been before I can remember."

"But when did you start learning all this?"

"As soon as I could read—normally, I mean—my master put me to work. I bound my first creature when I was seven."

"Seven!" Alice said. "You fought some kind of monster when you were *seven*?"

"It was only a sort of lizard-fish," Isaac said, almost apologetic. "I hit it with a stick."

"But you already had a master?"

"I've had a master all my life," Isaac said. "I think most

Readers do. The old Readers have gotten pretty good at finding children with the talent as early as they can. It's less . . . disruptive all around."

"But then nobody ever gave you a choice!" Alice said. "They just took you and said you had to be a Reader? How is that fair?"

"It's not a matter of fair," Isaac said. "I *am* a Reader. So are you. You don't get to choose, any more than you get to choose to be a fish instead of a person."

Geryon gave me *a choice.* Not much of a choice, really, but at least he'd offered. Alice didn't say it, though, partly because she didn't want to argue but mostly because Isaac had stopped short, staring down at the map in his hands.

"This is the edge," he said. "Now what?"

"Is there something on the other side?" Alice suggested.

Isaac turned the map over, but the other side of the parchment was blank. He held it up to his glow-wisp, trying to see through it, then shrugged and handed it to Alice. She looked at the creased rectangle and thought for a moment.

Unfolding it got it to work the first time. So maybe . . .

She tried creasing it back up again the way it had been, but it only flopped open. Then she bent it the other way, folding the section of the map they'd already passed through underneath the section they were standing in. At once she felt *something* happen. The page twitched under her fingers. With mounting excitement, she ran her hand around the edge and found that it would open in a new direction, at right angles to the first. She unfolded another section with that faintly sticky sensation to reveal the continuation of the path.

She held it up for Isaac to see, unable to help a triumphant smile, and he grinned back.

"Brilliant," he said, and Alice found her cheeks unaccountably flushed.

She held the map out in front of them, orienting herself, and led the way into the depths of the library.

Before they reached the end of the second square of map, the library started to change. Shelves appeared at odd angles to the rest, forming squares or triangles facing inward or outward. The pathways started to curve, then lost themselves altogether and became only the spaces between shapes and clusters. At the same time, the books themselves started to thin out, until each bookcase bore only a couple of lonely-looking volumes or none at all.

It was the place Alice remembered from her first night

in the library, what Ashes had referred to as Geryon's back rooms. Seeing it again made her a little nervous, and she found herself tracing the scar on her cheek with one finger. Isaac seemed perfectly comfortable, though, and she was determined not to show any hesitation in front of him. She kept her eyes on the map and her feet moving forward.

The groups of shelves they walked by started to change. She passed one cluster that exuded frigid gusts of air tinged with the smell of new-fallen snow, and another that gave off a rumble like distant thunder and had the metallic tang of ozone. Flickering lights within one octagonal ring played green and purple against the ceiling. An enormous triangle smelled of new-mown grass, and from within an oval she could hear the faint cheering of multitudes and the ring of steel on steel. A pentagon leaked a sullen red glow and the vile stench of brimstone.

When they reached the edge of the map again, she showed Isaac how to fold it and open it again. This time, the green line didn't continue off the end of the page, but led to small dot in the center of a hexagonal ring of shelves some distance ahead of them.

"That must be it," Isaac said. "That's where the book is hidden."

Alice nodded, oriented herself from the map, and pointed the way. They passed a rectangular set of shelves that leaked steam from every gap, from which Alice could hear the squeal of squeaky bearings and the low thump of an engine. She longed for a little peek at what was inside—*how could just a peek hurt?*—but Isaac pressed onward.

This is all probably old hat to him, I suppose. Alice tried to imagine *growing up* with all this, with magic in every corner and the knowledge that you were different from everyone else.

"Alice," Isaac said, after a long silence. There was a hint of nervousness in his voice. "Did Ending tell you anything about what we would have to do to retrieve this book?"

"Only that it was lost." Alice thought back. "And that it was guarded. If it's called the Dragon, does that mean there'll be a dragon guarding it?"

"No," Isaac said quickly. "That means there's a dragon *inside* the book. Whatever guards it will be on the outside."

"Whatever it is, it must be something awful," Alice said, "since Ending thought it would take both of us to get past it."

"That makes sense." Isaac sounded as though he wished it didn't. "Those little . . . things of yours—"

"I call them swarmers."

"Right. Can they fight, do you think?"

"I haven't tried," Alice said. "Except for poking Mr. Black in the ankle."

"Have you tried using them internally?"

She shook her head. "Geryon mentioned that, but I don't really know what it means."

"If you pull the creature into yourself, rather than out into the world, you can take on some aspect of it. Even turn yourself into it entirely, if you're good enough."

Turn myself into a swarmer? Alice was dubious. *It wouldn't be big enough. Where would the rest of me go?*

"I don't think we've covered that in my training." She shifted uncomfortably. "What about you? Is that lizard-fish good for anything?"

"I can use it to breathe underwater," Isaac said. "But no, not for fighting."

"What about—"

"I think this is it," he interrupted, reaching in front of her and tapping the map. "That group there, you see it?"

Alice did see it. A set of ancient bookcases stood in a hexagon, their wooden shelves cracking or rotted away entirely. Light spilled out of the cracks between them, a pale, cold radiance that looked like moonlight. Alice and Isaac walked up to it, and Alice waved her hand experimentally in one of the beams and watched her fingers make huge shadows on the floor.

"Want me to go through first?" Isaac said. "To make sure it's safe?"

Alice snorted. She shoved her fingers into the crack between the shelves and pushed, wedging herself little by little into a space that seemed much too small to hold her. As before, she had the feeling the bookcases were bulging out, creating a passage just wide enough for her to pass through. When she thought too hard about that, it made her nervous, so she just kept moving.

From the inside, the ring of shelves looked like enormous monoliths, giant slabs of rock arranged in a circle around a grassy glade. Alice stepped from between two of them, out of a passage full of clammy mist, and found herself standing in bright moonlight under a starry sky. The glade was much larger than the group of shelves had looked from the outside, but after everything she'd seen in the library, Alice was hardly surprised by that now.

Ashes said the books . . . leak. That they make a little bit of our world into a little bit of theirs. If that was true, then the world on the other side of this book was a reasonably pleasant one. The moon gave more than enough light to see, and a refreshing breeze rustled the long, silver grass, blowing away the dust-and-paper smell of the library and replacing it with the smell of soil and growing things.

In the center of the glade was a small, weathered stone pedestal, a bit like a sundial without the point in the middle. Alice looked over her shoulder and found Isaac emerging from the mist, brushing a few clinging drops of moisture off the sleeves of his coat.

"No guards so far," she said. "At least that I can see."

"They wouldn't be out here," Isaac said. "We're still inside the library, even if it doesn't look like it. This is still part of Ending's labyrinth. If the Dragon book is here, it's somewhere inside another book—that'd be the only way to hide it."

"The best place to hide a book is inside another book?" Alice shook her head. "Sometimes this business makes my eyes cross."

Isaac smiled. They walked to the middle of the glade and found that there was indeed a book resting on the little pedestal. It was a large, thin volume, with a green canvas cover that was stained and worn ragged in places. If there had been a printed title, it had long since faded away.

Isaac stepped forward and laid a hand on it. He closed his eyes and cocked his head, as though he was listening to something.

"Well," he said after a moment, "it's a portal-book, not a prison-book."

"What does that mean?" Alice said.

"It means there's a matching book on the other side, so we can come back without any special conditions." He frowned. "But I can't tell anything about where it leads, except that I don't think it's on Earth."

"Only one way to find out, then. How do we go through together?"

"Hold my hand."

Alice took Isaac's hand in her own gingerly. The sleeve of his coat flopped over and rested on her arm. They stepped forward, and with his free hand Isaac flipped the book open to the first page. Alice saw the same confusing mass of characters that she had when she'd opened *The Swarm*, and then, as before, they twisted before her eyes into recognizable letters. She read:

Alice stood hand in hand with Isaac on a windswept, moonlit plain that stretched as far as the eye could see . . .

Chapter Eighteen
THE LONELY COTTAGE

ALICE STOOD HAND IN hand with Isaac on a wind-swept, moonlit plain that stretched as far as the eye could see in every direction. The grass dipped and bowed in waves, like the movement of an ocean. In front of them, rising out of the sea of grass, was a rocky hill, with a path on one side that looped laboriously back and forth several times. A small stone cottage with a peaked wooden roof stood at the top, with a curl of white smoke drifting lazily up from the chimney.

All in all, it was not nearly as bad as Alice had been expecting. She gave a little sigh of relief.

"Would you mind letting go of my hand?" Isaac said. "If you squeeze any harder, I might lose a finger."

Alice let his hand drop, cheeks burning, and fumbled furiously with the map. This time, she discovered, it was prepared to fold up along the crease and open again to display their new surroundings. Apart from the outline of the hill and the cottage, it was mostly blank. The green line led up the switchback path and ended in a green dot somewhere inside the house.

"It's in there," Alice said. "Or the map thinks it is, anyway."

"At least we won't have any trouble finding our way back." Isaac gestured behind them, and Alice looked over her shoulder. Another pedestal, twin to the one in the library, held an identical-looking book. It stood out amid the grass, the only feature for hundreds of yards in any direction.

"All right," Alice said. "So do we just go up and knock on the front door?"

"You're the one who told me we should expect something nasty," Isaac said.

That was true. But there was something inexplicably *cozy* about the cottage. A big mound of firewood was stacked against one wall and an empty straw basket hung upside down beside the door. It had the look of a place where people lived, full of little repairs and small touches to make their lives easier.

"I'm not sure," she said. "Maybe if we . . . explain?"

"If there's someone in there guarding the book, they're not going to just give it up for the asking," Isaac said.

"Let's get a closer look," Alice said. "We can hide in those rocks."

The moon was bright enough that it was easy to see their way up the switchback path, but they were both breathing hard by the time they got to the top. Alice was secretly pleased to see that Isaac seemed to be having a harder time than she was. They knelt behind a pile of loose stones, and while Isaac panted to get his breath back, Alice summoned a single swarmer and regarded it critically. Its dark hair would make it hard to detect, as long as it kept to the shadows, and she thought it would be able to approach the cottage unnoticed.

A moment later, the rickety front door opened, casting a merry rectangle of firelight across the silver grass. It was followed by a splash as someone emptied a pot into the dirt. Alice saw a figure outlined in the doorway— human-shaped, but even in that brief glimpse, recognizably *not* human—but after a moment it stepped away, leaving the entrance clear.

There's no percentage in hanging about. Alice's lip curled in a smile even as her heart gave a little lurch.

She signaled Isaac to be quiet, then closed her eyes and slipped into the swarmer's senses. It sped from their hiding place to the cottage door, then peeked around the door frame and looked inside.

The cottage consisted of a single large room. The stone walls were mostly covered with colorful cloths, and a patchwork of overlapping rugs on the floor that gave the whole place a warmer feel than the outside. A pair of wooden benches sat in front of a massive stone fireplace where a steady blaze crackled. Against one wall, looking somewhat out of place, was a heavy-looking chest bound with leather straps, like something a pirate would keep his treasure in.

The creature Alice had glimpsed sat in front of the fire, at work with a needle and thread. The swarmer leaned forward for a better view, and Alice felt her breath catch in her throat. The thing was slender and graceful, with pale mauve skin and a thin, elfin build. In place of hair a velvety river of thin purple strands ran from the crown of its head, in a tight bunch down the back of its neck, and then spread broadly across its shoulders like a fall of silky hair. It wore only a pair of ragged shorts, held up by a bit of twine wound around and around its waist.

He—Alice decided the creature must be male, based

on his attire, though his skin was as smooth and hairless as a porcelain doll—had his face to the fire, concentrating on his work, and Alice took the opportunity to run the swarmer around the door frame and take shelter in a convenient pile of kindling. One of the sticks snapped under its feet, and the creature looked up. His face was the least human part of him, a perfectly symmetrical oval with a lipless slash of a mouth, a tiny button nose, and two enormous eyes the color of amethysts, with huge, owl-like pupils. They sparkled in the firelight as though they were made of crystal.

Alice made the swarmer stand stock-still amid the kindling. There was another one of the creatures sitting on the floor in front of the fire. This one was much smaller, half the size of the other, but it looked less like a child than a reproduction in miniature, down to every detail but the color of its skin, hair, and eyes, which were shades of sapphire blue.

The small one made a sort of hissing squeak, and to Alice's surprise the larger one spoke. His voice had a lilting, musical tone.

What he said was, "Hungry, are you? And why not, with a third log burned and Mah-Li not yet returned. I warn you, though, all the lamb is gone, and all the squirrel as well. We're down to lizards, and not very fat ones at that."

The little creature made a complaining sort of noise.

"You don't have to tell *me*," the other one said. "I wasn't the one who made the bargain. 'It's a place to hide until all this blows over,' Mah-Li said, 'and it won't be for long, anyway. You and I should know better than anyone that the Readers always get what they want in the end.' And here we are, stalking lizards in the long grass instead of *proper* food." He gave a very human-sounding sigh. "Do you want the lizard?"

The little one nodded. The other put his stitching down, got up, and crossed the room to a corner where a number of barrels sat. On the way he passed the big chest, and gave it a reflexive, resentful kick.

"What could be worth the bother," he muttered, "that's what *I* want to know. Eating lizards, indeed. Oh, for the old days." He lifted the a lid off of one of the barrels, peered down, then bent over to reach inside.

A moment later the creature screeched, and a remarkable thing happened. The purple stuff he had in place of hair, thick fibers like threads of yarn, all went rigid at once. Violet spikes suddenly jutted out from his skull, a foot or more, and a crest of them encircled his shoulders, making him look a bit like an agitated purple porcupine. That comparison was more than merely casual—even from floor level across the room, Alice could see that the spines came to wickedly sharp points.

He muttered something that sounded impolite, groped further in the barrel, and came up with a droopy-looking green lizard about as long as his arm. He held it around the neck with thumb and forefinger, and though it thrashed and scrabbled desperately at the air, it couldn't make any progress. The creature glared at the lizard with his huge purple eyes.

"It bit me! Stupid vicious thing. Here."

The creature tossed the lizard across the room, and the little one picked it out of the air with impossible grace. His tiny mouth turned upward in a smile, and then as Alice watched in horror the smile spread, wider and wider, until it split the thing's head almost in half. In the light of the fire, Alice could clearly see hundreds of teeth like little needles, row on row of them, and a long, nimble blue tongue. The small creature crammed the lizard into his maw whole, ignoring its terrified scratching, and bit down on it so hard, the swarmer's ears could hear the crunch.

Isaac tugged on her sleeve, back at her real body. She

ought to be telling him what she could see, but she found herself rendered temporarily speechless, watching in awful fascination as the little creature slurped up the lizard's tail that stuck out of his mouth like a stray noodle. His jaw worked from side to side for a moment, and then he spat something small and white onto the hearth. It was a tiny bone, licked clean of flesh, and it was rapidly follow by another and another, a rain of neat white vertebrae rolling across the stone.

"Alice!" Isaac hissed.

Alice let the swarmer's senses go and opened her eyes. She found her heart was hammering fast. "I think," she said, a little shakily, "we may not want to try explaining."

Isaac grabbed her shoulder and jerked her around to face the path. Standing there was another one of the creatures, green skin silvered by the moonlight, regarding them with his huge, sparkling eyes. He had a dead sheep in one hand, dangling it by its hind legs over his shoulder.

"I think," Isaac said hoarsely, "we're in trouble."

CHAPTER NINETEEN

DINNER

Humans," said the green-skinned creature. He let go of the sheep, and the carcass thumped to the ground. "Honest to goodness humans!"

He took a step closer, and a wave ran through the spines on his back, as though they were rippling in the wind. Isaac edged between the thing and Alice, and raised his hands, palms out.

"Wait," Alice said, voice only a little shaky. "Listen. We don't have to—"

"Do you have any idea how long it's been," the thing said, "since I've tasted a human?"

His thin mouth spread across his face in a horrible

grin, jaw hinging open to reveal row after row of needle teeth with a flickering green tongue lurking at the back.

"Run!" Isaac shouted. The air was suddenly full of the sharp scent of new-fallen snow as a cold wind rose from nowhere. "Alice, run!"

"What?" Alice scrambled up the pile of rocks. "But—"

Tiny shreds of white ice, like bits of torn cloud, sprayed from Isaac's hands and blasted the green-skinned creature full in the face. The thing gave a whistling shriek and spun aside, graceful as a dancer, his spiny mane extended and quivering. Isaac shifted his aim, ice blasting from his hand like water from a fire hose as frost formed across the rocks underneath him. But the creature was too fast. He ducked low, then sprang into the air like a cricket, clearing Isaac's head in a standing jump and landing behind him in an easy crouch. Before he could turn, he grabbed Isaac around the elbows, dragging his arms back and pinioning them painfully behind him.

"Now, now. That's enough of *that*," the creature said, needle-fanged mouth still gaping wide. Looking over his shoulder for Alice, he added, "And you had better keep still, if you want your friend's arms to stay attached."

But the rocks were empty. Alice was gone.

She'd crossed the little clearing, diving behind the sheltering bulk of the woodpile, and waited for a count of five before risking a peek to see if the creature was following. It took her a moment to find him, aided by a human-sounding shout of pain. The creature had Isaac by both arms, twisted at an uncomfortable angle, and he used this grip to force Isaac to stumble toward the cottage or dislocate his own shoulder.

Alice found her mouth hanging open for a moment as she realized the sheer depths of Isaac's stupidity. When he'd said "Run!" she'd assumed that he had some sort of a plan, that he was going to get away from the awful thing himself with one of his bound creatures. Now it dawned on her that he'd had no idea *what* he was doing, and he'd told her to escape out of some kind of misplaced chivalrous impulse.

"Idiot, idiot, idiot," Alice muttered. If she hadn't been running, she could have *helped.* She fought down a flush of shame in her cheeks; from an outsider's point of view, it would look very much like she'd taken off at the first sign of danger and left him to fend for himself. *I assumed he was being sensible. How was I supposed to know he was so stupid?*

The creature frog-marched Isaac through the door, and Alice considered her options. She had to rescue him, obviously. It would serve him right if he got his head bitten off, but that wouldn't get her any closer to the book they'd come to find. *And he* did *help me with Mr. Black.* But if the creatures were going to eat him—and, judging by the fate of the lizard, they liked their meat raw—she didn't have much time.

She realized she still had the Swarm thread in her mental grip, which meant that her swarmer was still in place in the pile of kindling. Hurriedly she slipped back into its senses, and saw that all three of the creatures were now clustered excitedly around Isaac, who was backed against

their table. The little one was hopping from one foot to the other in excitement, while the purple one leaned over him and ran his long, thin tongue over his teeth.

"A human," he said. "A real, live, human. I must say, Mah-Li, you never cease to surprise me."

"Serendipity, Sah-To," said the green one, who Alice guessed was Mah-Li. "He was hiding just outside the cottage. Probably lost, poor thing."

"Can't have been lost for too long," said Sah-To. "He's plenty plump." He leaned closer.

"Careful," said Mah-Li. "He has a little magic."

"Even better. It adds to the flavor." Sah-To straightened up. "You don't think he's a Reader, do you?"

"If he is, he's a pretty feeble one," Mah-Li said.

"Fair enough. Let's get him out of that nasty coat."

Isaac jerked, but Sah-To held his arms securely. Mah-Li pulled his trench coat down from his shoulders with thin, delicate fingers.

"There's another one too," Sah-To said. "She ran away, but she can't have gotten far. I'll track her down when we're done with this one."

"Better and better," Mah-Li said. "You hear that, Van-Si? We're going to have a feast."

The little creature hissed his approval. Alice blinked

away the swarmer's vision and got up from the woodpile, absently brushing dirt from her knees.

Now what? She could send the swarmers at the three of them. But the problem was Isaac—they already had him in hand, and it would be easy for them to hurt him before the swarmers could accomplish anything.

If I could start a fire, they might come running out . . . But she hadn't brought matches, and the cottage was mostly made of stone. And it would take too long. She was already taking too long, they could already be tearing him to pieces.

There was only one thing that would distract them from their meal, she realized. Alice looked down at her hands and was pleased to find them shaking only slightly. *No percentage in hanging about.*

All three of the creatures were visible from the doorway. Mah-Li, the green one, had gotten Isaac's coat off and was sniffing it with distaste, but to Alice's relief they didn't seem to have hurt him yet. Little Van-Si worried at one of his boots, carefully undoing the laces. When he noticed Alice, his spiny mane bristled, and he let out a warning hiss.

"The other human!" Mah-Li said, big eyes going wider. "Fascinating."

"I thought you said she ran away," Sah-To said.

"I thought she had."

"Alice," Isaac said. His face was tight with pain; Mah-Li was bending his arm behind him at an awkward angle. "What are you doing?"

"Please." Alice tried to put a pleading, sobbing note into her voice. It was not something that came naturally to her, but she hoped the three creatures would not be familiar enough with human mannerisms to notice. "Please let him go."

"Let him go?" Mah-Li said, sounding genuinely puzzled. "Whatever for?"

"They're not going to listen, Alice!" Isaac said, then doubled over as Mah-Li twisted his arm even further. The green-skinned creature pushed him forward to sprawl on the floor and took a step toward Alice.

"Take me instead," Alice said. "You don't need both of us, surely. Let him go."

Mah-Li flowed toward her, another step, like someone trying to approach a wild animal without startling it. Alice forced herself to look directly in his huge green eyes, ignoring the needle-filled mouth and the licking, snaky tongue.

"I suppose," Mah-Li said, "we could make do with one human for tonight—"

He leaped forward, fast as a cobra, and grabbed Alice by both shoulders. For all their thin dexterity, his fingers were inhumanly strong.

"— and save the other one for tomorrow." His horribly broad mouth curved up into a toothy grin.

Alice kicked him in the stomach. It wasn't a very good kick, since she was at an awkward angle, but it was unexpected enough that it connected, and the breath went out of Mah-Li with a *woof.* If she had been expecting it to get her out of the creature's grip, however, Alice would have been disappointed, as Mah-Li's fingers only tightened painfully on her shoulders.

Fortunately, this was not what Alice had been expecting, though she tried to jerk backward as though it had been. At the same time, she tightened her grip on the Swarm thread, pulling it *inward*—not toward the world, to call the swarmers into being, but inside herself.

Mah-Li gave an angry, hissing shriek. He pulled Alice toward him and closed his needle-filled jaw around her throat. Distantly, Alice heard Isaac shout her name. Mah-Li tried to bite down—

—and stopped. Alice could feel the pressure of his jaws. But the Swarm thread coiled inside her had changed Alice's flesh to the same rubbery consistency as the swarmers themselves, and Mah-Li's teeth could only dimple the surface of her skin, like a dog trying to bite down on a rubber ball. Alice twisted, and then came free with a sharp *ping* as several needle-teeth snapped. Mah-Li screeched in pain, clutching at his mouth and staggering backward.

"Isaac, *now*!" Alice shouted.

She pulled the Swarm thread back the other way, toward the world, and swarmers materialized by the dozen all around her. There were too many to control carefully, but the swarmers had instincts of their own, and once she'd set them to work, they went at it with a will. They nipped and slashed at Mah-Li and Sah-To with their beaks. Little Vin-Si tried to make a grab for Alice herself, but one of the swarmers put itself underfoot, and he slipped and tumbled as though he'd stepped on a tennis ball.

Isaac was on his feet too, and shards of ice flashed through the air on a blast of freezing wind. Mah-Li groped toward him, spines stiff and arms flailing, and Alice attacked his shins with a dozen swarmers. Their beaks left long, shallow cuts that oozed dark red.

"Out the door!" Alice shouted, and saw Isaac nod. She started herding the three creatures with her swarmers, even as Isaac blinded them with ice and pushed them backward. In a few moments the monsters were pushed toward the door, feet sliding on the ice-slicked floor. Isaac frowned, cheeks white with strain, and the indoor blizzard redoubled, the wind shrieking like a chorus of madmen.

All at once Vin-Si, holding on to the doorway with one hand, let go and tumbled out into the yard. Sah-To followed, and finally Mah-Li, his broad grin frozen into a rictus of pain, staggered back through the doorway. Isaac pushed the ice storm after them, and in the moonlight Alice could see the three figures loping away as fast as their legs could carry them. She let the swarmers vanish and stumbled to the door, slamming it closed and shoving the iron bolt into place. Isaac lowered his hands, and the wind died away. The little cottage went silent.

"Are you all right?" Alice said.

Isaac nodded, breathing hard. "You?"

"I think so." Alice ran a hand along her neck. She found half a tooth dangling from where it had cut shallowly into her skin, and tossed it aside with a shudder. "Just a few scratches."

There was another pause.

"You are the stupidest—" Alice and Isaac both began, almost simultaneously. Then, catching each other's expression, they both stopped, and equally simultaneously began laughing. Isaac doubled over, hands on his knees, while Alice leaned back against the door and shook with slightly hysterical giggles.

"Do you want to go first?" she said, when they'd calmed down a little.

Isaac took a deep breath, leaning against the table. "I thought he was going to tear your throat out."

"I was a little worried about that myself," Alice said. "I'd never tried using the Swarm like that before."

"You were *planning* on that? Your plan was to walk in here and get one of them to bite you?"

"More or less." It didn't sound like such a great idea, now that Isaac said it out loud. "I didn't have a lot of time to come up with it. What were you *thinking* when you told me to run? I thought you were coming too."

"I have no idea," Isaac said. "I just . . . I really don't know." He shook his head. "Thanks for not running too far."

"Well. I still needed your help. And you saved me from Mr. Black." Alice paused as something occurred to her. "Why didn't you use that . . . song when they grabbed you?"

Isaac sighed. "She's called the Siren. She can put people into a trance, and eventually to sleep, but it takes a little while to have an effect." His hand went to his trouser pocket and patted it to make sure something was still there. "It also takes a lot of energy. I'm not sure I could have gotten all three of them at once."

Alice nodded. Now that the hysterical relief was wearing off, she was realizing that their position was still precarious. The stone cottage didn't have any windows, and the door looked sturdy enough, but Mah-Li and Sah-To might have stopped running by now and come back to wait for her and Isaac to emerge. She glanced nervously at the door, then over at the big chest.

Isaac followed her gaze. "It's in there, if it's anywhere. Let's have a look."

The chest had a padlock, a huge, ancient-looking thing with a big old-fashioned keyhole. Isaac gave it an experimental tug and found it secure.

"Ending didn't mention this," he said. "Did she tell you about some kind of key?"

"No," Alice said. She knelt to examine the lock more closely, trying to see inside the keyhole. "You'd think she would have—"

As she took the lock in her hand, there was a *click*. Surprised, Alice let it fall, and it popped open. Isaac laughed.

"Apparently she gave *you* the key," he said, pulling the lock free and setting it aside.

"Apparently," Alice said, frowning.

Isaac lifted the lid. In the padded interior of the chest, looking ridiculously small, was a slim, weathered book bound in something like snakeskin. The title was picked out in gilt on the cover: *The Dragon.*

It was hard to imagine that this little thing was at the root of so much trouble.

She reached for the book at the same time as Isaac, and their fingers touched. He looked up at her and laughed, a little nervously.

"We're taking it back to Ending together, aren't we?" Alice said.

He nodded.

"Then you hold on to it for now."

An emotion she couldn't identify flickered briefly across his face, but he nodded. He brought the book over to the table, and he retrieved his battered coat from where Mah-Li had dropped it. It had acquired a few more rips, but Isaac seemed not to mind. He shrugged it on and tucked the book into an inner pocket.

"Okay," Alice said. "Now we just have to get out of here."

In the event, that turned out to be easier than Alice had worried. If the three creatures were still nearby, they were keeping their heads down, and no one emerged to challenge Alice and Isaac as they cautiously opened the cottage door and made a dash for the switchback path. The moon was still high, and they ran down the path together in a mad rush, skipping over rocks and jumping ruts in the dirt. When they stumbled to a halt at the bottom in a cloud of dust, it took Alice a moment to get her bearings, but she soon found the silhouette of the pedestal and pointed the way.

The portal-book was just where they'd left it. Alice held out her hand wordlessly, and Isaac took it. He flipped the cover open, and the letters did their now-familiar crawl into legibility. Alice's eyes went wide as she read:

Alice looked up from the book into the bearded, grinning face of Mr. Black. She tried to shout a warning . . .

CHAPTER TWENTY

THE SECOND TRIAL

ALICE LOOKED UP FROM the book into the bearded, grinning face of Mr. Black. She tried to shout a warning, but one huge hand was already on her arm, and the other was around Isaac's wrist. Alice jerked backward, reaching out automatically for the Swarm thread, ready to call a dozen of the sharp-beaked little terrors into being . . .

"Now, children," said Geryon. "Let's not make a scene."

Alice froze. Isaac did too, though in his case it seemed to be from sheer terror. He had the wide-eyed look of a rabbit trying to stare down a pair of headlights. Geryon stepped out from behind Mr. Black, hands in the pockets of his tatty old jacket, tutting like a disappointed tutor.

"I believe you can release our Alice, Mr. Black," Geryon said.

Reluctantly, Mr. Black let go of her, circling around to loom behind Isaac. Alice rubbed her arm—it ached where he'd grabbed her—and said, "Master. Sir. This isn't—"

"Do you have the book?"

"Wait. Listen," Alice said. She felt like she had this one moment to make him understand, before he made up his mind. She searched desperately for the words that would do it, but her mind felt blank and sluggish. A sob welled up from her chest, and she pushed down hard. "I can explain—"

"Do you have the Dragon?" Geryon said, and this time there was steel in his voice.

"No," Alice said. "He does."

"I see." Geryon nodded to Mr. Black, who patted Isaac's pockets until he found the book. He extracted it carefully and handed it to the old Reader, who put it under his arm without even glancing at the cover. "And you, boy. What's your name?"

Isaac set his jaw, in spite of the fear Alice could still see in his eyes. He said nothing.

"He's Isaac," Alice said. "And he was *helping* me. We—"

"Quiet, my dear," Geryon said. "If I want something from you, I'll ask."

"But—"

"I said *quiet*." Geryon glanced briefly in her direction, and something invisible slashed across the space between them.

Alice's jaw locked, clenching so tight, her teeth hurt, and she dropped to her knees, tears coming to her eyes.

Geryon, turning back to Isaac, said, "And whose pawn are you, young Isaac? You don't look like one of Grigori's. The Eddicant, perhaps? Gabriel?"

Isaac shook his head, lips pressed together. Geryon sighed.

"You must tell me, you know. How else am I to open negotiations with your master for your safe return? Assuming he wants you back, of course." Geryon bent slightly to look Isaac in the eye. "Come on, boy. Make it easy on yourself."

Isaac looked away, twisting in Mr. Black's grasp. Geryon chuckled.

"As you like," the old Reader said. "Mr. Black?"

Mr. Black did something to Isaac's arm, and Isaac screamed. Alice screamed too, or tried to, though it only came out as a muffled grunt. She pounded her fists on the grass and struggled to get back to her feet.

"Well?" Geryon said. "Are you going to make poor Alice watch such an unseemly affair?"

He gestured, and Mr. Black let Isaac go. He stumbled forward a step, pale and shivering, one arm cradled in the other.

"Anaxomander," he said, so low, it was almost inaudible. "My master is . . . Anaxomander."

"Oh dear," Geryon said. "My old friend, thieving from me in such a shameful fashion." He shook his head sadly. "What faithless times we live in. Mr. Black, take this young man to the vault and see that he's looked after." He turned to Alice. "As for you, my dear, you must be exhausted. I think you should get some sleep."

Alice gave another muffled shout. She'd caught sight of two yellow gleams in the shadows behind Geryon: Ending's feline eyes, glowing in the lamplight. She tried to point to them, but blackness slid down around her like a curtain. She felt her legs turn wobbly, and she toppled, but she was asleep before she hit the ground.

"Alice. Alice, wake up."

Alice opened her eyes, the morning light from her window chasing away mad fragments of dream. It was hard to breathe, like there was a weight on her chest, but this turned out to be because Ashes was sitting on her. He had his head held up, Sphinx-like, front paws idly kneading her blanket.

"Ashes?" she said blearily.

"Your powers of perception are, as always, acute," the cat said. "How do you feel?"

"Fuzzy," Alice said, though she found that her head was clearing rapidly. The events of last night came back to her in a rush, and she sucked in a deep breath. "Where's Isaac?"

"Under guard in Geryon's vault, I would imagine. Mother sends her apologies."

"Her *apologies*?" Alice sat up, forcing Ashes to spring to the floor, where he walked in a tight circle and began licking his paw in an offended manner. "They were waiting for us, and she was there! She must have led them right to us!"

"Apparently Mr. Black went to Master Geryon and warned him a thief had entered the library, and he compelled Mother's assistance. Her contract binds her to obey him, if he issues a direct command." Ashes looked as though admitting this lack of omnipotence on Ending's part pained him severely. "They were able to follow your progress and wait for you to emerge from the book."

"Wait until Geryon hears what that rat Mr. Black has been up to," Alice said, throwing off the sheets. "I'm going to—"

"Mother asked me to remind you," Ashes interrupted, "that if you accuse Mr. Black, Vespidian will undoubtedly flee, and we will lose any chance we might have left to interrogate him." His tail lashed. "Also, as it would be your word against his, there is no guarantee that Master Geryon would believe you."

Alice chewed her lip. While the cat had a point, the idea of just letting Mr. Black get away with his treachery rankled. *He was the one who told Vespidian about me in the first place!*

"All right," she said reluctantly. "But what am I supposed to do now? Geryon has the book, and I can't steal it from *him*." The very idea sent a shiver down her spine. Quite apart from whatever safeguards the old Reader had in place, stealing from him would be a rebellion against authority on a scale Alice wasn't prepared to accept. "And what about Isaac?" She hesitated. "Do you think he's really . . . what Geryon said? A thief who came to steal the book for himself?"

Ashes yawned, indicating disinterest. Alice shook her head.

"I don't believe it," she said. "If that was what he wanted, he wouldn't have . . . helped me. We can't just let Geryon keep him locked up."

"Are you planning a prison break, then?"

Alice paused again. If stealing the book would be bad, freeing Isaac would be infinitely worse. *But the way Geryon treated him . . .* She winced as she remembered the casual way he'd ordered Mr. Black to hurt Isaac until he got what he wanted out of him, and how he'd locked away her voice.

He's a Reader, Ending had told her. He is cruel, because that is his nature.

"For the moment," Ashes said, interrupting her thoughts, "the question is moot. Geryon wants to see you."

Alice froze. "Now?"

"When you've got a moment," Ashes drawled. "You know how patient he is."

Alice knocked at the door to Geryon's suite, and he answered it promptly. She was relieved to find that he seemed to be in a good mood, smiling genially.

"Good morning, Alice," he said. "I trust that a night's

rest has helped you recover from yesterday's exertions."

"Yes, sir. I feel much better."

"Splendid." Geryon stepped aside and waved her in, shutting the door behind her. "I'm sorry I had to treat you so roughly. Finding an agent of one of my enemies in my own library was a considerable shock to me, as you might imagine."

"Your enemies, sir?" Alice said. "I thought you said Anaxomander was a friend."

He chuckled. "I'm afraid that when you reach my age, child, the line between friends and foes becomes a little blurred. I have no quarrel with Anaxomander at the moment, certainly, but that doesn't mean he would hesitate to strike me should the opportunity present itself and he saw a profit in it. That's the way of things, with Readers. The only path to true friendship is endless vigilance."

"I see." Alice hesitated. She was strongly tempted to tell what she knew about Mr. Black, regardless of Ashes' warning, but she managed to hold back. *I can always tell him later.* Instead she said, "What about Isaac?"

"The boy? What about him?"

"What will happen to him?"

"Oh, I'll send him home eventually. His master and I

will work out some sort of bargain." Geryon's face darkened momentarily. "Not before he tells me how he got into my library, of course."

Alice swallowed. "And . . . me?"

"You?" Geryon pointed to the door to his sitting room, where two armchairs sat facing each other beside a hearth. There was a rich, warm scent of leather and old wood that reminded her of her father's office back in New York. "What do you mean?"

"You're not upset with me?"

"Oh! No, of course not." He gestured for her to sit, and took the opposite chair himself. "You couldn't have known what the boy was up to. I imagine he spun you some fantastic story. Consider it a lesson—being a Reader means learning whom to trust, and unfortunately the answer is often 'no one.' No, as a matter of fact, you are progressing more quickly than I anticipated!"

"Thank you, sir," Alice said carefully.

"That's why I've called you here today," Geryon said. "The time has come for your second trial."

"Trial?" Alice hesitated. "I thought you said I hadn't done anything wrong."

"Trial as in task or labor," Geryon said. "For a Reader, it means entering a prison-book and binding the creature within it to your will. You have succeeded at the first trial, with the Swarm, and the first is always the most dangerous for a new Reader. Now, with that power behind you, you will confront another. And eventually a third, and so on, until your power is sufficient to bind anything you wish."

"Oh." Alice looked around the study. "Now?"

"Now," Geryon confirmed. "Your duties will grow more dangerous, and you must be prepared. Anaxomander may be angry, and it's possible . . ." He trailed off, shaking his head. "In any event, I have selected the book for you. It will not be easy, but you should be successful if you use what you have learned."

"But . . ." Alice hesitated. "If I go into a book, I won't be able to come out again unless I kill whatever it is, right?"

"Unless it submits to the binding of its own accord, correct."

"I'm not sure I want to kill anything," Alice said. "Even monsters, if they've never done anything to me."

Geryon smiled thinly. "Poor child. I wish I could spare you this, I truly do. But believe me when I tell you it is the only way."

Ending's voice seemed to rumble in her ear. *His magic is based on cruelty and death.*

"Besides," Geryon went on, "it's not as though the prisoner can truly die, any more than a character in a novel can. You can always flip back to the first page, can't you? You've seen that with the Swarm."

Alice wanted to say that even if the prisoner couldn't die, they could still feel pain. But Geryon had a determined expression, and after last night she was afraid to test him.

"Are you allowed to tell me what's in the book?" she asked.

"Of course. It's a variety of tree-sprite, though an uncommonly strong one. A vicious little thing, truth be told, but I have every confidence in you." He picked up a thick, leather-bound volume from the floor beside the chair, apparently no different from those that lined the walls of the study. "Are you ready?"

What would happen, Alice thought, *if I said no?* Nothing good. She nodded.

"Something you may not know," Geryon said, "is that anyone touching the prison-book here in the real world can look inside, once someone has opened the way. So I will be able to observe your performance."

As if fighting for my life wasn't enough, I'm going to be graded as well.

He held out the book, and she accepted it and settled back in the armchair, old leather creaking around her.

"Good luck," said Ashes, from under the chair.

"Thanks," Alice said. "Here goes nothing."

She opened the book. There was a moment of eye-twisting incomprehensibility, and then she read:

Alice found herself on a grassy hill, overlooking a little valley with a stream . . .

CHAPTER TWENTY-ONE

THE TREE-SPRITE

ALICE FOUND HERSELF ON a grassy hill, overlooking a little valley with a stream that splashed and burbled through a racecourse of mossy rocks. She could see for miles in all directions, across rolling grassland spotted with small forests. Mountains, blued with distance, lined every horizon, as though she were standing at the bottom of an enormous basin. The air smelled sweet with growing things, and a warm sun beamed down from overhead.

Long green-and-yellow grass stalks rustled all around her, reaching up under her dress to brush against her thighs. She brushed them away, wishing idly that she'd worn trousers, and turned in a careful circle. Not far away, on the highest point of the hill, there was an enormous willow tree so perfectly circular, it resembled an overturned bowl.

That had to be where she was intended to go. Alice felt a brief, rebellious spark, and wondered what would happen if she turned her back on it, just walked out across the beckoning fields and never went anywhere near the tree. But Geryon was watching, and in any event he'd told her that the world of a prison-book wasn't *really* real, only real enough to contain the prisoner. She wondered if she'd eventually walk into a painted backdrop, like an incautious actor on a movie set.

Reaching out for the silver thread that led to the Swarm and keeping it firmly in her mental grip, Alice walked toward the tree.

She reached the curtain of hanging leaves, and parted it with one hand. The inside was shadowy and quiet. The willow's overhang had smothered the grass, leaving bare, hard earth underfoot, broken here and there by the knots and gnarls of the great tree's branches. Overhead, the branches of the trees stretched in all directions.

On one of those branches sat a . . . thing. When Geryon had said "tree-sprite," Alice had pictured something that looked like Vespidian, only painted in delicate greens and browns instead of yellow and black. This was a different sort of being altogether, vaguely ape-like in shape and massively bulky, covered all over in thick, dry bark. It had no head, only a slight bulge above its shoulders that showed two deep-set eyes. Enormous, outsized arms ended in heavy, gnarled fingers tipped with ragged claws, and short but similarly massive legs sported long, finger-like toes. It really was made of wood, Alice saw—here and there along its barky surface, she could see thin, protruding twigs and even a few hanging leaves.

It sat motionless for a while, glaring at her with its brilliant green eyes. Alice wasn't quite sure what to do. She was supposed to kill the thing, Geryon had said, but she had never deliberately started a fight with anyone in her life, and hadn't the least idea how to go about doing it. Instead she cleared her throat and held out her palms in what she hoped was a non-threatening manner.

"Hello," she said. "I'm Alice."

The tree-sprite made no reply, other than to shift slightly on its perch. Encouraged, Alice took a step closer.

"Can you understand me? I don't want to hurt you."

Well, she thought, *it's true. I don't* want *to hurt anyone.*

The thing made a noise, halfway between a grunt and the dry sound of a dead branch snapping. Alice took

another step forward, until she was almost underneath it, looking upward.

"If you can understand me," she said, "come down, and we can talk about things."

The tree-sprite leaped, swinging completely around the branch and hurling itself toward Alice with astonishing speed. It came at her face-first, arms extended, ragged-edged claws spread wide. Alice jumped backward just in time as it hit the ground with the force of a cannonball, rebounded neatly into another leap, and landed on its haunches a few feet away.

Alice backed away, tugging hurriedly on the silver thread. A dozen swarmers popped into being in front of her, lining up like a football squad.

"We don't have to fight," Alice said nervously. "If you would just listen to me . . ."

Geryon's voice suddenly filled her skull. "You can't reason with it, Alice. If it could be talked to, it wouldn't be in a prison-book in the first place."

The tree-sprite raised one hand to touch a low-hanging branch, as though preparing to fling itself back into the canopy. Alice, looking over her shoulder at the sound of rustling leaves, saw the willow fronds behind her twitch and reach inward as though pressed by a strong breeze, then spread out toward her like a mass of writhing tendrils. She gave an involuntary shriek and backpedaled, away from the sprite and the searching leaves, only to back into another hanging branch. The tree-sprite's clawed fingers, nails now sunk smoothly into the bark of the branch, twitched as though they were manipulating a marionette, and the limb behind Alice twisted out of place with a mass of rustling, groaning sounds, curving around to embrace her.

She quickly lost all desire to talk to the thing. She ducked away from the circling branch, and at a mental command the swarmers charged beak-first like a tiny squadron of lancers. They pecked the tree-sprite around the legs, ripping viciously at its wooden skin and tearing it away in strips. This appeared to bother the thing not at all, however, and it swept its free paw down to scatter the little creatures, grabbing one that was unable to get its beak free in time and hurling it against the trunk of the tree. Alice expected it to bounce, but instead it simply sank into the wooden surface as though into muddy ground, the wood rippling and closing over it. An instant later, she cried out with the little creature's pain as it died, remorseless wood closing all around it with the strength of an industrial press.

The rest of the swarmers closed in again, but the tree-sprite took hold of the branch with both hands and lifted itself off the ground and out of their reach. More tree limbs were bending inward, the perfect dome of the willow folding in on itself in a cacophony of tearing leaves and splintering twigs. Willow fronds spread out all around Alice, cutting her off in three directions and forcing her back toward the tree trunk. The ground under her feet writhed, roots shifting and groping as they tried to trip her.

Alice ducked the flailing limbs and dodged backward, rapidly running out of room. The groping branches were clumsy and easy to avoid, but the willow fronds were much more agile. A look over her shoulder told her that she had only a couple of feet left before she came up against that deadly trunk, and a curtain of leaves surrounded her almost completely. It didn't reach *quite* to the ground, though—

There wasn't time to think about it. She ran forward, feinting left, then right, then throwing herself to the ground in a roll that she hoped would take her past the curtain and out into the open. She felt a moment of exultation as she felt the leaves brush by her, straining but unable to reach. A bare instant later, her headlong tumble ended hard against a clump of roots that had risen in her path, sending a jolt of pain through her shoulder. She scrabbled to get over it, but the whole patch of dirt she lay on was rising, and before she could get past, she felt the willow fronds winding around her.

Desperately, Alice called on the Swarm. First a dozen and then more of the little creatures popped into being, stabbing and slashing at the willow switches with their beaks, trying to hack their way to the knots that were already winding around Alice's limbs. The sharpened edges of their beaks could cut the fronds, but for every one they severed, two more snaked into place. After a moment of confusion, the willow was fighting back, reaching out for the swarmers and wrapping around them or grabbing their legs. The swarmers tried to stay clear, surprisingly agile, but first one and then another were caught. The dangling fronds hurled them into the trunk of the tree, like a zookeeper flicking morsels into the mouth of a waiting lion, and their dying pain exploded in the back of Alice's skull.

In spite of her efforts, the willow branches had a solid hold around her waist, arms, and legs, and they lifted her into the air. The edges of the leaves, stiffened until they were as hard as glass, could cut like razors. They'd slashed her sleeves to ribbons and were threatening to do the same to her skin. Alice let the swarmers vanish and drew their thread inside herself, thickening her skin to the same rubbery consistency as theirs while the branches tightened their grip with bone-cracking strength.

The tree-sprite itself approached, riding a twisting tree branch, one hand still buried in the wood and twitching as though the myriad limbs were extensions of its fingers. Its green eyes regarded her coldly as the thick ropes of twisting fronds tightened and the razor-leaves pressed tighter. She wondered if it was curious why she was still struggling; certainly anything made of ordinary flesh and blood would already have been crushed to a gooey paste. As it was, her Swarm-infused flesh resisted the pressure, but the tight press made it difficult to draw breath, and spots were already dancing in front of her eyes.

After a long pause, the tree-sprite twitched its buried fingers, and the willow fronds responded. Alice found herself turning helplessly, branches groaning around her as she was pressed toward the thick tree-trunk. Even the Swarm's power wouldn't help her survive *that*, as several poor swarmers had already demonstrated. She struggled, but she might as well have been trying to push over a tree with her bare hands. The air was full of the sound of splintering bark and twigs as the branches bent nearly double, and she could smell the sweet tang of sap.

If Geryon was going to rescue her at the last minute, she thought, surprisingly calm, then that minute was rapidly approaching. The trunk of the tree loomed in front of her, as menacing in its stolid immobility as the slavering jaw of a monster and just as deadly. She tried not to picture being fed into it, a little at a time—

Geryon would let it happen, she realized. He would sit there, in his comfortable study, and let it happen. It would save him the trouble of dealing with her failure and erasing her memories. She felt a sudden, frantic rage, cutting through the terror like a knife. *No*, she thought. *I am* not *going to die. Not today.*

She pulled on the Swarm thread, as hard as she could. There was a *pop*, like the sound the swarmers made, but a hundred times louder.

Alice *became* the Swarm.

The willow fronds sprang apart, taken by surprise by a sudden lack of resistance, like a man leaning against a suddenly open door. Swarmers poured between the fronds, a cascade of them, dozens and dozens. They pattered and bounced on the root-gnarled ground like a strange, hard rain, rapidly righting themselves and huddling together into a nearly solid mass. When they moved, they ran in a bunch, parting to clear roots or flailing branches and flowing back together afterward, like a school of minnows.

Alice had a hundred tiny hearts and two hundred legs, all moving at once. In the first instant, the pain of so many fragmented perceptions overwhelmed her, and she thought she would go mad. She wanted to back away, release the Swarm's perceptions as she did when she peered through their eyes, but this time there was nowhere to go. She wanted to scream, but didn't know how.

It was that first instinct, the terrified desire to curl up into a ball until the horror went away, that saved her. The swarmers took over, flowing around the clumsy, reaching branches like a tide. She didn't need to control the little bodies, like a puppeteer jerking their limbs about. The swarmers *knew* how to move, just as her human body knew how to walk or jump or run.

No sooner had she gotten the hang of this than her perceptions resolved as well, snapping into place like a *trompe l'oeil* painting into its component parts. Alice realized in that moment that she had never really understood the Swarm. She'd thought of it as a pack of creatures, like a bunch of wolves running side by side, but it wasn't like that at all. They were *one* creature in a hundred bodies, one mind—her mind. And those bodies knew how to use their multiple eyes, just as well as Alice's own body could use her two. She could see all around her, see all *sides* of a branch as the swarmers split up to run past it. The sudden rush of understanding was such a glorious sensation, she forgot her pain completely.

The willow branches, recovering from their surprise at suddenly grasping nothing but air, bent back down to block her path, fronds writhing and twisting into a living wall of greenery. But Alice-the-Swarm was a hundred times more agile than Alice-the-Girl had ever been, and she slipped through gaps in the barrier in a hundred different places. Where there wasn't a hole, she made one, her sharp beaks nipping and slashing at the hanging tendrils. Then she was through, leaves and branches boiling furiously behind her. Her tiny legs blurred, and she felt grass underneath her claws.

The willow branches pulled up short, stretched out as far as they could go, fronds straining after her horizontally as though whipped by a hurricane. They fell back, finally, exhausted by the effort. The swarmers huddled together outside their range, a mass of beaks and rubbery dark fur.

There was a moment of flowing, melting confusion. Then, in place of a hundred tiny creatures, there was one girl lying in the grass, bloody and panting for breath.

CHAPTER TWENTY-TWO
A DECISION

"Geryon!" Alice shouted, as soon as she had her breath back.

Her heart still hopped and jumped in her chest, though she couldn't say whether it was from fear or exhilaration. That first moment of dissolution, her body dissolving into dozens of different pieces—Alice was certain she'd have nightmares about it until the day she died, if she lived to be a hundred and ten.

"*Geryon!* I know you can hear me." She sat up, feeling a little wobbly. "It's over, all right? I can't do it. Get me out of here."

There was no answer. She hadn't really expected one. She wasn't even sure if he *could* get her out, once she'd gone inside, but she didn't think he would even if it was in his power.

All around her, the wind whistled gently through the grass, sending silver, rustling waves all the way down the hill and through the distant valleys. Beyond that, the mountains loomed, distant and somehow *vague*, as though they weren't quite completely defined.

It's not real, Alice thought. *None of this is* really *real, except this hilltop and that tree. And that* . . . thing. *There's no way out, except through there.*

"But how am I supposed to kill something like *that*?" she said aloud.

It had seemed impossible even before the entire willow tree had turned on her. She'd caught it off guard and gotten away, but she wasn't sure if she could manage it a second time. She wondered what would happen if *some* of her was caught while she was the Swarm. Would she reassemble herself without a finger, or a big toe?

Alice laughed, a little giddily. She clambered to her feet and shook out her arms and legs. The air here was just cool enough to be bracing. She'd lost her shoes during the transition, somehow, and the grass and soft earth were gentle on her bare feet. She stretched, taking several deep, calming breaths, and turned back toward the tree.

The tree-sprite was watching her, sitting on a single thin limb folded down from the tree's crown to stretch as far as it could from the trunk. It still had one hand thrust inside the wood, and its green eyes burned maliciously. There were scores and notches in its hide where the Swarm had attacked it, but they were already starting to fill in and scab over. Alice glared back at it defiantly, only a hint of color in her cheeks.

"We wouldn't have to do this," she shouted, "if you would be reasonable!"

Another tree limb unfolded, club-like and massive. It raised itself up to a great height, then plunged downward with shocking speed, hitting the ground hard enough to raise a mighty *crunch* and a puff of dust, like a giant pounding the earth in a tantrum. Alice couldn't help but jump backward, and she thought she saw satisfaction in the vicious creature's eyes.

"You're not going to scare me like *that*," Alice muttered.

She started walking in a circle around the tree, just beyond the thing's striking distance. It followed her, leaping from branch to thin upper branch when they'd stretched as far as they could. The willow fronds rustled and reached out as she approached, as though they could scent prey.

But not the whole time, she thought, watching them carefully. There's a moment—

It wasn't much of a plan, really, but it was more than she'd had the first time she found herself in a prison-book. She tugged on the Swarm thread as far as it would go, summoning as many of the little creatures as she could manage. They tumbled from the air around her with a susurrus of *pops*, until a huddled crowd of several hundred of the things surrounded her. Meeting the tree-sprite's gaze, she gave it a slow, deliberate smile, and then extended a finger and a mental command.

The swarmers charged. The willow fronds rustled, spread wide to receive them, but the little creatures were too fast when they were running full tilt. They shot through gaps in the leaves or pushed the thin tendrils aside, ignoring the razor-sharp leaves. When they were past the perimeter of hanging branches, they converged on the tree trunk.

Alice had realized, at some point during her wild, multi-bodied flight, that the swarmers could climb trees. They were heavy for their size, but extremely strong, and the sharp-tipped claws on their feet could dig through bark and get a solid grip. More importantly, they could work *together*. They hit the tree trunk and swarmed up it like an army of angry ants, the ones still close to the ground helping to support the weight of those farther up. Many of them didn't make it, especially once the trunk started twisting in an effort to rid itself of its uninvited guests, but those that fell simply bounced a few times, rolled over, and ran back to the fray. Within moments they had reached the lower branches and were running along them, beaks slashing at the hanging fronds, while gangs of them worked to hoist themselves farther into the canopy.

The tree went berserk, like a dog suddenly assailed by an army of fleas. Every branch bent inward, fronds reaching and grasping in a leafy chaos, trying to grab the persistent little parasites and pull them free. A few were yanked off and sent spinning across the fields, but when a frond grabbed one, a half-dozen others descended at once, chopping the offending tendril with their beaks and freeing their trapped compatriot. Alice could almost hear the scream of rage as the tree flailed frantically at itself.

She never could have done it before this. Individual

control of the swarmers would have overwhelmed her in a chaos of multiple legs and eyes. But her brief moments *as* the Swarm had taught her a great deal about them, including what she could safely leave them to handle on their own. Each swarmer knew where the others were, all the time, and they could look through each other's eyes as easily as she could see through theirs. They needed only the lightest prodding to do what she wanted, and once she'd sent them off, they set to it with a will.

She had enough concentration left over to wave at the tree-sprite as she walked deliberately forward, past where the cordon of hanging fronds had been.

"Hey!" she told it. "You want me? Here I am!"

The creature turned to face her, the branch it rode twisting around like a snake. Its green eyes flared malevolently. All around Alice, other branches arched toward her, and she could feel the ground writhing beneath her feet as roots worked their way upward.

She stuck out her tongue at the tree-sprite and ran, staying within the willow's reach but a comfortable distance from the trunk. The branches twisted around to follow, as did the tree-sprite itself. She saw it reach the end of its branch and leap to a new one. And, through the countless eyes of the Swarm, she caught something important: The tree stopped moving during the brief moment the sprite was out of contact with the wood.

More branches quickly curved in to block Alice's path, and she had to dodge and weave to avoid them. The swarmers ran along the tree limbs, snipping and snapping at any fronds that looked like they might get ahold of Alice as she passed. Even so, she had several near misses that left her with stinging cuts, and the fronds in front of her were getting thicker. She didn't look over her shoulder—she didn't need to, the Swarm could see everything—but she kept as much attention as she dared on the tree-sprite itself. The branches it leaped to were mostly the very highest on the tree, as they could stretch the farthest, but as it closed in behind her it jumped down, swinging from a suddenly still limb and landing on one of the lower branches directly in Alice's path. She pulled up short, skidding to a halt in a cloud of flying dirt, and the glow in the sprite's eyes seemed to brighten with triumph. Fronds raced in toward her from all directions.

It didn't notice the swarmers piling onto the branch behind it. How could it? Alice thought, almost pityingly. It only had one pair of eyes.

The little creatures raced out along the limb to where it thinned, then attacked it with their beaks like a swarm of maddened woodpeckers. Chips of bark flew. The tree-sprite spun, perhaps feeling some echo of the tree's agony, but it was far too late. Two dozen swarmers were already slashing at the weakened branch, and before the sprite could jump free, the wood gave way under its weight with a mighty *crack*. It fell almost directly toward Alice, who had to duck backward to avoid it.

The sprite's left hand, with its ragged, bark-like claw, was still sunk deep in the wood of the branch. But the branch was no longer connected to the tree. As Alice had observed, without that connection, the willow was just a willow, not a multi-limbed engine of destruction. All the branches stopped at once, swaying gently with suddenly halted momentum. All the fronds twitched and fell limp, hanging in gentle curtains like willow fronds ought to, and there was a shower of dislodged leaves and twigs.

If the tree-sprite got its hand back on the tree, Alice was certain, it would all start back up again. The fall seemed to have stunned it, and she didn't intend to give it a chance to recover. The swarmers dropped from the branches like a rain of strange-shaped fruit, bouncing and rolling across the uneven ground, then homing in on the ape-like thing. They charged beak-first, burying the points into its skin, slashing and cutting. Alice, recalling the vicious sharpness of those beaks, quailed at the sight, but there seemed to be no flesh or blood in the tree-sprite. Chunks of bark came away with dry cracks and pops.

The thing started to move, freeing its hand from the broken branch and swatting feebly at its tormentors. Alice directed the swarmers to pin it to the ground, driving their beaks into it and holding it fast with their combined weight. Soon they had it spread-eagled, face-down, and Alice herself cautiously approached.

"It's over," she said. "Can you understand me? You've lost, all right?"

Something was happening to the creature. Its skin seemed to be drying out, cracking and hardening into old, dead bark, while in the chest of its ape-like body something continued to twist and writhe. Alice watched, still tense, as a great plate of bark cracked in half and fell away. A mop of pale green hair emerged, straight up out of the tree-sprite's back like a shoot growing out of a fallen timber. It was followed by two slender hands, their skin the color of fresh buds in spring.

They scrabbled on the bark armor until they found a handhold, and then a child-like creature no taller than Alice's knee levered itself out. It was naked, genderless as an undressed doll, with a painfully thin body and slender, delicate limbs. All it shared with the ape-like armored thing were its eyes, which were the same brilliant, burning green. Alice had a sudden image of this fragile little thing sitting cocooned in bark and wood like a medieval knight in his plate-mail, looking out at the world from a slit in its visor.

It was trying to get away, clambering over the wreckage of its bark-suit, but when it reached the edge it lost its footing and slid heavily to the ground. One of the swarmers ran up to it and took a tentative peck at its leg, and its beak left a curving, ugly wound that leaked thick, sticky sap. The tree-sprite's mouth gaped in a silent scream, showing teeth the pale color of birch wood.

"Stop," Alice said aloud.

A ring of swarmers halted, all around the little creature, which clutched at the cut just like a human in pain. It rolled over, face-down, knees pulled up under it, and huddled there like a child awaiting punishment. The swarmers surrounded it, razor beaks gleaming and dangerous.

She tried to think back to what Geryon had told her. He'd mentioned, offhandedly, that a creature could surrender rather than fight to the death, but he'd never said *how*.

"You have to . . . submit," Alice said uncertainly. "Then

I can go away and leave you alone. Do you understand me? I don't *want* to hurt you. But otherwise I have no way to get out of here."

Was this enough? The fight was clearly over. But she was still here. She tried to remember what had happened when she'd escaped the world of the Swarm, but she'd been freezing and nearly unconscious at the time, and recalled only waking up in bed.

"Geryon!" she said. He could hear her, she was certain. And he'd already spoken once. "What do I do?"

"Kill it," Geryon said, inside her skull.

"What?" Alice looked down at the creature, pathetic and in pain. "I can't. Not now."

"It has not submitted to your will. You must destroy it to escape the prison."

"I don't think it understands."

"Whether or not it understands is immaterial," Geryon said. He sounded irritated. "It is bound, and can choose only submission or destruction."

"But I can't seem to *talk* to it," Alice said. "If I could explain things, I wouldn't have to—"

"Just because a creature has a human face does not mean it has a human mind," Geryon snapped. "Submission may be beyond its comprehension. It matters not. Strike."

"No," Alice said. "I'm not going to hurt someone just because it's more convenient for me!"

"I do not understand your reluctance," Geryon said, getting angry. "It is not 'someone.' It is not *human*. What does it matter?"

Alice ignored him. She bent beside the little thing, swarmers shuffling aside to let her through, and put her hand on its shoulder. Its skin was cool to the touch, and smooth as a fresh-grown twig.

"Listen," Alice whispered. "I don't know if you can understand me, but please try. I'm not going to hurt you. Whatever Geryon says, I'm *not*. But it's over, you know? You don't have to fight anymore."

A shudder ran through the huddled thing. Slowly, it began to uncurl, and it turned its head to look up at her. It had a narrow, triangular face, with thin lips and a tiny button nose, but its green eyes were enormous. They flashed and sparkled with a light of their own, like gemstones in the sun, and once again Alice could almost feel what the creature was thinking. Rage, and hatred, and fear, and—satisfaction?

One of the tree-sprite's hands had scratched out a hole in the dirt, burying itself to the wrist. Between its tiny fingers, Alice could see something pale white and wormlike, twisting and writhing. The very tip of a root.

The willow shuddered back into motion with a thousand creaks and rustles that merged into a triumphant roar. Alice turned in time to see one of the largest branches bend back until it nearly touched the trunk with its tip. It snapped forward like a bow with the tension released, whistling through a wide arc. The end of it caught her in the stomach with the force of a baseball player's swing, hard enough that it lifted her off the ground entirely and sent her flailing through the air like a tossed ragdoll. There was a moment of disorienting flight, and she got a glimpse of the tree trunk looming in front of her, with only time enough to close her eyes and cringe.

Instead of the bone-crushing impact she'd expected, she hit the wooden surface and sank inside it like it was made of thick syrup. Darkness enveloped her, and her ears were full of the creaks and pops of moving wood. Her breath wouldn't come, and something in her chest felt broken and *wrong*. She tried to scream, but nothing emerged. The tree began to press on her, a giant's fist tightening its grip, and Alice felt the *pop* and *crunch* of bone before her consciousness fled and her body fell away behind her.

Chapter Twenty-three
THE *GIDEON*

A LICE OPENED HER EYES, gasping for breath. She was standing at the rail of a ship, looking out at the sea. The setting sun filled the sky with gaudy colors, and the highlights on the gentle swells faded from gold to crimson.

When she worked up the courage to examine herself, she was doubly surprised—not only was her body intact, but she was wearing a dress she distinctly remembered leaving behind in New York. It was a blue silk-and-satin affair her father had given her this Christmas past, a bit fancy for Alice's taste, but she'd always loved it because *he* did. Just the sight of it brought tears to her eyes, and she reached up to wipe them away. Her hand froze, midway through the gesture, and rubbed tentatively at her cheek. The thin, slashing scar she'd gotten from the Swarm was gone.

The color drained out of the sky, and the ocean went from red to purple to a deep, impenetrable black. Stars began to emerge through the shredded clouds overhead, one by one. Alice turned around. The wall behind her was pierced by a set of round portholes and a single door, looking very nautical with a round handle set in the center. Standing by the door—

That, Alice thought, is impossible. It's a trick, and a cruel one. It's—

Her traitorous legs were already in motion, paying no attention to her rational brain. She ran as though through molasses, slow and clumsy, expecting that at any moment the apparition would vanish and be replaced with something painful and awful. Then she was there, throwing herself forward, and her father's arms wrapped around her. He was warm, and *real*, and as she buried her face in his chest he smelled of everything she'd ever thought of as safe and home.

"Hello, Alice," he said. His familiar voice tipped her over the edge, and she began to cry great, wracking sobs. He patted her head and ran his fingers through her hair,

and Alice felt six years old again, crawling into his bed in the middle of the night because she'd read something scary and had bad dreams.

She cried for a long time. When she stopped, she felt empty inside, hollowed out, but it was a good feeling. Like something she'd been bottling up, under pressure, had finally been allowed to escape. She felt lighter, and *clean.*

Alice rubbed her stinging eyes and mopped ineffectually at the mess she'd made of her father's clothes. She stepped back, composing herself, and said, "Hello, Father. It's good to see you."

He smiled. He looked just as she remembered seeing him last, in a gray suit and his favorite battered hat, standing with his hands in his pockets while she waved from the shore.

"It's good to see you too," he said. "You're looking well."

"I'm not sure I *am* well," Alice said. "I'm not sure—"

She stopped. She wasn't sure of *anything*, but she couldn't bring herself to ask, lest too close an examination disturb something and make her father vanish like a popped soap bubble. But she *wanted* to say—Are you dead? Am *I* dead? Is this a dream, or another book, or is this the boat that takes us to heaven?

Her father seemed to be able to read all this in her face.

He'd always been able to do that. Alice had never been able to keep any secrets from him.

"Has it been hard?" he asked.

"Yes," Alice whispered. She tried to swallow the lump in her throat. "It's not all bad. But . . . I don't know if I can do it anymore."

"I'm sorry," he said. "I love you, Alice. More than anything. You know that, don't you?"

"I do," Alice said. "Of course I do."

He put a gentle hand on her shoulder. "Come on. I want to show you something."

He went to the door and gave the handle a few spins, then pulled it open. Inside was a long corridor, with an elegant green carpet underfoot. Alice followed her father inside, and noticed the row of portholes that looked out over the walkway and the rail. Her father closed the door behind her and walked to the first of these, beckoning her to follow.

"You should see this," he said.

Alice frowned. "But—"

"Shhh," her father said. "Listen."

A bit confused, Alice bent and put her face to the glass. Instead of a slightly distorted view of the outside of the ship, she found herself looking down into a richly appointed bedroom. She recognized it, after she got over the strange angle. She'd woken up there once before, after her encounter with the Swarm. In the bed, practically buried under thick covers, lay a girl with dark hair, freckles, and a delicate white scar on one cheek. She looked pale and exhausted, with dark circles under her closed eyes. Only the faintest trembling of the blankets indicated she was breathing. A gray cat lay beside her, pressed against her arm.

Alice looked back up at her father. "Is this—"

"Shh." He indicated the porthole again, and she put her face back against it.

Geryon entered the room. He looked like he had been up all night, his face thin and drawn beneath his drooping whiskers. He went to the bedside and poked the cat, who raised his head and looked up at the old man reproachfully.

"Nothing," Ashes said. "No change."

"That counts as good news, under the circumstances," Geryon said. He found a high-backed chair, dragged it to the bedside, and sat down heavily.

"How long, do you think?" Ashes asked. "Before she . . ."

"It's hard to say," Geryon said. "A considerable time, I

should think. Maybe never. Having another Reader force himself into the book alongside you is a traumatic process, you know. Something so antithetical to the purpose of the book . . ." He sighed. "We shall see."

"I'm surprised you bothered," Ashes said. Alice imagined she could hear a hint of bitterness in the cat's voice. "I mean, she failed your test."

"I didn't have much time to ponder it," Geryon said. "It seemed better to keep my options open."

"Options?" Ashes flicked his tail. "So you're not going to make her forget?"

"I will wait," Geryon said firmly, "upon events. But I will do what is necessary. A Reader cannot be . . . soft."

"No," Ashes muttered, almost too low to hear. "I suppose not."

Alice looked up from the porthole at her father, then down at herself. "That's me in there. So—who am I now? Where are we?"

He shrugged. "It's not for me to say."

"But . . ." Alice bit her lip experimentally. The pain *felt* real enough.

"Come on," her father said.

He walked down the hallway a bit farther, stopping beside the next porthole. Alice looked at him curiously, then bent and put her eyes to the glass. Once again, the scene beyond was not the outside of the ship, but the interior of the room in Geryon's suite. She was lower down now, closer to her—body, or whatever it was, lying on the bed. Geryon was gone, but Ashes was still there, climbing across her as he walked around in circles, looking for a comfortable spot. His tail lashed. Finally he settled down on her chest in his familiar Sphinx-like posture, staring down at her sleeping face. His paws kneaded gently at the blanket.

"Might be better for you if you never wake up," he said. "You don't know what happens when Geryon makes a Reader forget. What's left over isn't what you'd call bright. You'd be walking and talking, after a fashion, but alive? Maybe. I don't know."

There was a long pause. The cat laid his head across his paws, eyes hooded.

"I'd like the chance to apologize, though. Even if you wouldn't remember it afterward. After all, if it weren't for me taking you into the library, you'd never have gotten involved in this in the first place." His tail flicked, irritated. "That's just talk, though. You and I both know it isn't true. Between Geryon and Mother, they'd have gotten to you, one way or the other. But it didn't have to be me doing it."

He sounded so miserable that Alice wanted to reach out for him and tell him it was all right. She tried, but her hand found only the wallpaper beside the porthole, and her body on the bed remained stubbornly inert.

The door swung open, and Emma entered, carrying a tray with a steaming bowl on it. Ashes' head snapped up, then sank down again when he saw who the intruder was. Emma set her tray down on the side-table, then stood waiting, her eyes vacant.

"Go on," Ashes said. "Get out of here. Go back to your room."

Emma nodded politely and left without a word. Ashes sighed.

"You see?" he said. "Not very bright."

Alice stepped away from the porthole and straightened up. The lump was back in her throat.

"Geryon wouldn't really . . . destroy my memory, would he?" she asked her father.

Is that *what happened to Emma?* The thought that a normal, living girl could be turned into something like that filled Alice with a sudden, crawling horror.

"I know I didn't kill that tree-sprite when he told me to, but it was just a helpless little thing." She reflected and added, "All right, maybe not helpless. And maybe it wasn't the smartest thing to do. But it felt right."

"It was the right thing to do," her father said. "Whether Geryon thinks so or not."

Alice felt a warm rush of pleasure at his approval. "I thought so. But now he's going to do something horrible to me."

"You'll find a way through," he said. "You always do."

Alice swallowed again. "Thanks."

He smiled. "Come on. There's one more to see."

This time, the porthole looked out from just above the sleeping form on the bed. Alice could make out the door and the bookcases, along with a sofa and a couple of armchairs. Ashes was nowhere to be seen.

The gas lamps were out, and the only light came from the moon, which threw a pale square across the floor through a window. The rest of the room was in shadow. Alice watched her body breathing, slowly but deeply, and thought it looked a bit better than it had through the last porthole.

A pair of yellow eyes opened in the darkest part of the room, cat-slitted and glowing faintly. Below them was the faintest gleam of ivory, as though of moonlight catching sharp, white teeth. After a moment, two more pairs of eyes joined them, one huge and round like a startled hare's, the other faintly green with weird, horizontal pupils.

"This is the girl?" said a voice, reedy and whispering.

"Hmm," said another voice, so deep and resonant, it made Alice's teeth buzz, even through the glass. "She doesn't look like much."

"It's not a matter of what she looks like." The third voice was Ending's dark, feminine purr. "She's the one we've been waiting for."

"So you say," said the first voice. "And yet you plan to risk her against our brother?"

"It's a good point," the second voice said. "She is nowhere near strong enough. And Geryon has the Dragon. If he's able to bind it . . ."

"I have been forced to . . . improvise," Ending said. "Too many powers were on the trail of the Dragon. It will be safer under Geryon's protection, and he is cautious to a fault. It will be some time before he dares make an attempt. But the girl learns rapidly. In a year, perhaps two, she will be strong enough to defeat our brother and bind him to our cause."

"If she lives," said the first voice.

"Hmmm," said the second. "He's right. If Geryon catches the scent, he will not let her survive."

"She may not," Ending admitted. "I'm doing my best. But if she does—"

"If she lives," the second voice rumbled, "I'll be ready."

"Hmph," the first voice said. "*If* she survives, then . . . we'll see."

Two pairs of eyes closed and vanished. Ending remained, two luminous yellow circles in the shadows.

"Perhaps I am a fool," she said. "It has been such a long time. But . . ."

The eyes half closed.

"Good luck . . ."

Alice stepped back from the porthole. For some reason her heart was beating fast, and she looked up at her father for reassurance. He smiled, but she thought he looked a little sad.

"Who were those things?" she said. "Do you know?"

"You'd know better than I would," he said.

Before she could ask him anything further, he was continuing down the corridor. Instead of another porthole, there was a door, identical to the one they'd come in by. Alice's father gave the central wheel a few turns, grunting with the effort, and pulled it open a few inches. Beyond it was darkness, as heavy and complete as black velvet.

"We're going in there?" Alice asked uncertainly.

"You are," he said.

She thought about that for a while.

"I have to ask," Alice said. "I know it's—it doesn't make any sense. But I have to ask." She took a deep breath. "Are you dead?"

His expression went flat. "What do you think?"

Alice looked back along the corridor. She looked down at herself, in her father's favorite dress, and up at him, just as she remembered. She ran a finger across her cheek, where the scar ought to be.

"I think . . ."

He cocked his head, waiting.

"I think this is a dream," Alice said.

Her father smiled. "I always said you were the smart one in the family."

Alice went on tiptoes and wrapped her arms around him, feeling his weight, his warmth, the familiar scent of his after-shave. She kissed his cheek softly, and he ruffled her hair in a way that made her feel like a little girl.

"I love you," she said.

"I love you, Alice," he said.

She smiled against his cheek. "I know."

"And I believe in you. Whatever happens, I have faith that you'll get through it."

Alice nodded. Pulling herself away was cruelly hard. She brushed down her dress where it had gotten rumpled, wiped her eyes with the back of her sleeves, and turned to the doorway.

"Through here?" she said.

"Through there."

There was nothing but blackness. And something else—barely audible—music? She could hardly be certain she'd heard it, but the tiny scraps she could make out sounded somehow familiar. A tune she'd heard once before, and forgotten.

She looked back at her father, at his smile, and tried to burn the image into her memory. If everything else faded, as dreams had a tendency to do, she wanted to keep this.

Then she turned away, blinking back tears, pulled open the door, and stepped into the darkness.

CHAPTER TWENTY-FOUR
SLEEPING BEAUTY

ALICE OPENED HER EYES.

She lay in the bed in the room in Geryon's suite, covered in blankets up to her neck. The lamps were out, and the faint silver glow of moonlight outlined the sofa, the chairs, and bookcases.

Her hand came up automatically and brushed her cheek. There was a long, thin scar there.

She sat up carefully, expecting protests from her much-abused body. Somewhat to her surprise, she felt quite well. She was wearing a pair of sky-blue pajamas that were a bit too large for her. Alice threw back the blankets and wiggled her toes, which responded satisfactorily.

She closed her eyes and reached out for the Swarm.

The thread was there as always, shining and silver, but it had been joined by another. This one was a deep brown in color, as though it were made of wood, but it bucked and twisted like a living thing. Experimentally, Alice took hold of it, and it thrashed in her mental grip for a while before settling down.

That must be the tree-sprite. Geryon must have come in to rescue me and killed the sprite himself. He'd never told her such a thing was possible, or that he could help her fight and bind a creature. *He let me think I was going to die in there!*

Opening her eyes again, she looked around the chamber. No one was in evidence, but that didn't mean much. She cleared her throat and called softly.

"Ashes? Ending? Is anyone there?"

There was no answer. But music filled the air, very faintly, as though from a phonograph playing in a distant room. It was a simple, repetitive melody, and though Alice couldn't quite place it, she found it maddeningly familiar.

She swung her legs off the bed and stood up. There was a bad moment as the world turned sickeningly around her, but she closed her eyes and counted to ten, and when she opened them again it had settled into more or less its usual orientation. She padded across the carpet in her bare feet to the door, which was closed but not locked.

On the other side of it she found Ashes, curled into a tight ball. She waited for him to acknowledge her, and when he didn't, she gave him a tentative prod with her foot. Nothing happened.

"Ashes?" Alice bent over him, beginning to worry. "Are you all right?"

She lifted him off the floor entirely. His whiskers twitched, but he hung bonelessly from her hands like a stuffed animal, eyes still firmly closed.

Geryon must have done something to him, Alice thought. She hoped he wasn't being punished for her sake.

She set the cat down carefully and looked around. She was in the main hall of Geryon's private suite, a shelf-lined room with a couple of fantastical statues matching those in the main hall. Four doors opened off it, two on each side. Apart from the one she'd come out of, only one was open. The carpet by the doorway was blackened and stained with mud.

Something felt wrong. The proper thing to do was obviously retreat to the bedroom, bar the door, and wait for Geryon to deal with it. Instead, Alice padded forward, skirting the stained carpet, and shifted her mental grip to the Swarm thread, ready to yank swarmers into being all around her. Beside the doorway, she stopped for a moment to listen, but there was no sound except for the faint, frustrating music.

Finally, she leaned over and looked inside. She'd been expecting another bedroom, or perhaps a study, but this looked more like a vault. The carpet stopped abruptly, replaced with slate flagstones, and the walls were unpaneled oak set with iron braces. There were shelves built directly into the walls. Sitting on these, at intervals, were a number of small chests of various sizes and shapes, constructed of more or less outlandish materials.

Many were ordinary trunks, or fancy-looking leather-lined cases, but there were also metal lockboxes and elaborately carved all-wood carrying cases. A few looked as though they were made of *glass*, or transparent crystal, blurry contents barely visible. They were all locked, in some cases more than once. One case bore a complicated-looking set of dials that could be set to a combination of numbers, while another was wound about with an intricate chain of cut flowers.

In the center of all of this lay a creature roughly as long as Alice was tall, huddled in a heap. It was a bit like a dog and also quite a bit like a spider, with a mastiff's build and a wild combination of scales and thick, wiry tufts of hair across its hide. Six long legs, heels tipped with vicious, bony spurs, lay tangled underneath it. Its head was flattened and disturbingly human-like, but with long, knife-like fangs and a lolling purple tongue.

It was also asleep, and apparently as unwakeable as Ashes, because something had happened to the glass casket just beside its head that probably had made quite a bit of noise. This had been one of the larger chests, complete with a glass padlock with visible brass inner workings. The glass lock must have been more formidable than it appeared, since whoever had broken into the chest had bypassed it by simply smashing through the top. Whatever had been inside the chest was gone. Spots and speckles of blood were all around the broken casket on the shelf and edging some of the jagged shards, making a trail to the doorway where Alice stood and out onto the carpet.

Alice spent a few moments considering this. The trail of dirt and blood led quite clearly to the door back into the main hall, and after a while she padded over to this, skirting the mess, and pulled it open. Aside from the music, everything was still silent.

In the hall lay Emma, slumped against the base of one of the marble statues. A tray was overturned on the floor beside her, with a smashed bowl of sticky oatmeal. Alice hopped over the muddy carpet and hurried to the girl's side, and found that she was just as deeply asleep as Ashes.

It clicked, finally, and Alice remembered where she'd heard the music before. Her breath caught in her throat. Breaking into a run, she followed the trail back into the kitchens and confirmed that it led to the back door. From there, she was certain, it would go out, around the garden, and into the library.

If everyone in the house was asleep, there was no one to go after Isaac but Alice. She hesitated, her hand on the doorknob, then turned around and dashed up toward her room. She'd gone charging off into the library by herself twice now, and if those experiences had taught her anything, it was that it was better to dress warmly and bring along a decent pair of boots.

A few minutes later, Alice trotted down the gravel path toward the library. The music was still just on the edge of hearing, growing no louder or fainter wherever she went.

He lied to me. The thought burned large in her mind.

Isaac had told her that his Siren wasn't strong enough to put the three needle-toothed creatures to sleep at once, but now he'd used it to entrance the entire *house*. She hadn't been able to find Geryon, but he must have been caught as well, or he would have responded to the pilfering of his vault. *He was just playing with me, the whole time. He could have gotten away from those things easily, if he could do* this. *He never needed my help.* Alice rubbed the back of her hand against her lips unconsciously, as though trying to wipe away a stain.

The full moon provided a good illumination. The trail of blood was down to a few drops, and not always visible in the silver light, but it didn't matter. Alice knew where she was going, and finding the bronze front door of the library slightly ajar confirmed her suspicions.

She slipped through, stopping only to retrieve and light a lamp, and headed inside. There was something different, something *wrong*, down at the very edge of perception. Like a noise she hadn't realized was there until it stopped, the library felt different. It was, she thought, as though even the shelves and the building were asleep, somehow. There had always been a sense of presence, as though something was watching her from the shadows with cool, unblinking eyes, but now those eyes were closed. She passed a half-dozen sleeping cats, curled up in corners or lounging astride the shelves.

It wasn't long before she could see the glimmer of another lantern, up ahead. It didn't seem to be moving, and Alice slowed her steps as she approached, suddenly uncertain how to proceed. She thought about trying to sneak around, behind a shelf, and then pop out unexpectedly, but that would only make Isaac run, and she wasn't certain she could outrace him. He might even attack her. Her stomach roiled, reminding her that all she'd had to eat in who-knows-how-long was honeyed oatmeal, and her legs gave a warning quiver.

Alice pulled herself together and marched forward. If she could see his lantern, he could probably see hers, so there was no point in trying to be sneaky. She raised the hurricane lamp over her head and called out.

"Isaac! It's you, isn't it? I know you're there!"

She rounded a bank of shelves and found herself at the low table Mr. Wurms usually used. The scholar was nowhere to be seen, but another lantern was sitting on the table. Behind it, rising slowly from a crouch, was Isaac. He was still in his dirty, tattered coat, and his hair was limp and heavy with sweat. He had crude bandages around both his hands and halfway up one arm, and Alice could see spots of blood already soaking through the linen.

"*Alice?*" he said, and all the tension went out of him in one breath. "Oh, God. Of course." Isaac flopped down onto one of the benches beside the table. "I thought I'd had it when I saw someone coming after me."

"You," Alice said. She didn't know *what* to think. A half-dozen things to say crowded toward her tongue, but the one that finally escaped was, "How did you get out?"

"Geryon puts too much faith in his guard dogs." He sounded a little smug.

"You lied to me about the Siren."

"Oh." Isaac had the decency to look a little bit embarrassed. "I didn't lie, exactly. I just didn't mention this."

He dug in his pocket and produced a small piece of jewelry, a red stone in a silver setting, like a broach or a necklace. The stone was dull and plain, and a wide crack ran most of its length.

"It's a sort of . . . battery," he explained. "My master gave it to me. It let me feed enough power to the Siren that it caught even Geryon off-guard. But it only works once, and I knew I'd need it—"

He stopped, looking puzzled at Alice's expression.

"You'd need it to escape," Alice said. "Because you're a thief."

"You don't need to say it like *that*. It's nothing personal. The book is just something my master wanted, so he sent me to get it." He shook his head. "Anyway, Geryon didn't even know where the Dragon was. I can hardly be stealing it from him if he didn't know he had it, can I?"

"We were supposed to get it back for Ending," Alice said. She didn't mention her own goal of using the book to trap Vespidian.

"Ending told me we could make a deal for the book," Isaac said. "My master wants the book, and he'd be willing to bargain generously for her help in getting it. But she *betrayed* us, Alice. No one could have led Geryon to us except for her!"

"She didn't have a choice," Alice said.

"She told you that, I assume?" Isaac snorted. "You should know how much that's worth."

"And what about me?" Alice said.

"What about you?" He stared at her, and a strange expression came over his face. "Ending promised *you* the Dragon, didn't she? You thought *I* was there to help *you* get it." He shook his head. "She's played us both for fools.

I imagine she was following Geryon's orders the whole time."

"I don't . . ." Alice hesitated. "I don't believe that."

Isaac sighed, and sat down heavily on the bench beside the table. His hand bumped the tabletop, and she saw him wince.

"What happened to your hands?" Alice said, in spite of herself.

"Just a couple of cuts from the glass," Isaac said, frowning at his bandages. "I'll be all right."

"You should have told me," she said, trying to hold on to her anger. "We could have worked something out."

"Alice . . . if you're going to be a Reader's apprentice, you need to understand what that means."

"What, that I have to be awful? That I should lie and cheat and steal like you?"

"It's more complicated than that." Isaac looked up at her. "Did you have any brothers and sisters, when you were growing up?"

"What?" Alice paused, taken aback. "No. It was just me and my father. My mother died when I was very young."

"I had a brother. I don't think he was really my brother, actually, but he was as good as one. We grew up together in my master's fortress. He was a Reader too, about three years older than I was. His name was Evander." Isaac paused. "We used to do everything together. It was all they could do to pry us apart for lessons."

Alice heard the significant past tense. "What happened to him?"

"When I was six, and he was nine, my master came to some kind of deal with one of the other old Readers. I have no idea what it was about, but this other Reader must have needed an apprentice, and my master felt like he had one to spare. He told us that Evander was going to live somewhere else from now on, and that was that. I cried and cried, but he just left me in my room until I got over it."

"That's horrible," Alice said. "They just . . . traded him? Like he was a box of chocolates?"

"That's how they think. We're all just *stuff* to them. I even understand how they feel, a little. When you've lived a thousand years, can you take the feelings of a six-year-old seriously? It would be like you and me trying to understand an ant."

"Did you ever see him again?"

"Oh, yes," Isaac said. "That's the point, really. The next time I saw him, he tried to kill me."

"*What?*"

Isaac laughed. "That's unfair, I guess. I don't know if he would actually have killed me. But my master sent me to get something he wanted, and Evander's new master sent him for the same thing, and we . . . fought. In the end I ran away. My master was very angry with me.

"But the *next* time we met, we were working together. My master and his had made an alliance with a couple of the others, and they sent a bunch of us to some awful jungle world to try and find . . . well, it doesn't matter. We didn't find it, in the end. But I got a chance to talk to Evander, and he explained everything."

Isaac leaned forward. "The old Readers fight each other in a hundred little ways, and one of them is always sending his apprentice to steal this or defend that. None of us has any choice, you see? For us it's like a . . . a game, or something. You try your hardest, because you don't want to be punished, but there's no use in taking it *personally*. The person fighting you today might be on your side tomorrow, and stealing from you the day after."

Alice shook her head. "But that's awful."

"It's who we are. It's who *you* are. All we can do is try to make the best of it, and live long enough to become old Readers with apprentices of our own." Isaac shook his head. "Then maybe we can treat them a little differently."

He brushed some of the dust off his coat and got to his feet, flexing the fingers of his injured hand.

"Anyway, my job here is finished," Isaac said. "You can believe what you like, but you'll learn soon enough." He gave her a thin smile. "Who knows? Next time, maybe we'll be on the same side again."

He turned to leave, in a swirl of dust. Alice took a step toward him and said, "Where do you think you're going?"

Isaac looked back at her, over his shoulder. "Excuse me?"

"I'm Geryon's apprentice," she said coldly. "I can't just let you walk out of here with the book, can I? Give it back, and I'll let you leave. Just to show that it isn't *personal.*"

There was a long, fragile moment of silence. Slowly, Isaac turned back to face her, long coat dragging in the dust.

"Or what?" he said.

Alice wanted to say "Or else" in the manner of a pulp radio action-hero, but she couldn't quite bring herself to do it. She found herself unaccountably blushing instead, and shook her head violently. Isaac snorted.

"Go back to bed," he said. "It'll be a while before everyone wakes up, you'll have plenty of time. Then you won't get in trouble for letting me go, if that's what you're worried about."

"I'm not worried about getting in *trouble.* I mean it, Isaac. Just give it back."

"If I come back without it, I *will* get in trouble." A shadow passed across Isaac's face, as though he'd remembered something unpleasant. "I don't plan to risk that."

"I'm not going to let you leave."

"I don't want to hurt you, Alice."

He shifted his stance slightly, and spread his arms like a wrestler. Alice could feel something change in the air, a kind of thrumming tension, like a guitar string vibrating just on the edge of hearing. She realized he'd taken hold of his threads, leading back to some distant prison-book. A sharp, cool breeze cut through the stagnant air of the library, and the crisp smell of fresh snow briefly overwhelmed the ancient scent of dust.

Alice's eyes narrowed. No matter how tough he acted, he was still just Isaac. She grabbed the Swarm thread, then hesitated. If she unleashed the little creatures, she really *would* hurt him, and for all that he was being an idiot, she didn't really want to. Instead, she drew the thread inward, hardening her skin, and leaped.

She jumped to the bench, then to the table, then cleared the distance between them with a knee-wobbling leap that brought her down nearly on top of him. Isaac, startled, backpedaled and brought his hands up in front of his face, but Alice went around him instead, grabbing great handfuls of his long coat and yanking him off his feet. He fell heavily on his stomach, and before he could turn over she kept him there by the simple expedient of sitting on the small of his back.

Alice had never had any siblings, so she had no experience with casual children's scuffles. But Isaac had the disadvantage of a certain amount of built-in chivalry. The kind of person who had saved her from Mr. Black, Alice suspected, was not the kind of person who would easily punch a girl in the nose, and while she felt a little bad about taking advantage of that, she told herself it was no worse than his taking advantage of her good nature. Besides, with the Swarm thread wrapped around her, she outweighed him considerably, and the occasional awkward blows he did manage to land simply bounced off her rubbery flesh.

Before too long he'd stopped squirming. "Alice," he said. "Come on, Alice. Don't be—ow—stop kicking me!"

Alice ignored him and began methodically going through the many pockets in the inner lining of his trench coat. "Stop squirming," she told him severely. "You should have just given me the book."

After a few more moments of searching, she found a rectangular bulge in one pocket and triumphantly produced the Dragon.

"Give it back!" Isaac moaned.

"Let everyone go," she said. "Then we can talk to Ending together."

"Don't be an idiot. She'd just give it back to Geryon!"

He braced one arm against the floor and twisted underneath her, managing to get her off balance and toppling sideways. Squirming out from under her, he made a grab for the Dragon, in the process planting a knee in her stomach that knocked the wind out of her in spite of the Swarm's protection.

Somehow, Alice kept one hand on the book, while the other pushed at Isaac's face in an extremely undignified manner. He had her by the wrist, and they flopped and wrestled on the floor, raising a billowing cloud of dust that made it hard to breathe. Red-faced and sweating, Isaac refused to let go, until Alice finally got her legs between them and planted both her feet in his chest. That gave her the leverage to push him away, but he squeezed her wrist hard enough that the book slipped free, and in the ensuing scuffle one of them gave the Dragon a kick that sent it skittering across the dusty floor.

Alice and Isaac separated, both sweating and panting, and spent a long moment staring at each other. Then, as though a starting gun had gone off, they both rolled over and scrabbled toward the book on their hands and knees.

Alice got a hand on it at the same moment Isaac did. They both pulled, in opposite directions, and the little book flopped open between them. In her flustered state, it was a second or two before Alice thought to avert her eyes, and that was a second or two too long. The writing curled and shifted under her gaze, and she read:

Alice screwed her eyes shut, but she could tell by the breath of wind on her face that she'd been too late . . .

CHAPTER TWENTY-FIVE
THE DRAGON

Alice screwed her eyes shut, but she could tell by the breath of wind on her face that she'd been too late. The air smelled of wet rock and growing things, not the ancient dust of the library. They were inside the Dragon.

"Oh, no." This was Isaac, speaking not inside her head as Geryon had, but from somewhere nearby, which meant that *he* was inside the book too. "No, no, no, no, no. How could you . . . you stupid . . . !"

Alice opened her eyes. Isaac stood beside her, ragged coat flapping in the slight breeze, staring around with a rage that was rapidly transmuting into terror. He rounded on her, fists clenched at his sides. Alice could see a set of parallel scratches on his cheeks, where she'd caught him with her fingernails.

"Of all the stupid things you could have done, it had to be *this*!" he shouted, his voice echoing off the surrounding rocks. "I should have—oh, God—"

They stood on a wide, flat stone, looking out over a landscape like a giant's toy box. Enormous, craggy boulders were everywhere, piled up in heaps. Bushes and even a few small trees sprouted from between bare stones. Roots grew out over the edges, groping blindly in search of somewhere to burrow, like worms. A mountain loomed in the distance.

Isaac shifted to a language Alice didn't understand, though she thought he was swearing. She straightened her dress and dusted herself off.

"This wouldn't have happened if you had just given me the book, like I asked," she said. "Or better yet, not stolen it in the first place. Now we're here, and we'll have to deal with it."

"'We'?" Isaac shouted. "I think I have had about enough of working with *you*!"

He raised his hands, and Alice caught the scent of snow again. Little swirls of white whipped out from

Isaac like ocean foam. He extended his arms, palms out, and a blast of wind hit Alice in the face, freezing cold, as though she'd opened a door into a blizzard. Tiny hailstones bounced off her with painful, stinging impacts, and she had to squeeze her eyes shut.

Blindly, she reached out and pulled a dozen swarmers into being all around her. Borrowing their vision, she saw Isaac in the center of his self-created gale, and sent the little creatures running at him. The first to arrive pecked at his legs, not deep, but enough to cut his trousers and draw blood. Swearing again, Isaac lowered his hands, directing the blast of freezing wind toward his feet. The swarmers scrabbled for purchase, finding claw-holds on the bare rock or else rolling over the side to carom off the rocks below.

Alice pulled harder on the thread, and more swarmers materialized. She opened her eyes to find Isaac staring back at her, his lip set in a snarl.

"Don't you think—" Alice began.

She was interrupted by a tremendous roar.

Alice had heard a lion roar once, in a circus, and at age ten it had made her squeal and clap her hands over her ears. This was another class of sound entirely, as if it had issued from some vast mechanism, like the engines of a steamship groaning into life. It rattled her skull from the inside, and the rocks themselves shook and shifted alarmingly. Alice lost her grip on the thread, and the little swarmers vanished. Isaac was on his knees, hands pressed to his head.

The sound died away slowly, amid rumbling echoes. Alice's ears still rang with the force of it. She looked around wildly, but there was no obvious source for the tremendous noise.

"We're dead," Isaac mumbled. "Oh God. We're dead, we're dead, we're dead . . ." He lapsed into the other language again.

"Isaac." This produced no response, so she strode over and grabbed him by the collar, jerking him to his feet. "Isaac! What the . . . What *was* that?"

"The prisoner. This is a prison-book, after all." He glanced up at her, then closed his eyes again. "The Dragon."

Alice let him go, and he slumped forward.

"A dragon?" she said. "*Really* a dragon?"

"*The* Dragon," Isaac said.

"There's only one?"

"Nobody knows where it came from. Some Reader caught it in a book a long time ago, and nobody has ever been able to find another one. And even the book has been lost for centuries."

Alice felt a hint of fear, clutching like a cold hand at her chest, but she pushed it ruthlessly away.

"If it was lost, how come you came looking for it?"

"My master found a hint that it had been hidden somewhere in Geryon's library, and he talked Ending into sneaking me in to try and find it." He looked accusingly at Alice. "And *you* got us stuck inside it!"

Alice scanned the horizon. There was no sign of a dragon.

"If this is a prison-book," she said, "that means we've got to find the prisoner, and force it to submit. How much do you know about the Dragon?"

"Nothing!" Isaac said. "I wasn't supposed to go inside. My master didn't tell me anything about it!"

"We've got to do *something*."

"We're going to get eaten, that's what we're going to do," Isaac said. "We—"

"You sound like Ashes," Alice said. "He was certain we were going to die too. But we didn't. So would you quit—"

The rocks shifted underneath her, this time more violently. The one they were standing on, a huge, flat-topped boulder, *jumped* as though something had struck it hard from beneath, then sagged on one side until it was canted like the deck of a sinking ship. The movement shocked Isaac out of his hypnotized immobility, and he scrambled for the high end of the rock, looked down, and leaped over the side.

"Isaac! Wait!" Alice hurried to the edge and found him scrambling up the face of the next boulder. "Where are you going?"

He didn't have the chance to reply. Ahead of him, rocks crunched and exploded in a great shower of dust and debris, sending shards zipping and pinging in all directions. Isaac nearly lost his grip, and the stone he was clinging to tilted violently backward, leaving him hanging by his fingertips against the nearly vertical surface.

Something was moving inside the cloud of dust, something enormous, shouldering aside tons of stone like a human might kick off a constricting blanket. *Where* to run suddenly didn't seem nearly as important as just being somewhere else. Alice had a clear shot down the slope of her boulder, and a solid leap would take her to another flat surface. But just ahead of her, Isaac struggled to pull himself up with his bandaged hands, long cloak flapping absurdly behind him, his thin arms shaking with the effort.

Alice said a word her father would have been shocked to hear and knelt on the lip of the rock, just above Isaac. She yanked the Swarm thread into her body and held out her hand.

"Isaac!"

He risked a look over his shoulder, saw her hand, and clung even tighter to his perch.

"It's coming!" Alice shouted. The rock-crushing sounds were getting louder. "Just—push off a little. You'll make it!"

"I . . ." Isaac took one hand off the rock hesitantly, then grabbed it again when his foot slipped a couple of inches. "I can't."

Alice wanted to scream with frustration. She dropped flat on her stomach and reached out with both hands, and her fingers nearly brushed the back of his head. "Come on. Now!"

He reached for her again, and this time she grabbed his hand with both of hers and pulled. His footing slipped, pebbles sliding and clattering below him. For a moment he swung free, all his weight on Alice's wrist. The edge of the rock dug deep into her forearm, and she was certain her bones would have snapped without the power of the Swarm hardening her flesh.

It didn't lend her additional *strength*, though, and light as Isaac was, he was still too much for Alice to lift. Fortunately, the fear that had paralyzed Isaac had washed out of him again, and he got his other hand on her elbow and braced his legs against the overhang. Between the two of them, Alice on her knees pulling backward and Isaac climbing up hand over hand, they were able to get back over the edge and onto the rock. Isaac flopped down face-first, panting, and Alice ended up spread-eagled on her back beside him.

"You . . ." Isaac wheezed. "You saved . . ."

"Again," Alice managed, fighting for breath. "Don't mention it."

The noises had stopped. Alice sat up cautiously, hoping whatever it was had gone back to sleep.

It hadn't. The dust was settling, and there, in the center of a crater of shattered boulders, was the Dragon.

If she'd seen a picture of it in a book, Alice thought she would have sniffed and said it didn't look like *her* idea of a dragon. She liked dragons that were lithe and graceful, more like scaly cats with fairy wings, who could dart about and be clever and help little girls defeat vicious ogres and so on.

This was not that sort of dragon. It didn't have wings,

and it didn't seem disposed to offer any kindly wisdom. It was a lizard the size of a small house, with eight legs each so thick that Isaac and Alice could not have linked hands and put their arms around it. It had a long, canine snout with a serious overbite and two enormous fangs like a serpent's sticking out like tusks on either side of its lower jaw. On each side of its arrowhead-shaped skull were three eyes, huge hemispheres that gleamed like black diamonds in the weak sunlight. They were lidless and unblinking, and reminded Alice more of some kind of insect than a reptile.

Its scales were gray-white, and two long black stripes ran down its back. Its tail, as long as the rest of it put together, coiled behind it in an elaborate S-shape and was never still, even while the rest of the beast was perfectly at rest.

Alice was struck momentarily dumb. She could see herself reflected in all six of those eyes, the distorted image compressed to a tiny dot amidst the endless rock-field. All six tiny Alices shifted in unison as the Dragon took one step forward, then another. The way its legs moved was *wrong,* too fluid, as though they had extra joints. Its sinuous tail lashed and coiled from side to side.

It spoke without moving its jaw, like Ashes, but in a

voice so deep and resonant, it rattled Alice's skull. It was the voice of a mountain crag, or an ancient, secret cavern.

"Pathetic," the Dragon rumbled. "*This* is what my sister sends against me, after so many years? Children? And the little bones always stick in my teeth . . ."

It opened its mouth in a long, slow yawn. A black, snaky tongue licked out and tasted the air.

Alice opened her mouth to speak—or perhaps it had been hanging open anyway—and realized she had no idea what to say, or how to address a dragon. She stuttered lamely for a moment, and settled on, "Hello."

"What are you doing?" Isaac said. He was crouched beside her.

"Trying to talk to it," Alice whispered. "Shh."

"You can't talk to it," Isaac said. "It's a *dragon*."

"If it can speak, it ought to be able to understand."

"Who says it can—"

"Hello, yourself," the Dragon said. "A brave little girl, I'll give her that."

"Thank you," Alice said. "But nobody sent us here, and I don't think I know your sister. I expect I would remember if I'd met her."

There was a long silence. Alice was no great judge of dragon expressions, but she thought it looked surprised.

"Alice—" Isaac began, tugging at her sleeve. She stopped him with a gesture.

"You . . ." the Dragon said, drawing out the word. "You understand me?"

"I think so."

"But . . ." It turned its head, examining her with one set of eyes and then the other. "She did it, then. After all these years."

"I don't know who you're talking about. I came in here by accident—"

"Of course you didn't," it said. "You happened to fall into *this* book, of all books? Don't be foolish." Its tone was getting angrier. "You came here because she wished you to come. But why? She can't honestly expect you to triumph. Does she think I will show *mercy*?"

The last word came out as another roar, drowning all other sound. Isaac tugged hard at her arm, but Alice needed no urging. She took off running as the Dragon uncoiled and started toward them. Alice held on to the Swarm thread and leaped to the next boulder, letting her rubbery legs absorb the impact. Isaac landed just behind her.

The Dragon surged forward. All eight legs moved at once, rising and falling in opposing pairs like pistons of a steam engine. Boulders crunched and groaned under its weight. One huge foot hit the rock they'd been standing on and flipped it into the air, tumbling end over end like a child's toy. Alice jumped to the next boulder, slipped on a patch of mossy earth, and caught herself before she fell between the rocks and stuck there. Isaac, moving more carefully, got to the top of the boulder but made the mistake of turning to look behind him. The sight of the oncoming Dragon froze him in his tracks, and Alice had to grab his arm and pull him away by force. They jumped again, this time hand in hand, moments before the creature lunged over the stone they'd been standing on, one huge foot coming down hard enough to raise a cloud of rock dust.

A tiny part of Alice's mind—the part not concentrating on her footing, or trying to figure out what the Dragon had meant, or screaming in silent terror—was busy assessing their prospects. They couldn't outrun the Dragon. Quite apart from its size, its eight triple-jointed legs gave it an easy grace on the uneven footing that the two humans couldn't hope to match. She didn't think attacking it with the Swarm would do any good, either, except possibly as a distraction, and maybe not even that. The swarmers were barely the size of lice in comparison.

That left one route to safety. She tugged the Swarm thread inside her, as far as it would go, then glanced back at Isaac. *Really*, she thought, *I should just leave him. This is all his fault, anyway.*

"Come here." It was hard to hear over the sound of the Dragon, so she tugged on his hand as well. Before he could start squirming, Alice wrapped herself around him in a bear hug, gripping her own wrist behind the small of his back, her head alongside his. He smelled musty and old, like the library—probably the coat—and she could feel the trip-hammer beat of his heart pressed against hers.

"Alice?" he squeaked, right in her ear. "What are you—"

"Just hold still!"

The Dragon had turned, slewing to a halt in a spray of bouncing boulders and rock fragments, gathering all eight legs underneath itself for a lunge. Alice tightened her grip on Isaac, lifted him an inch off the ground, and took a tottering step backward over the edge of the boulder.

CHAPTER TWENTY-SIX
HUNTED

I T WASN'T SO MUCH a fall as a descent, caroming off
one rock after another. Alice did her best to control it,
and to keep her body between Isaac's unprotected form
and unforgiving stone. She caught her head a couple of
nasty cracks, which in her Swarm-charged state made it
rebound like a tennis ball but produced surprisingly little
pain. Sharp edges and spires of rock snatched and cut at
her as they fell, and more than once she heard the sound
of tearing fabric, but her rubbery skin remained unbro-
ken.

She just had time to wonder if there *was* solid ground
underneath all these rocks before she landed on something broad and flat, rump-first. Isaac sprawled bone-

lessly in her grip. A small cascade of pebbles and dirt she'd dislodged on her way down showered all around them, raining into Alice's hair and forcing her to keep her eyes shut.

Far overhead, she could hear the Dragon moving. Rocks shifted and ground against one another, but nothing nearby moved. After a moment, the noises diminished, moving away, and Alice let out a long breath. She released Isaac, letting him slip to the ground beside her, and brushed the dirt from her eyes.

It wasn't completely dark in the fissure. Enough light filtered through the cracks and crevices up above to provide a shadowy twilight, with an occasional brilliant spot where a lucky beam of sunlight made it the whole way unmolested. Alice gave her eyes a moment to adjust and looked herself over. Her clothes were a mess of rips and tears, but other than that she seemed to be more or less all right. She breathed a silent thanks to the Swarm and the protection its rubber-ball body provided. Then, dreading what she would find, she looked at Isaac.

He was breathing, and didn't seem to have been battered too badly about the head, which dispelled the worst of her fears. His long coat had kept his skin mostly intact, though it had been shredded into strips and rags in the process. The only serious injury she could find was a long gash on his shin from a sharp-edged rock, which was bleeding profusely but didn't seem too deep. The sum total of Alice's medical knowledge was that blood was supposed to stay on the inside, but she tore a couple of strips from the tattered greatcoat and tied them into a crude bandage. When she pulled this tight, a hiss of pain escaped from Isaac's lips, followed by a groan.

"Isaac?" she said. "Can you hear me?"

"Are we . . ." He swallowed, and raised his head a fraction. "Are we dead yet?"

"Not yet."

He treated her to another long string of foreign curses, and took a deep breath. "What were you thinking? It's a miracle you didn't crack your head open!"

"It's only a miracle *you* didn't," Alice snapped. "I have protection. Besides, I didn't see any alternatives."

"Kind of you to warn me."

"There wasn't time." She gave the bandage an extra twist, which made him groan again. "Next time I'll just leave you for the Dragon!"

She got to her feet and stalked away, looking for a way out. They were in a small clear space where a pair of boulders had formed a crude arch, but the big stones were irregular enough in shape that there were plenty of spaces to wriggle between, albeit at the risk of losing a little skin. Alice selected the largest of these gaps, a couple of feet off the ground, and started to climb.

"Wait!" Isaac said. "Where are you going?"

"Somebody has to get us out of here, doesn't she?" Alice said, with more bravado than she felt. "You can just wait here."

"Don't be stupid." He sat up, wincing. "You can't—"

"I can't do it? I'm at least going to *try*. You're welcome to sit around under these rocks until you starve."

"You can't go after it by yourself," Isaac finished quietly. "We should . . . figure something out."

"All right," Isaac said, after Alice reluctantly backtracked and sat down cross-legged beside him. "Talking to it didn't work, obviously."

"It talked to *me*," Alice said. "It might calm down if we leave it alone for a while."

"It didn't say anything *I* could understand," Isaac said. "Are you sure you're not just hearing things?"

"Of course I'm sure. I'm not in the habit of imagining conversations with giant lizards."

"All right, all right." Isaac paused. "What did it say?"

"Something about its sister. It thinks she sent us to fight it."

"Its sister? Another dragon?" Isaac scratched his head. "I've never even heard of another dragon."

"That's what I was trying to tell it."

"We are going to have to try to . . . convince it, though. If we want to get out." Isaac shook his head. "What about magic? What did you call those little bird-things?"

"I'm not sure I should tell you," Alice said, still a little grumpy. "You were trying to kill me a minute ago."

"I wasn't—I wouldn't have *killed* you," Isaac said. "And anyway, I think we can agree to a truce, as long as we're stuck in here with the Dragon."

Alice sighed. "I told you, they're called the Swarm." She felt as though she ought to stand up for them. "And they've saved my life more than once. Yours too, when we fell—"

"When you pulled me over the side?"

"When you froze like a gawking idiot, and I saved you from being eaten by a dragon," Alice finished. "Yes."

"Do they do anything else? Besides protect you and . . . what, bite things?"

"Not really." Alice held out her hand and pulled a swarmer into being. It sat placidly on her palm, staring at Isaac, and gave a little *quirk*.

"They're sort of cute," Isaac said. "When they aren't trying to eat me."

"I don't think they eat anything, to tell the truth. They drink blood, though." Alice turned her hand over and let the swarmer vanish before it hit the ground. "Anyway, I'm not sure they'll be much good against the Dragon. It's too *big*. Maybe if they could get to its eyes . . ."

"It's a thought. Have you got anything else?"

Alice shook her head, then paused. There *was* another thread, a wooden one, at the back of her mind. When she touched it, it still felt jittery, but she was able to get a grip on it. Trying to pull it outside herself, to summon the creature, met strong resistance, but she was able to loop it around herself a few times fairly easily.

She opened her eyes to find Isaac looking at her intently.

"There's . . . something else," she said. "I've never used it before, so I'm not quite certain, but I think it's a tree-sprite."

"How can you not be certain? Either you went into a prison-book or you didn't."

"I did," Alice said, "but I don't remember coming out again. It nearly killed me, but I think Geryon came in and stopped it."

"Oh." Isaac was quiet for a moment. "Can you summon it?"

"I don't think so. It feels like something's wrong with it. I have an idea, though."

She stood up, dusting off her tattered dress, and looked around the little hollow until she found a single, pencil-thin root, snaking all the way down from some desperate little tree on the surface. Alice put her hand against it experimentally and closed her eyes.

She could feel . . . something. A sense of light, and heat, and the vague feel of wind rustling through scraggly leaves. Her mind could follow the root all the way to the surface, where the gnarled trunk of the tree hunched in a bowl of thin soil, and back down a dozen other questing roots that forked and spread through the rock-pile.

Isaac poked his head in the end of the crevice. "Did you find something?"

Concentrating, Alice focused her will on the root. With a faint sigh like an old man forced to leave his comfortable chair, it pulled itself away from the rock and looped into the air in front of her, vibrating gently. Alice kept it there for a few moments, then let it drop.

"I think that's about it. Trees."

"I see." Isaac scratched the side of his nose. "Not terribly useful in our present circumstances, then."

"All right," said Alice defensively. "What have *you* got? Can you use that Siren to put it to sleep?"

"I don't think so. I don't have the power-charm anymore, and the Dragon is too big. Besides, she's still singing out *there,* and I'm not sure what would happen if I tried to pull her in here with us as well."

"What about the one you used on me?"

"The iceling?"

Isaac extended one hand toward the rock wall and frowned. Cold wind whipped for a moment, and tracks of frost spread out from a central point like the rays of a star.

"It can freeze water and move the ice about a bit," he said. "And I have a couple of little ones, like the glow-wisp and the lizard-frog."

"That's it?" Alice said, with a bit too much satisfaction. "I'm not sure that's very useful in our present circumstances."

He gave a wan smile, which she hadn't expected. "No, I'm afraid not. I told you, I never expected to have to *fight* the Dragon."

"There's got to be *something* we can do." Alice felt the flutter of fear again, and balled up her fists. "What do we know about the Dragon?"

"It's big?" Isaac offered. "And it has big pointy teeth."

"It moves like a snake," Alice said. "It's fast, and agile."

"It—"

"Shh." Alice held up a hand. "Did you hear something?"

Isaac went silent. A moment later, the air was filled with an enormous rending crash, and one wall of their little hollow vanished upward. Brilliant sunlight flooded into the shadowy underside of the rock-pile, and Alice automatically raised her hand against the glare and blinked furiously. She could see the black shape of the boulder, and a long, snake-like protrusion wrapped around it.

It was the Dragon's tail. It lifted the multi-ton stone out of its way with sinuous ease, flicking it away to crash with a rumble out in the rock-pile. The thing's arrowhead-shaped snout filled the gap, blocking out the sun and plunging them back into shadow. The hot, fetid wind of its breath washed over Alice like a wave. She stared back at the two closest eyes, and found she could see something moving inside the smoky black hemisphere. Inside an enormous iris was a pupil, contracted to a pinprick but slowly expanding in the sudden gloom.

"Hello, little wizard," it said. "I can smell you, you know."

"I don't want to fight you," Alice said. "Please. If we could just talk—"

"Were you fighting? It looked to me like you were hiding under a rock." It snorted, a geyser of hot breath all around her. "Is this the best you can do?"

Alice found her hand closing around a fragment of stone. Before she could tell herself what a bad idea it was, she threw it as hard as she could, right into the Dragon's eye. It bounced off the black casing as though from thick glass, causing no apparent harm, and the huge pupil swiveled and struggled to focus. A moment later the Dragon's head lunged forward like a striking snake, thrashing against the rock just beside Alice.

A deep crevice ran away from the newly exposed hollow. Alice grabbed Isaac's hand and ducked into it, flattening herself sideways to pass a narrow point in the rock. The crevice branched, and branched again, threading through the boulders. Alice, terrified of finding a dead end with the beast so close behind them, summoned a dozen swarmers and sent them on ahead, checking with their monochrome vision to make sure there was enough room for the two humans to pass through. Isaac followed her willingly enough, glancing frequently back over his shoulder toward where the Dragon was tearing their brief resting place to pieces.

When they'd come what felt like a safe distance, Alice paused for breath, the swarmers forming around them like a bodyguard. Isaac let go of her hand and leaned back against a rock, puffing hard.

"It's . . . too strong," he said. "Did you see the way it lifted that rock?" He coughed for a while, then spat a thick glob of dust on the ground. "I thought maybe we could . . . I don't know, drop rocks on it, but anything we could lift wouldn't even slow it down!"

Alice nodded weakly. "The eyes are no good either. Maybe if we could get up close and bash it with stones, but . . ."

"We're dead," Isaac said. "There is no way—"

"Don't start that again," Alice snapped.

"I'm open to suggestions," Isaac said. He slid down the rock, tattered coat bunching at his shoulders. "God, I'm thirsty."

Alice's own lips were cracked, but she'd been trying to ignore them. She was about to scold Isaac again for complaining when something occurred to her.

"Your iceling can make . . . ice, can't it?"

"It doesn't really *make* it. It can freeze water that's

already there, and there's always a little bit in the air." He frowned. "Maybe we could scrape up the slush and have enough for a drink? It'd be dirty, though, and it wouldn't be much in any case."

"How much water can it freeze?"

Isaac laughed. "Quite a bit. One time, I was out with Evander, and we froze a lake solid so we could go skating at mid-summer." He sighed. "Of course, once it melted, all the dead fish came floating to the top. Master was not pleased."

"Water." Alice looked upward. Far overhead, atop the rock-pile, the sun filtered down in a dappled pattern through the sparse leaves of another scraggly tree. "Somewhere, there has to be water."

They climbed cautiously back to the top. The Dragon was visible a ways off, still apparently searching around where it had last seen them. Boulders occasionally flew in long parabolic arcs as it hurled them away in a rage. Alice led the way again, picking her way through the top layer of rocks rather than climbing over it, and always keeping something between them and the beast. It made for slow going, and it felt like hours before they found what they were looking for.

A little stream of muddy water trickled down the side of the boulders, and Alice led Isaac along it until she found a little spring-fed pool on top of a great round rock. A couple of shallow depressions had gathered a small bed of soil, and a tree grew from one of them, many-branched and a bit taller than Alice.

The water was so cold that it hurt to touch, but she and Isaac slaked their thirst from cupped hands until they started going numb. Then, sitting cross-legged with the tree between them and the Dragon, Alice jammed her fingers in her armpits and explained the plan. Isaac seemed impressed and dubious by turns, especially when she came to her part in it.

"Are you sure you can *do* that?" he said. "I mean—"

"I did it once before," Alice said.

"What if you get lost?"

"I won't get lost."

"All right." He thought for a moment. "I'm still not certain the ice will do what you want it to do, though."

"Let's give it a shot, then."

They went to the edge of the pool, where it trickled over the side of the little hillock and down among the field of boulders. Isaac reached down to a spot where it flowed between two of the enormous rocks and dipped his fingertips in the water. Patterns of frost spread out instantly, like blossoming flowers, and in a few seconds milky-white ice began to form.

For a while Alice worried that Isaac had been right. The boulders were too heavy, or too close together, or else the iceling simply wasn't strong enough, whatever Isaac claimed. Then, with a faint groan, the huge boulder *shifted,* just a fraction of an inch, as the expanding ice forced it upward. Tons of rock shivered, letting fall a rain of dust and pebbles. It moved a little farther, perhaps an inch, and Isaac pulled his hand away. Instead of lying directly against the neighboring boulder, the rock was now resting on an inch-thick layer of dirty ice.

"I didn't know it could do that," Isaac said.

"At home," Alice said, "we once had a hard freeze right after a rain. Some of the piping on the roof burst. Father brought it down to show me afterward. Solid iron, but the ice broke right through it. It expands when it freezes, you see, and . . ." She shook her head, not wanting to think about her father. "All right. It works. Now, let's get ready before that thing comes looking for us."

CHAPTER TWENTY-SEVEN
THE TRAP

THE STRAIN WAS EVIDENT on Isaac's face by the time they were done. He had the look of a man struggling under some enormous weight, brow furrowed, teeth clenched, hard-pressed but determined not to let it fall.

"Are you all right?" Alice said.

"I can hold it," Isaac said. "For a while, anyway."

"If it gets away from you," Alice said, "for God's sake say something. I'd rather not end up buried under a thousand tons of rock."

"I'll hold it." He puffed a breath between his teeth. "I'm more worried about you. Will you have time to get away?"

"I think so." Alice thought about the huge eye trying to focus on her. "I don't think it's very good at going from light to dark and back again. I should have a few seconds before it can even see me."

"That's a thin guess to bet your life on."

"If you had any better ideas, you should have said so earlier."

Isaac shook his head. They stood in silence for a moment.

"Well," Alice said. "Let's get started."

She left Isaac on the little hillock, beside the spring, while she climbed down to the base of their prepared section of the rock-pile. A touch of the Swarm thread kept her from skinning knees or elbows on the stone, but did nothing for the chill, which pebbled her skin to goose bumps. Waves of cold washed over her whenever the wind gusted from the direction of all the ice Isaac had laid down.

The Dragon had quieted down some. The huge cloud of dust had dispersed, and she could see the enormous thing pawing methodically through the rocks, occasionally lifting a boulder out of the way with its tail.

Wouldn't it be a laugh, she thought, *if we went to all this trouble and the thing decided it was bored with us?*

She could feel a touch of hysteria, bubbling under the surface of her determination, and she forced it down ruthlessly. Reaching the rock she wanted, she looked over her shoulder toward the hillock. It was invisible behind a small mountain of boulders. From here, they looked just like any of the other small rises in the rock-field, but Alice couldn't help imagining what would happen when the mass of stone got loose.

I wouldn't even be a smear on the rocks, she thought, before forcibly derailing that train of thought. She turned around, facing the Dragon, and cupped her hands to her mouth.

"HEY!" Alice screamed. "YOU WANT TO FIGHT? I'M ABOUT READY!"

Her voice carried and echoed oddly across the field of stones. The Dragon looked up, head cocked, like a dog hearing a rustling in the bushes.

"Impudent wizard," the Dragon rumbled. "Quit your scurrying about."

"Come on, you ugly thing!" Alice shouted. "What are you waiting for?"

The enormous tail lashed back and forth. Slow at first, but accelerating quickly, the Dragon headed in her direction. Eight multi-jointed legs carried it smoothly across the broken, irregular surface of the rocks.

Alice backed up, first to the edge of her rock and then,

climbing slowly, onto a large boulder that leaned against it. She could feel the cold of the ice all around her, and she had to clench her fists to keep from shivering.

"That's right," she went on, throat already raw. "Come and get me. Dinner is served . . ."

It had gotten sight of her now, and its legs were a blur, moving faster than a charging horse. Alice hoisted herself up onto a ledge and scrambled backward, tightening her grip on the Swarm thread. She would have only a few seconds, at best, before everything came crashing down.

The Dragon hit the edge of the pile of rocks, but Alice had crawled back in and among them. The creature's huge head pushed in after her, between a pair of boulders. Alice could see it lose its bearings in the sudden gloom, enormous snout sweeping back and forth. When she moved, it swung toward her, drawn by the sound of her shoes on stone. The great mouth opened, letting loose a hot wind that smelled of dead, rotting things. Alice could see past its teeth into the bottomless recesses of its throat.

God in heaven, she thought. *I wouldn't even be a morsel.*

"Isaac," she shouted hoarsely. "NOW!"

At the same time, she yanked the Swarm thread into herself, wrapping it around her essence over and over until her body started to change. There was a weird, frag-

343

mented moment of dissolution, flesh flowing and melting in a way that made Alice want to vomit. She tasted bile at the back of half a hundred tiny throats, as the swarmers spilled forth in a wave. They—she—dashed off, up through the rocks, leaving only a pair of shoes to mark where she'd been standing.

The swarmers couldn't climb stone as well as they could trees, but the slopes weren't as steep, and they were excellent jumpers. Alice's consciousness expanded as she raced through the pile of rocks, dodging the icy bonds that held them in place, racing away from the Dragon and up toward the hillock. The swarmers leaped from boulder to boulder and stormed through the crevices, working their way through passages too small for any human. Below, the Dragon swung its head back and forth, hunting for some sign of the prey that had suddenly vanished.

As soon as she'd shouted, if everything had gone according to plan, Isaac would have released his grip on the iceling. They'd spent the better part of an hour directing the little stream into carefully iced-over channels, growing discs and pads of ice between the boulders, feeling the whole structure twist and complain at every shift. Now he threw that process into reverse, drawing the cold away, melting the ice much faster than the chilly air could. The hill of boulders, padded with planes of slippery, half-melted ice, began to move.

Alice nearly didn't make it out before the avalanche began. Her leading swarmers had reached the firmer ground of the hilltop, beside the tree and the trickling spring, but the rest of her felt the rocks begin to slide underfoot. She jumped, leaping from rock to rock even as they began to move, and the last couple of swarmers hurled themselves blindly into space as they lost their footing, trusting to their rubbery physique to keep them relatively intact.

The collapse picked up speed as more of the boulders slipped free of the ice and began crunching down toward the Dragon. The first rock bounced off another boulder in a cloud of dust and struck the creature a glancing blow on the flank, and the Dragon jerked its head up from where it had been searching for Alice and emitted another ear-shattering roar. By then boulders were coming down all around it, though, bouncing and tumbling and smashing themselves to bits in sprays of flying stones.

Alice soon lost sight of the Dragon in the cloud of dust, but she could hear it bellowing. It was too much to hope that the rock-slide alone would kill it, but she thought that much stone should pin it in place, at least for a while.

She let the Swarm thread slip out of her mental grasp, and the cluster of gray-brown swarmers flowed together, losing their definition until they became a girl, lying gasping on the hilltop beside the spring. Alice sucked air desperately, until she had enough strength to roll over. She groped with one hand until she found the base of the tree that stood beside the little pool, and gave a yank on the other thread that coiled through her mind.

This tree was much stronger than the ragged one she'd felt before. The tough little trunk with its leafy branches was only the tip of a much larger plant—its roots extended down into the rocky piles and burrowed in wherever they found purchase.

Alice grabbed hold of the tree, bending it to her will, forcing it into a frenzy of activity ten thousand times faster than anything nature had intended. The fronds trailing in the little pool thickened and multiplied, filling with water like fire hoses, drinking in everything the pond had to offer.

At the other end, one root-tip began to *grow*, stretching down into the settling avalanche with single-minded purpose. It burrowed into the cloud of dust, snaking around and beneath the boulders, which rocked and shifted as the Dragon struggled. Alice could only sense the creature as a vague warmth, and then as a hard, scaly presence as the root slid along the side of its pinned snout.

Grow, Alice urged. *Grow, grow, grow.* The tree itself was rapidly wilting, leaves turning yellow and falling away as Alice diverted its energy to fuel the one berserk root.

The Dragon shifted, but the mass of rock pinned it in place. All it could move was its tail, but that would be enough, eventually. Alice heard a *crunch* as a boulder came free, then another. She closed her eyes and concentrated on the root, guiding it by sense of touch down the Dragon's body, curling around the thick neck in front of the first pair of shoulders, wrapping around it once, twice, and then curling over and about itself in a living parody of a hangman's noose.

The root began to thicken, changing from a pale tendril to the solid, bark-skinned limb of a mature tree. She could feel, through the tree, the Dragon's attempts to struggle, but the root held on with patient vegetable strength, and the huge creature couldn't get any of its legs free to claw its way out.

For a moment, the contest hung in the balance, the Dragon struggling to draw breath, the dying tree tightening its grip, notch by remorseless notch, even as the rest of its body collapsed. Alice found herself holding her

own breath, teeth clenched, fists closed so tight, her fingernails were four points of pain against her palms.

"Well played, child," the Dragon said, voice unimpeded
by the vine wrapped around its throat. "But we both know
it's not going to be enough."

Alice held on for all she was worth.

"Then," she growled, "I'll think of something else."

A deep, rumbling laugh echoed through her mind.
"You still claim to have come here by accident?"

"I *told* you," Alice said. "No one sent me."

"Fierce. Small, but fierce." A long moment passed.
"Perhaps my sister has gotten more than she bargained
for. In which case, there may be a chance . . ."

The Dragon's voice echoed hollowly around the inside
of Alice's head.

"Very well," it said. "I submit."

No sooner had it said the words than the world began
to dissolve around them. The sky went gray, then black,
and the rocks underfoot fuzzed out into a gray mist and
disappeared. It was like looking through a camera as it
lost focus, but for sound and touch and smell as well as
vision. For a moment, Alice felt like she was falling, alone
in an infinite void. Then reality snapped into being all
around her, and she was lying on her back on the dusty

floor of the library, next to Isaac, one hand still gripping the cover of the ancient leather-bound book.

A last echo of the Dragon's voice buzzed at the back of her mind.

"And I will be interested, little sister, to see what you can do . . ."

She took a deep breath, inhaling half a pound of dust, and regretted it immediately. A coughing fit turned her on her side and doubled her over, raising more dust all around her. Some instinct made her keep ahold of the book, which she clutched to her stomach like a drowning man grabbing a rope.

Alice could hear Isaac coughing as well, and as she brought her spasming lungs under control she realized he was hiccupping and laughing too, all at once. When Alice had regained sufficient breath to sit up, she found him lying on his back, the rent and torn remnants of his coat spread beneath him, with tears of laughter squeezing out onto his cheeks.

"You did it," he said, when he caught sight of her, followed by a word she didn't understand. "You really did it. The Dragon."

"You helped," Alice said.

"Only after you convinced me not to lay down and die." Isaac sat up, rubbing his eyes with the sleeves of his coat, which left dark stains of dirty grit across his cheeks. "I would have . . . I don't know. I didn't think it was possible."

"Neither did I," Alice said truthfully. "But my father always said there's no percentage in hanging about."

They fell into silence. Isaac's eyes went to the book, which Alice still clutched tightly to her chest. He looked away, sighed, and rolled to his feet, groaning like he'd aged sixty years. Alice levered herself up with one hand, unwilling to release the book even for a moment. Her feet—bare again, she noticed—swept up the dust of the library floor.

Behind them was the table, still bearing the hurricane lamp. Above it, faint and spectral, Alice could see the wraith-like Siren, and a faint hint of her music still pervaded the air. Isaac found the other lamp lying where he'd dropped it in their scuffle. He picked it up and made a futile attempt to pat the dust off his trousers.

"Well?" Alice said. "What now?"

"I'll go back to my master," Isaac said. "I haven't got the book, but I *have* got the Dragon. That ought to count for something." He hesitated. "You've got it too, haven't you?"

Alice felt around at the back of her mind. There were three threads there now—the silver one belonging to the Swarm, the wooden tendril of the tree-sprite, and another, black and shining like obsidian. Even without touching it, she could feel it *thrumming* with power. Taking hold of it sent a thrill through her essence, like licking a live battery, but when she gave it a tentative tug, it barely shifted.

"We were both in the book when it submitted to us," Isaac said. "I don't think I'll have the power to use it if I live a thousand years." He sounded a little in awe. "But..."

Alice was silent. She could *feel* Isaac, she realized, feel his touch on the thread. It ran through both of them, and back to the book she clutched under her arm. It wasn't a connection of minds, or even voices; just a sense of contact, like sitting side by side on a bench with their hands intertwined. She found herself smiling, a little inanely, and realized he was doing the same.

"And you?" Isaac said. "What will you do?"

She shook her head. "I don't know."

"I know I didn't tell you . . . the whole truth," he said. "But I meant what I said about Geryon. He's the worst of the Readers. All the other old ones hate him, even more than they do each other."

"He took me in," Alice said. "He didn't have to."

"If he did, then there's something in it for him. And Ending is just as bad. You can't trust either of them."

"Even if you're right," Alice said, "which I don't admit, what can I do?"

"I don't know." Isaac shook his head. "Be careful."

This, Alice thought, was not the most helpful advice she had ever received. But she tried to take it in the spirit it was meant. "I will."

"All right." Isaac looked around. "I'd better go. I don't know how much longer Siren's power will last."

Alice nodded, a little uncertainly. She felt like there was something else she ought to say, but she didn't know how to say it, or even what it was.

Isaac took a step toward her, putting them nearly face-to-face. Alice's fingers curled around the edges of the book, drawing it tighter against her side, and she fought her automatic urge to back away. Isaac's face was a mess, scratched, bruised, and smudged, but looked at up close she thought it wasn't a *bad* face, all things considered.

"Alice?" he said, very quietly.

Her voice was barely a whisper. "Yes?"

He leaned in and kissed her. His lips were dry, and tasted of gritty stone and dust. Alice's fingers curled so hard against the book that they ached, and after a moment or two she closed her eyes.

It seemed like an age before he pulled away. Her lips tingled, as though he'd passed along an electric charge.

"I'm sorry," he said, with a lopsided grin. "It's part of the spell."

Alice had a single moment to be furious before the music of the Siren rose all around her, a quiescent orchestra building to an unexpected crescendo. As her mind drifted away on that exquisite, all-encompassing melody, the last thing she felt were his hands on hers, gently tugging the book from her slackening fingers.

CHAPTER TWENTY-EIGHT

A BIT OF BLACKMAIL

I THINK HE'S STILL TRYING to figure out what happened," Ashes said. "And who to blame."

"Who can there be to blame besides himself?" Alice said.

"This may come as a shock to you," the cat drawled, "but while Geryon has many sterling qualities, accepting blame is not one of them. I think he would like to blame Mother, but he can't quite figure out how."

"I just hope he doesn't take it into his head to blame *me*," Alice said.

"I think you're off the hook," said Ashes, rolling onto his back and batting playfully at nothing. "Blaming you would be like admitting that the great and powerful

Master Geryon needs a little apprentice girl to defend his domain, and I'm sure I don't have to tell you how he would feel about *that*."

Alice fell silent, leaning against a bookshelf and watching the dust dance and sparkle in the light of the hurricane lamp. They were in the relatively well-ordered part of the library, out of sight of Mr. Wurms' table. Alice was supposed to be retrieving a particular volume for the scholar, but she'd found her mind wandering.

It had been a week since the break-in. Alice had awoken back in her bed in the house, and had stayed there for twenty-four hours, bruised and exhausted. During that time, according to Ashes, Geryon had shut everyone up in their rooms and ransacked the entire estate with a pack of vicious creatures at his heel. He'd discovered the rogue book that had given Isaac a way in and had a long talk with Ending, then stomped back into the house as unsatisfied as ever.

Alice, on waking, had given him an abbreviated version of her story. She'd left out any mention of friendship or cooperation with Isaac—not that he *deserved* any protection, she thought, cheeks burning—and said only that she'd woken up to find everyone under the Siren's spell, had chased the thief, and ended up inside the Dragon's book. This last had given Geryon pause, and he'd spent a long time examining her afterward.

After that there had been no more talk of erasing her memory. Life had gone back to normal, or what passed for normal under the circumstances.

"It's not here," Alice said to Ashes, dragging her finger along the spines of a shelf's worth of books. It came away gray with dust. "I'll go and check the other side."

Ashes was still sprawled on a shelf, all four legs in the air. His tail twitched aimlessly, and he directed a lengthy yawn at Alice.

"Go ahead," he said. "I'll be right here."

There was a gap in the shelves a little farther on, and Alice slipped through into the next aisle, then counted bookcases until she found the one opposite where she'd been looking. It was stacked full of dusty volumes, and she sighed and knelt down to start looking at the bottom.

A moment later, she felt the odd twisting sensation of the library shifting around her. Alice straightened up slowly, keeping her eyes on the shelf.

"I was wondering when you'd turn up," she said.

The sound from behind her was halfway between a chuckle and a purr.

"Oh, Alice, Alice," Ending said. "I hope you're not *angry* with me."

"I have every right to be. You lied to Isaac, and you lied to me."

"Now, that's not fair." Alice could hear the feline smile in Ending's voice. "I told you both you could have the book. I could hardly be lying to *both* of you."

"Unless you planned to turn it over to Geryon all along."

"Believe me when I say that was the last thing I wanted." Ending heaved a rumbling sigh. "You must understand our position, Alice. I—and all my kind, my brothers and sisters—are bound to serve the Readers. They hold tremendous power over us, and we cannot defy them openly. So we are forced to meddle and scheme in the shadows, out of sight."

"You once told me you did that because it was your nature," Alice said.

"When you are as old as I am," Ending said, "one's nature is largely a product of habit."

Alice turned around. There was an alcove in the shelves that hadn't been there before, deep in shadow, and all that her lantern was able to pick out was a pair of slitted yellow eyes.

"You said 'brothers and sisters,'" Alice said. "And

when I spoke to the Dragon, he talked about his sister. Did he mean *you*?"

"If he was angry, I'm afraid he did," Ending said. "He was one who refused to serve, long ago, and was thrown in a prison-book for his troubles. He blames me and the others for not coming to his aid." Ending cocked her head. "He is, I think, a bit mad. Who wouldn't be, after so many years alone? But I have tried to care for him as best I could, and make sure none of the Readers had a chance to bind him."

But he called me . . . Alice shook her head. Ending's soft purr of a voice was beguiling, and she had to keep reminding herself that she couldn't trust her. *Best not to tell her everything.*

Instead she said, "But now this Anaxomander has the book, and the Dragon ended up bound to me."

"Far from the worst of all possible outcomes," Ending said. "Anaxomander is weak, compared to Geryon. I doubt he will dare a confrontation with my brother soon. As for you . . ." There was a gleam of light on sharp, ivory-white teeth as Ending smiled. "I have hopes that you have it in you to be better than the others."

Alice felt a little flush of pride, and berated herself for it. "Be that as it may," she said, "you still owe me. I want your help with Vespidian."

"Whatever I can do, of course," Ending murmured. "But without the book . . ."

"No one knows it was stolen except for me and Geryon. And you and Ashes, I suppose. But Mr. Black doesn't know, and that means as far as Vespidian is concerned, Geryon still has it. And that means we still have a chance."

Alice paused in front of the door to the basement steps, took a deep breath, and rapped loudly.

"Mr. Black!" she said. "I'm coming in."

The last time she'd been here, she and Isaac had crept down the stairs, dreading every creak. Now Alice marched down as if she owned the place, doing her best to ignore the fluttering in her stomach.

Mr. Black was crouching in front of a squat round furnace, orange light flooding through a grilled window and painting the room with twisting shadows. Alice could feel the blast of heat even from the door. She cleared her throat conspicuously.

Slowly, the huge man got to his feet and turned around. His jaw worked from side to side, rustling his bushy black beard.

"I didn't think I'd see you in here again for a while," he said. "Awful *bold,* if you ask me."

"I wanted to talk to you," Alice said.

"But I don't care to talk to you," Mr. Black said. "So get out, while you're still able."

"I know you've been working with Vespidian," Alice said, as calmly as she was able. "I know you tried to sell him the Dragon. And I know you told him where to find me."

There was a long pause. Something in the furnace popped with a shower of sparks.

"That's a dangerous thing to say," Mr. Black rumbled. "If you know so much, why haven't you gone to the master? Unless you don't think he'd take your word over mine." He smiled, showing blackened teeth.

"He wouldn't have to take my word for it," Alice said. She swallowed hard. This was the crucial piece. "I still have the map we used to find the Dragon. If I give that to him, and he started looking into where it came from . . ."

Bingo. The narrowing of Mr. Black's eyes was all she needed to see. His breath rasped, and a tiny curl of smoke oozed from one nostril and lost itself in his beard.

"Let's say that's the case," he said, after an obvious effort to master himself. "I ain't admitting anything, but let's say you're right. Why would you do a foolish thing like coming down here to tell me about it?" He balled his hands into fists. "After all, a man you've backed into a corner is a dangerous man indeed."

Alice forced herself to stand her ground and fixed him with her most withering stare.

"I bound the Dragon, Mr. Black," she said. "I'm not afraid of you."

Mr. Black's lip twitched, but he'd lost, and he knew it.

"Besides," Alice continued. "I need you to do something for me."

Another long silence. Finally he shifted his gaze to glare over her head and muttered, "What sort of thing?"

"You must have a way of getting in touch with Vespidian. I want you to set up a meeting, in the library. Tell him I can get him the Dragon book, and I'm willing to make a deal."

Mr. Black met her gaze again. "If you turn that little flying rat over to Geryon, it's as good as turning me in."

"You don't have to worry about that," Alice said. "I just have some questions of my own for him."

One huge hand came up and scratched the bristly black hair on his chin as Mr. Black pondered.

"So that's it?" Mr. Black said darkly. "Just send him a message?"

"More or less. And I need you to answer one more question . . ."

CHAPTER TWENTY-NINE
VESPIDIAN

THE PLACE ALICE HAD chosen for her meeting with Vespidian was a cluster of shelves that, according to Ending, hosted a portal-book to a world of endless forests and vicious, six-armed monkeys. On the library side, the book's atmosphere had leaked out, creating a humid tropical air. A huge banyan tree dominated the circle of shelves, with the book nestled somewhere in its upper branches. Vines webbed it together with half a dozen smaller trees, creating an interlocking network of tendrils and creepers.

Alice sat on a ridge in the banyan's complicated root system, tapping her foot and trying not to jump up and pace. Technically, she was sneaking out after hours again—Vespidian had agreed to meet her at midnight— but somehow the looming dread of breaking the rules had lost some of its sting. Instead, she was worried that the fairy would smell a trap and not turn up at all, and she was worried about what she would say to him if he did.

And whether my "friend" will do her part. Alice strained her eyes staring at the shadows, hoping to catch a glimpse of movement. *She said she'd be here.* It irked her that, after everything, she had to put her trust in Ending once again.

A flicker of color caught her eyes. Yellow-and-black striped wings, the bold, ugly colors of something poisonous and unpleasant. Vespidian pulled himself out of a crack between bookcases and took to the air with a drone, looking around with a curious, unhurried attitude. He was just as Alice remembered him from that night in the kitchen, in what seemed like another lifetime: a few feet high, with a flat, nose-less face and huge wings that beat so fast, they were an insectile blur.

He caught sight of her and drifted over, threading his way easily between the hanging fronds and vines. Alice got to her feet, and Vespidian stopped in midair slightly above her head, so she was forced to crane her neck to look at him.

"Well, well, well," he said, in the nasal voice Alice had heard a hundred times in her dreams. "Here you are. Not such a goody two-shoes after all."

"You don't know anything about me," Alice snapped. "But I know that you want the Dragon. And I know how to get it."

"So I'm told," Vespidian drawled. "My friend Mr. Black informed me that you wanted to make a deal."

"Something like that." Alice put one hand on the tree, steadying herself.

"So what is it you want? Charms? Books? I can be very generous, I assure you."

"What did you offer Mr. Black?"

Vespidian cackled. "Him? All he wants is a way out of his service to Geryon."

"That's it?" Alice frowned. "Just freedom? Are you going to give it to him?"

"Of course not. He couldn't deliver what I asked for. Besides, turn him loose on the world and the next thing you know he'll be snatching children from their beds and devouring them whole. Some people have no grasp of the modern world." The fairy sniffed. "That sort of thing is so old-fashioned. But don't be shy, girl. What do *you* want?"

"I want you to answer some questions."

Vespidian frowned, and hovered a little lower. "I'm not sure I like the sound of that."

"I don't care," Alice said.

"Now listen to me, *girl.* Just because Geryon has taken you as his apprentice is no reason to put on airs. You have a long way to go before you're a proper Reader." He backed away from Alice. "I think this was a bad idea. I wouldn't trust you to steal a book, anyway. Tell Mr. Black—"

Alice yanked on the tree-sprite thread, wrapping it around herself until she could feel the vast bulk of the banyan tree beside her, pulsing with life like a beating heart. Compared to the tiny, bedraggled thing she'd used in the Dragon's realm, the banyan was a monster, huge and bursting with energy. It was the easiest thing in the world to force a few of the hanging tendrils into action. They lashed out like whips, wrapping around the fairy's midsection and holding him fast.

Vespidian jerked to a halt, wings straining but unable to make any headway against the vegetable strength of the vines. He struggled, spitting and cursing, and she gave him a moment to calm down.

"Look," he said, after a few moments. "This isn't going to get you what you want."

"You don't know what I want," Alice said, willing the

vines to pull him down toward her. "The night you came to my house, I saw you speaking to my father."

There was a long pause. It was hard to read much expression on the fairy's small face, but Alice thought he looked worried.

"So that's it, is it?" he said. "This is something . . . personal."

"You turned up in my kitchen," Alice said. "Four days later, my father was dead."

"I didn't have anything to do with that!" Vespidian protested. "I was only delivering a message."

"A message for *who*? Who are you working for, and where can I find them?"

"I can't tell you that," he said, sounding offended. "Do you have any idea what he'd do to me?"

"Fair enough." Alice stepped forward.

There was a copper band hanging loosely around Vespidian's left ankle. It looked out of place, and Mr. Black had confirmed her suspicion. This was the charm that gave him the run of the library, protecting him from Ending's near-omniscient oversight. His eyes stayed fixed on Alice and she put her hand up and grabbed it.

"Wait," he said. "What are you doing? That's nothing important, I don't know what you—"

Alice pulled the charm free. It was a tawdry little thing, just a ring of beaten copper with some words inscribed on the inner face. But Vespidian's eyes instantly went wide with panic.

"Give that back." His voice had gone high and shrill. "Please. Put it back on."

"Answer my questions."

"I can't! You don't know . . ."

"You're right. I don't know what your master will do to you." Alice tapped the copper band against her palm. "I don't know what *Ending* will do to you, either. Which do you think would be worse?"

"I don't . . . You don't know what you're doing. Please."

"Tell me."

The fairy's mouth worked silently for a moment, then words burst out of him like a dam breaking. "Esau! My master is Esau-of-the-Waters."

"What did he want with me and my father?"

"To take you as his apprentice, the same as Geryon. We knew the others were watching you, so we couldn't just snatch you. I tried to convince your father to give you up."

"There has to be more to it than that. Father went off to try and *protect* me, somehow. What happened to him? What happened to the *Gideon*?"

"I don't know!" the fairy wailed. "All I did was make the offer!"

"Who would know?"

"Only the master would know for certain." Vespidian strained against the vines. "Please, put it back on. It's not too late . . ."

"Oh, yessss." Ending's voice rumbled around the tiny forest. "It's far too late."

She moved through the underbrush like a living shadow, black fur rippling momentarily in the light from Alice's lantern before slipping back into darkness. Only her eyes were always visible, yellow and shining.

"I'm sorry!" Vespidian yelled. "That's all I know! Please, girl, let me go—"

Alice willed the vines to release their grip. Vespidian wriggled free and buzzed into the air, zipping around the tree and away from Ending, gibbering madly all the while. He found a gap between bookshelves, pressed himself into it, and was gone.

"You're not going to chase him?" Alice said.

"I don't need to," Ending said. "Without his little toy, he has nowhere to hide from me. This is *my* labyrinth, after all." Her eyes went to the copper band, and disgust crept into her voice. "Give me that."

Alice tossed the trinket on the ground. A heavy black paw came down on it, and the metal broke with a *crack*.

"Vile thing," Ending said. "I will make him tell me where he got it."

"Remember that you promised to let him go," Alice said.

She'd thought a long time about that. The banyan could have crushed Vespidian for her, if that's what she'd wanted. But Alice had eventually decided that he'd only been doing his job, after all, even if that job involved threatening people's families. Scaring him a little was one thing; killing him would be quite another.

If it had been him that hurt Father . . . But she was fairly certain he'd been telling the truth about that, and she was a little relieved she wouldn't have to face that particular choice. *At least, not today.*

"I will," Ending said. "Eventually." She padded off into the undergrowth, her voice slowly fading away. "But it can be so hard to find your way out of here, you know . . ."

It was the small hours of the morning before Alice returned to the house, passing by Emma standing as blank as ever in the front hall, and made her way to her bedroom.

She stripped down and got into her nightshirt, folding everything neatly and lining up her boots beside the door. One of the ancient rabbits had slumped over against the window frame, so Alice straightened it up and gave it a wistful pat on the head. After scrubbing her face with a tag-end of soap and the water from the basin, she blew out her candle and lay down on her small bed in the warm, dusty darkness.

She was desperately tired, but sleep wouldn't seem to come. Her mind kept going back to Vespidian's terrified face, and the feeling of strength in the vines as they'd coiled around him.

It hadn't gotten her very far. Another name, someone else who might know what had really happened aboard the *Gideon*. But this one was a Reader, and Alice had no idea how she was going to go about getting her answers out of him.

Esau-of-the-Waters. Alice didn't even know what the name *meant*, really, and she didn't know who to ask. Geryon would know, or Ending, or even Ashes, but she wasn't sure whether she could trust *any* of them. She felt suddenly, profoundly alone.

She closed her eyes and put a mental hand on the tight, unyielding thread that led to the Dragon. She'd told Mr.

Black that she'd bound the Dragon. But what she hadn't told him was that the Dragon thread remained unresponsive to any of her attempts to pull on it.

Once again, she felt the odd sense of connection, and she realized that somewhere, in some other hidden corner of the world, Isaac was reaching out to the Dragon thread at the same time. She trusted *him* least of all, of course, but somehow it was comforting, nonetheless.

Bit by bit, she felt herself relax. She had a direction to go in, that was the important thing. Once you had that, getting there was just a matter of hard work.

And then, on the very edge of sleep, she heard the voice of the Dragon. A memory, perhaps, echoing through her mind.

"Little sister . . ."

END

ACKNOWLEDGMENTS

This project started as something of a lark. Most of my writing to date has been in the genre sometimes called "doorstop fantasy," where something isn't considered a *real* book unless you could use it to deflect small-arms fire. After finishing one of these efforts, I decided to try and write something a little bit shorter and cleaner. Alice and *The Forbidden Library* were the result.

As usual, Elisabeth Fracalossi was my reader of first resort, keeping me encouraged and on the right track. Once the first draft was finished, my fearless cadre of beta readers jumped in. My thanks, in no particular order, to Carl Meister, Dan Blandford, Janelle Stanley, Amanda Davis, and Prentice Clark.

Special thanks are owed to Lu Huan, who not only did beta reading, but produced some spectacular artwork as well. (You can take a look at www.djangowexler.com.)

My agent, Seth Fishman, once again performed his standard set of miracles. It's begun to seem almost routine, as though I had Gandalf for a frequent dinner guest, so it's worth reminding myself from time to time what wonders he can accomplish. My thanks as well to the team at the Gernert Company: Will Roberts, Rebecca Gardner, and Andy Kifer, and in the UK Caspian Dennis at Abner Stein.

Kathy Dawson, my editor, deserves a double dose of thanks for this one. In addition to an editor's usual duties, she was faced with an author who didn't really know what kind of book he'd written, and wouldn't have known anything about it if he had. She handled it with aplomb, and showed a lot more patience than I would have in her shoes. Thanks for putting up with me.

Alexander Jansson's amazing cover blew me away, and I'm so happy to have his work in the interior of the book as well. He's done a wonderful job of capturing the feel of Alice and her world.

Finally, as always, my thanks to all the people who don't get to put their names on the cover but worked hard to make the book shine.

About the Author

Django Wexler graduated from Carnegie Mellon University in Pittsburgh with degrees in creative writing and computer science, and worked for the university in artificial intelligence research. An unrepentant geek, he migrated to Seattle to work for Microsoft, but eventually discovered that writing fantasy was a lot more fun.

He is the author of an epic fantasy novel for adults, *The Thousand Names*. *The Forbidden Library* is his first children's book. When not writing, he wrangles computers, paints tiny soldiers, and plays games of all sorts. He lives with two cats, Tomo and Sakaki, who generously assisted the writing process by turning part of one draft into confetti.

Learn more at djangowexler.com and djangowexler.com/forbiddenlibrary

Twitter: @DjangoWexler | Facebook: AuthorDjangoWexler